Dear Patron: You are invited to make a brief comment or two,
Signed or unsigned, after reading this novel. Your comments
May help other readers in their book selection. (Positive, as
well as negative, comments are requested.) Thank you.

Dead Float

Books by Warren C. Easley

The Cal Claxton Mysteries
Matters of Doubt
Dead Float

Dead Float

A Cal Claxton Mystery

Warren C. Easley

Poisoned Pen Press

Copyright © 2014 by Warren C. Easley

First Edition 2014

10 9 8 7 6 5 4 3 2 1

Library of Congress Catalog Card Number: 2014931635

ISBN: 9781464202667   Hardcover
        9781464202681   Trade Paperback

Poisoned Pen Press
6962 E. First Ave., Ste. 103
Scottsdale, AZ 85251
www.poisonedpenpress.com
info@poisonedpenpress.com

Printed in the United States of America

*In memory of my parents, Cliett and Virginia Easley
and Buddy, the Aussie*

Acknowledgments

Once again, deepest thanks to Marge Easley and Kate Easley for unerring advice and unwavering support, and to my incomparable critique group, LeeAnn McLennan, Janice Maxson, Debby Dodds, and Alison Jaekel. Many thanks to the talented crew at Poisoned Pen, and especially to Barbara Peters, whose sagacious edits helped shape the direction and tone of this novel. A special thanks to Sy Banaitis, who introduced me to the joys of fly fishing, and to owners Craig and Tina Hughson and the world class team at Rogue River Outfitters, especially guides Bob Bryant, Guy Billings, and Tim Conway, for countless hours of magnificent fishing on the Deschutes River. Long live *Onchryncus Mykiss Iridis*!

Chapter One

If I've learned one thing in this life, it's that trouble has a way of finding you, no matter where you go or what you do to avoid it. I moved up here from Los Angeles to get away from the big city and all that came with it. A one-man law practice in a small rural town—that was my plan. Start fresh, mind my own business, keep my head down. Oh, and my daughter, Claire, told me to get a dog and find a hobby. Well, I've done all that, but I can't say I've gotten the results I expected.

A case in point—the series of events that began early one morning last June.

I remember that morning distinctly because of the weird dream that woke me just before dawn. I was walking on a deserted beach. A gust of wind parted the fog hanging over the water just long enough for me to see Claire standing out in the surf on jagged rocks. As a huge wave gathered silently behind her, the mist closed again like a curtain. I ran up and down the beach waving my arms and shouting warnings. She reappeared. The wave was now nearly upon her. I cupped my hands around my mouth and screamed, but the wind blew the sound back into my lungs.

I awoke with the cry still rattling in my throat. I sobbed and my pulse hammered. Archie, my Australian shepherd, had left his corner of the bedroom to offer support. He stood with his head cocked to one side, his stump of a tail wagging tentatively. It had been a while since I'd had a dream like that. I used to dream about my wife, Nancy. But that's another story. This dream was about Claire, my daughter, my only child. She had taken a year off from her graduate studies at Berkeley to help dig wells in remote villages in the Darfur region of the Sudan. She was supposed to call me by satellite phone at least once a week. That was the deal.

She was now three days overdue.

Claire's presence in one of the most dangerous places on the planet had started innocently enough. She heard this guy speak at Berkeley—some high tech billionaire-turned-humanitarian—who'd founded a non-profit called Well Spring. Their mission was to help the poorest region on the planet. They would use simple, low-cost technology. They would not only dig wells, they would teach the Sudanese to dig their own. In so doing, they would transform a region where access to water is *everything*.

I'd seen enough of life to know that do-gooder schemes often have a way of going awry. But I wasn't about to let my cynicism get in her way, so I gave her my blessing. I knew deep down that what I thought wasn't going to influence her anyway. Claire was going to do what her conscience dictated. After all, that's how her mother and I had raised her. And, in truth, I was proud of what she was doing. So, apart from my usual separation anxiety, I wasn't particularly worried about her, at least not until she was late calling in. I sat on the edge of the bed, stroking Archie's head. I'll give it another day before I call Well Spring, I decided.

Archie and I jumped when the phone rang. I glanced at the clock as I picked up the receiver. It was a little before five.

"Cal?" a familiar voice said cheerily. "How are you, buddy?"

"Is that you, Lone Deer?" There was more edge to my voice than intended. I'm really not at my best before the sun rises.

"Yeah, it's me. You okay? You sound like I woke you up or something."

"Ah, actually you didn't wake me up, but you *meant* to. I was just hoping you were Claire is all." I instantly regretted having said that, because I didn't feel like discussing the situation, even with my good friend, Philip Lone Deer.

"Expecting her to call, huh? She doing okay over there?"

"Fine," I replied. "She's doing fine." I was relieved that Philip was apparently unaware of the ongoing situation in Darfur. At best it was being called a civil war, at worst genocide. This was a busy time of year for him, so I suspected reading the newspapers was not a high priority. "So, what's so important you have to call me before the damn birds are up?

Lone Deer chuckled. "Cal, you know I'm an early riser, man. I've been up since four. I need you on the Deschutes *tomorrow*, not Thursday. My clients moved their date up a day. Can you make it?"

"Hang on a sec. Let me check my calendar."

I slipped into my moccasins and padded down to the study on the first floor. Archie followed me with breakfast on his mind. The stillness of the morning was broken by the creaks and groans of the stairs and the sound of his nails on the worn treads.

Philip Lone Deer was a professional fishing guide. I had met him on a float trip Claire had given me as a birthday present. I was a fledgling fly fisherman and Philip a patient teacher. We hit it off, and soon, when our schedules allowed, we were fishing together as friends rather than as guide and client.

Last year one of Philip's guides hurt his back right at the beginning of the salmon fly hatch on the Deschutes River, as wild and unspoiled a river as there is in Oregon, and North America, for that matter. It was his busiest time on the river, so out of desperation, he asked me to fill in the three days it would take for him to get a replacement. I had such a great time that I offered to guide for Philip every year at this time, and since he was always short of personnel, he readily accepted. Tomorrow would be the first day of this commitment. For the next two weeks I was to shed my identity as small-town lawyer, and become Cal Claxton, fly-fishing guide.

I sat down at my desk, opened my calendar, and picked up the phone. "Yeah. Looks doable. My morning's full, but I can duck out this afternoon in time to be in Madras for dinner."

"Great, Cal." Then we're good to go. Look, Blake and I won't get in to Madras until late, so just meet us at the Trout Creek put-in at seven in the morning."

I was wide awake now and craving a cup of coffee. I went into the kitchen, fed Archie, and drew a double espresso shot using my stainless steel DeLonhi—one of my prized possessions—to which I added hot, frothy milk. The birds had begun to sing, and the Doug firs to the east formed sharply etched silhouettes against a deep orange sky.

My old farmhouse is perched like a lone sentinel on a high ridge in the Dundee Hills at the northern edge of Oregon's Willamette Valley. The view out the back of my place looks south, straight down the gun barrel of the valley, bounded by the Coastal Range to the west and the Cascades to the east. Pinot noir grapes thrive in the ferrous-rich soils up here, so the view below me is mainly undulating vineyards, although I can see fields of hazelnuts, hops, and even Christmas trees. Further out, the valley floor becomes a soft patchwork of cultivated fields narrowing to the horizon, a study in greens, yellows, and ocher.

Dundee, the nearest town, sits at the base of the hills a few miles away. Dubbed by some, mainly locals, the unofficial wine capitol of Oregon, the little town of eight thousand is experiencing growing pains brought on by the expansion of the wine industry and the split that inevitably develops between those who welcome growth and those who don't. As an L.A. native I know only too well what unbridled growth can do. But I felt safe in my refuge and figured it'd take a long time for the developers to find me.

After another jolt of espresso, I started packing so I could leave for the Deschutes directly from my office in Dundee. I loaded my traveling fly case with an assortment of caddis flies and bead-head nymphs and left room for the salmon flies that Philip had promised. He tied his own, and they were the best on the river. I screwed a fresh CO_2 cartridge into my fishing vest. The small bottle held enough pressurized gas to inflate the vest in case of an emergency. Activated by a ripcord, it would float me in case I came loose in the rapids.

As I loaded the car, I had this nagging feeling I'd forgotten something. I turned to Archie and said, "Okay, big boy, what is it?" His ears came forward and he whined softly a couple of times. Then it came to me. I'd lost the belt to my waders on my last trip. This wasn't just a matter of looking good on the river. I'd heard too many stories of good fishermen who'd drowned when their waders filled with water and dragged them under because they weren't wearing a tightly cinched belt. I went back in the house, grabbed a thick leather belt, and tossed it on top of my waders.

His chin resting on his paws, Archie lay on the porch watching me intently for clues—was he going with me or would he have to stay? When I packed his feeding dish, watering bowl, and a bag of kibble, he sprang up, wagging his tail. "Don't get your hopes up, Arch" I told him, "I can't take you with me." I would have left him at home, to be cared for by our neighbor, Gertrude Johnson, but Gertie was under the weather, so plan B was to drop him at the local vet.

When I finished loading the car I opened the back door and gave a slight nod. Arch vaulted into the seat in an instant, sitting erect with a doggie grin on his face. That dog of mine never listens to me.

As we rolled down my long driveway, a mass of dark clouds blotted out the sun. My enthusiasm faded with the sunlight. The vivid dream I had that morning came back to me, and I thought of Claire again. But something else nagged, too. Something I couldn't quite put my finger on. I won't say it was a premonition, because I don't believe in premonitions. But it was something pretty damn close.

Chapter Two

Eagle Nest Road connected my driveway with the main road. Some early settler just off the Oregon Trail probably named it, and aptly so, since bald and golden eagles hunt the area, although you're more likely to see a red-tailed hawk or a kestrel. At the intersection with the main road, I hopped out to grab the paper before heading down to Dundee.

Pritchard's Animal Care Center was located on the south end of Dundee in a small, white clapboard building that had once been a Baptist church. The cross on the belfry had been replaced with a large weathervane sporting the silhouette of a hunting dog, and a couple of the pews now served as customer seating inside the building. When we pulled into the parking lot, Archie let out two high-pitched squeals of joy. I clipped on his leash, and he led me into the building, his entire backside wagging. It was unusual, to say the least, for a dog to be so enthusiastic about visiting the vet. This was particularly true for Arch, who'd nearly died there. He'd been roughed up by a cougar and was limp in my arms when I rushed him into the center. Hiram Pritchard saved Archie's life that night, an act that had endeared him to both the dog and his owner.

Hiram was busy, so I handed the leash to the receptionist. Archie peered up at me, ears forward.

"It's okay, big guy, you stay with Doc."

He sat there a moment longer as if to say, *Are you sure?* Then he popped up and trotted with the receptionist down the hall like he owned the place.

My law office stands on the other end of Dundee, which consists of an eclectic collection of storefronts strung out along Route 99W. Upscale restaurants, a trendy inn, and numerous wine-tasting rooms offering "big, bold reds" were tucked in with taco and BBQ trucks, a tavern promising karaoke, and all manner of small shops. Not a national chain to be seen, and hardly an unfriendly person. At the north end of town, where the old barber shop had stood, was the only lawyer's office. A sign with letters carved in a slab of red cedar read "Calvin Claxton III, Attorney at Law."

My dad was called Junior his entire life. Like his dad, he practiced law in the San Gabriel Valley in Southern California. When I finished Law School at Berkeley, it was pretty much expected that I'd join his one-man practice. But I wasn't much for predictability and surprised everyone in my family by opting for a job as an L.A. prosecutor. I wound up as a Deputy DA in major crimes, riding herd on a large group of lawyers. I was in my twenty-sixth year with the city when my wife died. After that, well, let's just say I crashed and burned. Living up in my refuge in Dundee represented a fresh start.

At my office that morning, I managed to push some papers around on my desk while resisting the temptation to call Well Spring to inquire about Claire. I didn't want to act the nervous parent, and besides, Claire had warned me she might have trouble connecting with me on a regular basis.

In addition to my practice in Dundee I did some pro bono work in Portland. My clients were mostly homeless kids and adults who had been brought to their knees by the Great Recession, bad choices, hard luck, or some combination of all three. I'd postponed my meetings in Portland for the next two weeks and had finally talked my landlord, Hernando Mendoza, into fixing the leaks in the roof of his building in my absence. Nando was a good friend and a private investigator I used on occasion, but tight with a buck.

In truth, I welcomed the break, because every trip to Portland was haunted by the woman who'd convinced me to volunteer there in the first place. A passionate advocate for homeless kids, Dr. Anna Eriksen had run the health clinic in Portland's Old Town. We had grown close and even traveled to her native Norway together. But six months ago she left Portland to start a much larger clinic in New York City, where she grew up. I guess I always knew she'd put her homeless kids ahead of me, and I really couldn't fault her for it. But that didn't lessen the sting.

The women in my life, it seems, have a have a way of slipping away from me.

I closed up shop and left for Madras around three. It took John Coltrane's "Favorite Things" and half of Thelonius Monk's "Brilliant Corners" to reach I-22, which parallels the North Santiam River into the western side of the Cascades. Cresting Santiam Pass, I caught a glimpse of Mount Washington off to my left, its white volcanic cone etched against a cobalt sky. On the descent, the lush fir and cedar yielded to ponderosa and scrub pine and then to the chaparral and mesquite of the high desert.

I arrived in Madras around six. It was hot enough to convince an oil executive of global warming. The clerk at the motel managed to check me in without dropping the ash column from her dangling cigarette as I maneuvered to avoid her second-hand smoke.

I turned the air conditioner in my room on full-blast, changed into my swim trunks, and made for the pool. I swam forty laps in the tepid water and returned to my room, which was now cold enough to hang meat. The bed looked tempting, so I stretched out to relax for a few minutes. The air conditioner had a cyclic drone that became a mantra as I spiraled into sleep.

A phone rang and I sat bolt upright, frantically searching for my cell. On the fourth ring I realized it was coming from the next room. Claire, I said to myself, I wish you would call.

It was now nearly 8:30, and my stomach was rumbling. I found a restaurant tucked away in a new storefront mall. The place was cool inside, and the burnt umber walls looked inviting in the soft light. I requested a table at the back of the spacious room and sat with my back against the wall, gangster-style. I was in the middle of perusing the menu when three men and a woman came in and took a table near the entrance. A few minutes later a couple arrived and joined them. I glanced up and quickly lowered my face back behind the menu.

It was Alexis Bruckner and her husband Hal. I'd met them last fall in eastern Washington. They'd fished for salmon on the Klickitat River that day, using Philip as a guide. I'd driven over from Dundee that afternoon to join Philip for dinner. We were to fish the next day. I remember the exact date, September 3, since it was Philip's birthday. Philip had described the little restaurant where we planned to dine in such glowing terms that, at the last minute, the Bruckners decided to join us.

A man of few words, Philip seemed relieved I was there to carry the conversation. I'm not that garrulous myself, but spurred by the food and wine, to say nothing of the promise of good fishing the next morning, my mood became expansive. And I didn't mind that Alexis, a gorgeous woman by any standard, let her ocean blues rest on me as I moved the dinner conversation along. I hadn't been with a woman since Anna had left, which was the way I wanted it. But those looks from Alexis made me begin to question that decision.

I snapped out of my daydream when the waiter arrived to take my order. By this time, the group was absorbed in animated conversation, and to my relief, it seemed like neither of the Bruckners had noticed me.

My thoughts streamed back to that night on the Klickitat. We were on our second bottle of wine, and Philip had just finished telling Hal and Alexis about trout fishing on the Deschutes. He wasn't above a little advertising. After all, guiding's a tough business. He said, "You know, Cal likes the salmon fly hatch so much that he's agreed to put his law practice on hold next year and join me as a guide."

"It must be nice to have that kind of flexibility," Bruckner said almost wistfully. "I'd sure like to fish the salmon fly hatch one of these days."

Bruckner began to tell us about a fishing trip he and Alexis had taken to Alaska. They'd caught huge salmon and halibut the size of garage doors, and had even seen a couple of grizzlies in the wild. A trip of a lifetime.

As he finished, Alexis said, "Well, what I remember most about the trip was Hal's snoring. I remember lying there on the tundra freaking out. I figured the sound would attract grizzlies."

We all laughed and looked at Bruckner.

"Sleep apnea," he said. "It kicked in on that trip. Causes me to snore like a freight train," he added with a sheepish grin.

"That and drinking," Alexis added, her smile fading.

"Drinking?" Bruckner said with mock incredulity, as he held up his glass of pinot. "My dear, enjoying wine of this caliber does not qualify as mere drinking. This is *imbibing*, a much more refined way to get drunk." He laughed and drained his glass.

We said our good nights not long after that awkward exchange. I went up to my room and crashed on the bed, fully clothed. Thirty minutes later the buzz from the wine threatened to morph into a headache, so I got up for some aspirin. I'd just taken my shirt off when I heard a soft knock on the door.

"Who's there?" I said in a low voice.

"It's Alexis, Cal."

"Just a sec." Hastily putting my shirt back on, I opened the door and stood there holding the knob. She was barefoot in a gauzy blouse and jeans. Strands of blond hair were splayed on the ramps of her breasts, rising and falling with her breath. "Oh, hi," I said, "Uh, what's up?"

She looked at me and smiled in a way that said she found my awkwardness amusing. "Nothing, really. Hal's passed out cold and I'm bored as hell."

I continued to stand there, holding the doorknob like an idiot.

"Well, aren't you going to ask me in?"

I said, "Sure," and moved aside.

Alexis Bruckner and I had a brief affair. Not proud of it. It was over before Christmas.

I was jolted out of my reverie again when the waiter served my dinner. The restaurant had filled up, and Hal Bruckner still seemed oblivious to my presence. I doubted he would remember me in any case. But I caught Alexis stealing a couple of quick glances and figured my cover was blown. But she ignored my presence.

I couldn't leave without walking right past the group, so I ordered another glass of wine and slowed down on my meal to wait them out. Curiosity got the better of me, and I started sizing up the group. I wasn't too worried about being noticed. They seemed much too absorbed in conversation, or so I thought.

Alexis was dressed in white shorts, camp sandals, and a pastel tank top that did little to hide her ample cleavage. Her swept-back blond hair and deep tan accentuated the color of her eyes, a blue the ocean takes on far out to sea. The other woman stood out in contrast to her. She seemed a few years younger, small of stature but compact and athletic-looking. Her shock of raven hair and olive complexion enhanced an occasional smile below dark, almost brooding eyes. She wore a beige golf shirt tucked into faded jeans that bunched carelessly on her Nikes. She had this casual air of confidence about her I found intriguing.

Hal Bruckner was the oldest person at the table, the alpha male judging from the deference shown him by the three other men. There was a discernible pecking order among the men. The second-in-command was definitely the tall, dark-haired guy with the square jaw in the horned-rim glasses. He seemed to derive his position from a special relationship with Bruckner. The man with the retro crew cut, monolithic brow, and hefty body-mass index seemed a little too anxious to please. I guessed he had just recently been let into this inner circle and wanted desperately to remain there.

The third was tall and thin, sporting sandy hair, a bristly goatee, and John Lennon glasses with thick lenses. He carried his cell phone in a pouch on his belt. He was an integral member of the group, no doubt about it. The resident geek.

I managed to catch snatches of their conversation above the hum of the room. At one point I heard a fragment of a question the raven-haired woman asked Bruckner. I distinctly heard the words "guide service." My ears pricked up.

Bruckner replied, and I heard the words, "Northwest Experience."

The travel of my glass to my mouth stopped so abruptly that wine sloshed on the front of my shirt. *No!* I said to myself. *You've got to be kidding!*

I shouldn't have been so surprised. After all, chances were pretty good Bruckner would use Philip to guide a trip on the Deschutes. But damn it, I wasn't ready to spend the next three days fishing with my ex-lover and her husband. Talk about awkward.

And more than awkward it turned out to be.

Chapter Three

By the time Hal Bruckner signed the credit card bill covering the dinner for the group, I was about ready to sneak out through the kitchen. When I finally got back to my room, I tried to read, but restless, I got up and walked down by the pool. The night was desert cool, and the Milky Way lay across the sky like diamond dust. My thoughts inevitably turned to my affair with Alexis.

Put simply, it was about sex and ego gratification. What affair isn't? I was still dealing with the abrupt departure of Anna when Alexis showed up—a beautiful woman who wanted me. Sure, I tried to tell myself, the relationship might go somewhere. But it wasn't long before I admitted what I already knew at the outset—this was sex without commitment and intimacy without attachment. It would run its course.

I recalled the one time she came to my place. She'd come unannounced, to surprise me, she explained. Archie took an instant dislike to her, and Alexis, no fan of big dogs, sat fuming in her late-model Jaguar with the doors closed. "Jesus Christ, Cal, is that dog legal?" she screamed through a partially rolled-down window as Arch stood barking at her.

I quieted Archie down and coaxed her out of the car, then led her up the steps and through the front door. Her blond hair formed a mass of bouncing ringlets framing an oval face with fine, sculpted cheekbones and wide-set, deep blue eyes. She turned to me, clasped her hands behind my neck and pulled us together, our bodies meshing like precision machinery.

"*Now*, Cal. *Right now*," she said in my ear.

We made love all afternoon, and then she hurried off, the purring of her Jag barely audible as it pulled away. I vowed that would be the one and only time we met there. The Aerie was my refuge, after all. I was certain Archie would agree with that.

A woman's laugh snapped me back to the present. A young couple walked up to the edge of the pool. "Water warm?" the woman asked.

I'd been sitting with my feet dangling in the water. "Like a bath," I answered as I got up and headed back to my room.

I crawled back into bed. But sleep still didn't come. Memories of that time with Alexis kept coming back to me, especially the day I ended it between us.

It was mid December. The sky, I remembered, was a mottled mass of black and gray that day. I could smell the rain and see it in the distance, a soft mist churning between the clouds and the valley floor like smoke. Archie and I had jogged to the cemetery above Gertrude Johnson's farm before turning around and starting home. The rain met us halfway, a gentle pattering at first, followed by a hard shower that came in over the ridge from the vineyards. We had just taken refuge under a big Doug fir when my cell went off.

"Dad? It's Claire. How are you?"

"I'm fine, sweetheart." At the moment, Arch and I are holed up under a tree waiting for the rain to stop. We're on a jog."

"Oh dear! Is this a good time to talk?"

"Sure. What's a little rain to an Oregonian?"

"I wanted to let you know my plans for Christmas."

"Great." I secretly hoped they would include a visit north. I knew Claire loved our time together as much as I did, but I also knew that her PhD work at Berkeley came first.

"I plan to come up to Dundee on the Tuesday before Christmas, and I have to leave the following Saturday. Does that work for you, Dad?"

"Perfect! Just let me know when to pick you up at PDX."

"Okay. I'll email you my itinerary. Uh, there's one more thing." The tone of her voice alerted me that something important was coming.

"Uh, I'm going to be taking some time off from school, Dad—"

"You are? What for?" I interrupted, instantly regretting it. Shut up and listen, I told myself. She's an adult.

"I'm going to the Sudan, the Darfur region, in May to teach people how to dig wells. I'm volunteering with a nonprofit called Well Spring. They're doing great work over there, Dad."

Sudan, I thought to myself, *good God!* But I didn't want to come off as unsupportive, so I said, "What about school? Can you afford the time off?"

"Not a problem. Professor Hornseth wants me to go for it. He says Well Spring's a great organization. I've got my course work out of the way, so it'll be no sweat to pick back up."

I paused, trying to think of what to say. "Yeah, but, ah, is it safe over there? I mean, isn't there a lot of conflict in that region?" I read the papers. I knew damn well what the answer to that question was.

Claire exhaled loudly. "Well, there is some fighting, but we'll be working in safe areas. Clean water is everything to these people, Dad. I want to do this. If you google Well Spring, you'll see what I mean."

I struggled to catch my balance. "Okay, I'll check them out," but the tone came out decidedly unenthusiastic.

"Dad, it's a done deal. I want your understanding, not your permission. I've committed to go for six months."

Her words stung like a slap in the face. It hurt to be left out of the loop, even if she was twenty-three years old. But I knew my daughter. There'd be no changing her mind, so I swallowed my next point of argument. "Can't blame me for worrying. It's in my job description. Look, sweetheart, I'm damn proud of you. And I know your mother would be, too."

Brave words, but down in my gut I had an uneasy feeling, like things had just tilted away from me a little. Sure, I was proud.

Sure, I wanted her to have the courage of her convictions. But digging wells in Darfur?

Later that afternoon, I sat in the living room watching another squall sweep in. I thought about Alexis. I thought about her rings and diamond-studded bracelets, her powder blue Jag with the soft leather seats, her spoiled, self-centered poutiness. As the feeble December light died, I picked up the phone and ended it between us.

Chapter Four

The motel radio alarm buzzed at six the next morning. By 6:35, I was juggling a cup of acrid motel coffee in my car while I called Well Spring on my cell. I was relieved when a live human answered. I explained my situation to the receptionist, who immediately put me through to the director of operations.

"Chad Harrelson." He sounded young, too young.

"Uh, this is Calvin Claxton. I'm Claire Claxton's father. She's a volunteer on one of your teams in northern Darfur."

"Yes, Mr. Claxton." He paused for me to go on. This encouraged me in a sense. Apparently he had no shattering news. On the other hand, I sensed I wasn't going to get much from this guy.

"She's supposed to call me every Sunday. She's, uh, four days late. I'm wondering if you've heard from her team?"

"Just a moment, Mr. Claxton." I heard his chair squeak and the click of computer keys. "Yes, she's with Jerry Baker's team. Let's see, Jerry checked in last Saturday. Everything was copasetic." He paused again.

"So, I shouldn't worry that I haven't heard from her?"

"No. Not at all. It happens all the time with our field teams. Communicating in northern Darfur is difficult at best. Satellite phones are great, but they aren't very reliable."

I felt somewhat reassured, but not much. "I'm leaving on a three-day fishing trip and will only be in cell phone range tonight when we camp. I'm, uh, trying to decide whether to go or not."

"Mr. Claxton, I wouldn't worry about this. Go on your trip. We'll take good care of your daughter."

I paused for what must have seemed a long time to Harrelson. "I'd like to call you tonight to see if you have any news."

"Sure," Harrelson replied. "I'll give you my cell number. Call me anytime. Don't worry, Mr. Claxton. This isn't unusual."

Okay, I'm going, I decided. I should've felt better. After all, with any luck, word from Claire would be waiting for me tonight or at worst, when I got back. But I didn't feel better. Instead, I sat staring out across the mesquite-covered landscape, absently pulling at my mustache with my thumb and forefinger. The knot that had quietly formed in my gut tightened, and suddenly the coffee turned undrinkable. I opened the car door and poured it on the asphalt.

I headed north out of Madras and after a few miles turned onto a dirt road that angled off through a section of farmland made verdant by the water pumped up from the Deschutes River. Originating on the eastern slopes of the Cascades, the river traversed two hundred and fifty miles of high-desert terrain before emptying into the Columbia. I slowed to keep the dust down, thankful I wasn't following anyone in. When I saw the narrow, wooden train trestle with *Barlow Northern* stenciled across the top, I knew I was close to the put-in. The tracks that ran along the Deschutes connected central Oregon and California with the Columbia River and destinations north, east, and west.

As I pulled into the parking lot at the campground, I saw Philip's truck at the boat ramp and counted ten other rigs, at least. It's not going to be lonely out there, I thought. Hunched over, Philip was winching one of his aluminum drift boats into the water. The other was already in the river, lashed to the bank.

I stood there for a moment watching my friend. The only son of a proud Paiute Indian father and a white, social worker mother, Philip was someone you'd notice in a crowd. Narrow in the waist but thick through the chest and shoulders, he had his dad's high cheekbones, strong chin, and inky black hair, which was pulled back in a thick ponytail. Set against a coppery complexion, his jade green eyes were almost startling, and his narrow nose completed the break with classic Native American features.

Philip considered himself a Paiute first and foremost. He could be edgy around whites and had zero tolerance for patronizing do-gooders, to say nothing of outright bigots. It was as if the atrocities visited upon his father's people had been distilled down and poured into his consciousness, and the anger and frustration seethed, deceptively, just below the surface of his stoic demeanor. The death of my wife had affected me in a similar way, although my anger was self-directed. In any case, these similarities seemed to help us understand each other. I was proud to be his friend.

As I approached, I cupped a hand and called out, "Straight from central casting, Philip Lone Deer, fishing guide."

Philip stopped cranking and without looking up replied, "Sounds like the forked-tongued lawyer from the wine country." Then he raised his head, smiled broadly and said, "Glad you made it, Cal. Give me a hand with this damn boat."

With both boats in the water, we started loading the rubber raft that would carry our food and camping gear downriver. By this time, Blake Forman, the third guide, had joined us. Born and raised on the Sandy River outside Portland, Blake was only twenty-one but a top-notch boatman whose job was to navigate the heavily laden raft to our campsites. Judging from the number of rigs in the parking lot, we needed to get him on his way so he could secure our designated site downriver before it was snapped up.

We'd nearly finished packing the raft when a black Lexus and a canary yellow Hummer rolled into the lot and parked. Philip said, "That'll be our clients," and strode up the bank to greet them as Blake and I continued to pack.

Any hope I had that the new arrivals weren't the group from last night were dashed when Hal Bruckner came struggling down the bank in his pricey Orvis waders and boots. He was breathing hard, his belly sagged over his nylon wading belt, and a sheen of sweat glistened on his forehead. Wisps of blond hair protruded from a black ball cap with the name of his company—*Nano-Tech*—written in white script across the front.

"Good morning, fellas," he said. "My name's Hal."

Blake took his bag, and both of us introduced ourselves and shook hands with him. After wiping his brow with the back of his hand, he looked directly at me. "Of course. You're Cal, the lawyer from Dundee. Good to see you again. You know, the reason I'm here is that dinner we shared on the Klickitat last year. Couldn't get your description of this place out of my head." He hiked a thumb in the direction of the parking lot. "Decided to bring my management team along for a little team-building."

"Well, I don't think you'll be disappointed," I responded.

Bruckner mopped his brow again. "What's this heat going to do to us?"

I looked at Blake, since he'd been on the river the day before.

"The fishing was killer yesterday, and it was hotter. Cloud cover or a little rain's usually a good thing, but when the hatch's full-on like this, the weather doesn't matter much." He glanced out at the river. "It's an orgy out there right now." As if to underscore his point, Blake brushed a two-inch salmon fly off the back of his neck. It hit the river with a plop and drifted away, thrashing about in the current.

By this time, the other three men in the party had gathered around us. The dark-haired man with the horn-rimmed glasses offered his hand and spoke first. He was lean and trim, with a condescending smile and an air of confidence bordering on arrogance.

"Mitch Hannon. I'm here to see if this salmon fly hatch's all it's cracked up to be."

Bruckner laughed heartily and nodded toward me. "This is the guy I told you about, Mitch, who sold me on this river."

Hannon looked at me. There was something about his eyes, too small maybe, and set too far into their sockets. He allowed a thin smile. "Don't feel any pressure, Claxton."

Blake stifled a laugh that came out as a snort. I said, "Well, I hope I didn't oversell the river. The trout won't jump in the boat. You *will* have to fish for them."

Hannon introduced the nerdy-looking guy wearing a shirt decorated with drawings of artificial flies. His name was Duane Pitman, and he bent forward in the habit of tall people, his hand enveloping mine like a flaccid glove. He had a narrow face, like something off a Modigliani canvas. His eyes were alert and intelligent as they appraised me behind thick wire-rims.

Hannon introduced the guy with the Popeye forearms next. Andrew Streeter was a stocky hulk of a man. "Glad to meet y'all," he greeted us with a hard Southern twang—Georgia or Mississippi, I figured. His bushy eyebrows reminded me of weeds growing through cracks in a sidewalk, and his toothy grin seemed more nervous tic than an expression of friendliness. He handed me his bag. "When do we get to fish on this trip?"

I forced a smile. "Soon enough."

Pointing to the river, Hannon said, "Remember, Andy, those ain't your daddy's catfish out there."

Streeter smiled. "Shee-it, my daddy and me used to fish for tarpon in Boca Grande. Makes these trout look like minnows."

Pitman rolled his eyes. "Oh, God, no tarpon stories on this trip. You promised."

I glanced up the bank and saw the small woman with the raven hair but no Alexis. Another seed of hope germinated in my gut—maybe Alexis had decided to sit the trip out. Reasonable. After all, you could break a nail fishing on this river.

The small woman was struggling with her overstuffed bag. She smiled. "Okay, no comments about women bringing too much stuff. Guilty as charged." I thought I caught just a trace of an accent but wasn't sure.

I laughed. "Here, let me help you with that. I'm Cal Claxton, by the way."

"I'm Daina Zakaris. I can manage the bag. Just show me where to put the damn thing." I pointed at a spot on the raft, and after loading her bag she said, "So, did you enjoy observing our little get-together last night, Cal?"

Her comment caught me off-guard. I broke into a guilty grin despite myself. "Uh, yeah, I did. I didn't think you folks noticed me."

"The rest didn't, but I did. I could *feel* you looking at us," she continued in a tone suggesting this was an everyday occurrence for her. Her eyes were extraordinary—black and luminous, like dark globes with a lit match behind them. They were teasing me, but I knew she wasn't kidding about catching me spying at the restaurant.

"You know how it is—eating alone with nothing to do. Your group was quite a challenge for an amateur psychologist like me, but I think I've got you all figured out."

She raised her chin and laughed with genuine amusement. "We'll have to compare notes sometime." She looked almost comical in her oversized waders. But I sensed her legs were strong, an attribute I knew would hold her in good stead on the river.

"So, do much fly-fishing, Daina?"

She brushed a strand of hair from her eye. "I took a course last year in Seattle. Fell in love with the sport, but I only know enough to be dangerous."

I heard the scraping of feet behind me, then a familiar voice. "She's being modest. Actually, we're going to kick these guys' butts on this trip, aren't we, Daina?"

I turned around and found myself face-to-face with Alexis Bruckner.

Chapter Five

"Oh, hi, Alexis. How are you?" I hesitated a moment, then extended my hand.

"Hello, Calvin." Her hands remained resting on her hips.

"You two know each other?" Daina asked.

I glanced at Alexis, hoping she'd respond. But she merely looked back at me with a sardonic smile and folded her arms across her chest.

I stood there feeling Daina's gaze on the side of my face like a heat lamp. "Uh, yeah, we met last fall on the Klickitat River over in Washington. She and, uh, Hal were salmon fishing with Philip. I joined them for dinner."

"I see," said Daina. She looked at Alexis and then looked back at me. Her eyes were amused again, making it clear that she did, in fact, see.

"See you tonight at the campsite. Keep 'er dry." Philip's shout out to Blake as he shoved off with the raft interrupted the awkward scene. Philip waved me over to where he and Bruckner were standing, and after a brief huddle we decided I would take Daina, Hannon, and Streeter in my boat. Philip would take the Bruckners and Pitman in his. I figured Philip would opt for the Bruckners since Hal was paying the bill, and I was damn relieved when he did. While Alexis dallied on the bank meticulously applying sunscreen and threading her ponytail through the back of a NanoTech cap, I eased my boat into the current to the delight of Hannon and Streeter, whose competitive juices were already flowing.

"Atta boy, Claxton," Hannon said. "Let's put some distance between us and those bait casters."

"Yeah," echoed Streeter, "put your back in it, man. We need to bag the best fishin' holes."

Just my luck to get stuck with the type-A personalities. But I bit my tongue. "No worries, gentlemen, it's a big river, and there's plenty of trout to go around."

The day continued to warm and there wasn't a breath of wind. Insects buzzed and darted low over the water as the air filled with the scent of wild sage and mock orange. The river was glassy smooth, and I could see the telltale spreading rings of feeding trout along the banks. I rowed with the current for about twenty minutes until we came to the first section I planned to fish.

"Okay," I said after securing the boat, "the current's swift and the rocks are slick, so use your wading sticks and keep your wader belts cinched tight. The salmon flies are concentrated in the brush along the bank, so the fish will be in close. And remember, it's all catch and release on this river."

I had Streeter and Hannon fan out downstream and reserved a wide, riffling section that started at the boat and went upstream for Daina. Standing on the bank, I watched her fish, giving pointers now and then. She hadn't moved upriver more than thirty feet when a fish rose in front of her. I didn't think she saw it.

"Try casting at about one o'clock. Thought I saw something," I said casually.

She hit just above the spot on the second try, and I held my breath. Like it'd been waiting all day for it, the trout took the fly with a shattering strike that brought its body halfway out of the water.

"Whoa! Did you see that?" she screamed with pure delight as the fish dove and ran for the safety of the deep current. Line buzzed off her reel. Then the fish stopped abruptly. Daina's pole bent double in what was now a standoff. Just as suddenly the trout broke again, this time, toward her.

"Reel in!" I shouted.

Too late. Her line went slack, the fish jumped again, and with a flick of its head tossed the barbless hook.

"Oh, damn! I lost it. Did you see him? Wasn't he gorgeous? Those colors, my God. That was my first wild trout."

"Congratulations. That was a beautiful fish—fifteen, sixteen inches, easy. You hooked him on a good cast, and he gave you a helluva fight. Doesn't get much better than that."

"Thanks," she said, as she worked her way further upstream and began casting again. I was about to leave her to check on Streeter and Hannon when she said over her shoulder, "Somehow I get the impression this isn't your full-time job. What do you do when you're not guiding, Cal?"

I shrugged. "I'm a small-town lawyer who'd rather fish than practice law."

"I'll bet the story's more complicated than that." Her eyes were now studying me.

I laughed. "You're right about complicated, but long, too. The fish are biting, so my advice is to keep moving up this seam to the point. There should be plenty more action up ahead. Meanwhile, I need to check on your colleagues."

I spotted Streeter fifty yards downriver. He was working close to the bank in hip-deep water. I stopped behind him on the trail and watched him fish, thinking of water buffalo. He was nearly up to a hackberry tree whose branches formed a sizeable patch of shaded water. I knew there'd be at least one big redside feeding there.

He moved within range and squared up to cast. *Don't hang it in that hackberry*, I said to myself. But his cast was too strong, and disaster struck.

"Goddamn son of a bitch!" Streeter bellowed as his fly flew smack into the hackberry branches. "You dumb bastard," he screamed at himself, while frantically yanking on his line to free the fly. I was a good distance back, but I could see that the back of his neck was already beet-red with rage.

"Hang on, Andrew," I called out. "Let me give you a hand."

I slipped into the river and worked my way out to a spot directly below the snagged lure. Just managing to reach some leaves on the involved branch, I gently pulled it down and unhooked the fly, which now looked more like a plucked chicken than a salmon fly. I took his line in closer to the bank where the footing was firm and tied on another fly.

"You're good to go," I told him, tossing his new fly into the water.

He grunted something and started moving upriver, his face flushed and drenched with sweat. I found myself wondering about his blood pressure. It wasn't until I was halfway down to Hannon that I realized Streeter hadn't bothered to thank me.

I found Hannon working a stretch of deep water. As I approached, he snapped off a beautiful cast that took his fly out forty-five feet before dropping it on the river as softly as a flower petal. In the flick of an eye it vanished from the surface.

"Gotcha," he said as he expertly set the hook and brought the tip of his rod up. After a lengthy fight, he had the fish in front of him. Clamping his pole under his right arm, he reached down to release it. The trout still had plenty of fight in him and began to thrash about wildly. I smiled when it splashed him directly in the face, Top Gun aviator glasses and all. But my smile vanished at what happened next. Hannon reached down and grabbed the fish with his left hand and the nylon leader with his right. He yanked hard. The hook tore free and blood spurted from the fish's mouth.

"Hey! What the hell are you doing?" I yelled as I charged down the bank toward him with my fists clenched.

Hannon turned toward me and removed his glasses. He looked surprised for a moment, then defiant.

"Don't *ever* do that to a fish in this river!"

"Ease up, man. The little bastard splashed me. Whataya expect?"

I was aware this was Philip's paying customer, but I didn't care. "Listen, Hannon," I said, looking straight into his squinting eyes, "if you do that again on this trip you'll walk home."

"Okay, okay. You know damn well one dead trout isn't going to tip the ecological balance on this river, so cut me some slack." His smirk was intended to show he wasn't intimidated by my threat.

I turned on my heels and headed back toward the boat without saying another word. I knew Hannon's type. To him, catching a fish was an act of dominance, something to tally, stuff, and hang on the wall. It was the same mentality that led to shooting polar bears from helicopters or hunting cougars with dogs. I owed it to Philip to make nice with this guy, so I kept my mouth shut.

What a bunch of creeps, I muttered to myself as I walked away, wondering if Philip had fared any better that morning.

Chapter Six

I got the silent treatment the rest of the morning from Hannon, which was fine with me. He must have said something to Streeter at lunch, because after that neither of them said a word to me. Phillip had been right when he'd quipped over a beer one day that "being a fishing guide would be great if it weren't for the clients."

It was well past six when we stopped fishing for the day and headed for camp. The wind that had blown steadily all afternoon now swirled upstream in short bursts that danced along the surface in rippling bands like schools of fish on the run. The river, like a moving oasis, cut a lush, green swath through the arid terrain, and the Mutton Mountains closed in to form the deep canyon that would tower above us for the next thirty-five miles.

We swung around a broad bend in the river and caught a first glimpse of our campsite. Named Whiskey Dick after an early fishing guide who lived on the river for better than twenty years, the flat area is dotted with cottonwoods and junipers, sage, and mesquite. Sought after by those who know the river, it is spacious and even boasts a solar-powered chemical toilet, compliments of the eco-friendly state of Oregon. The only drawback is its proximity to a train switching area located about a quarter mile upstream. On most nights, this meant more than the usual train noise.

We'd arrived before Philip, but I saw our raft tied off at the bank. Blake stood next to the stack of bright orange boat bags we'd packed that morning.

I quickly squared away my gear and headed toward the train tracks that parallel the river behind the camp, at the top of a steep, scree-covered bank. This was the last spot with cell phone service before we plunged further into the canyon. I scrabbled up, keeping a sharp eye out for Pacific rattlers on the warm rocks. I checked my messages first. None from Claire. *Damn!* I fought back the disappointment. It was nearly 6:30, and I decided to call Chad Harrelson on the off chance he'd heard something but hadn't gotten back to me. He didn't answer so I left a message.

I sat on the tracks and looked down at the river with my chin resting on my knuckles. The wind had completely died, and the river looked like a band of freshly polished silver in the afternoon light. I hardly noticed. This trip—the fishing, the whole thing—suddenly seemed trivial and silly, and the thought of trying to be courteous and helpful to Philip's clients loomed as an impossible task. I hoped, for Philip's sake, that I'd find the energy and civility to see it through. After a few minutes of staring off across the river, I suddenly noticed that the entire NanoTech group was standing in the camp looking up at me.

"Hey, Claxton," Bruckner called, "Can you call out from there?"

"Yeah."

The group scrambled up the bank, and in no time they were spread out along the tracks dialing and chatting away on their smart devices. That is, with the exception of Streeter, who was using a dumb phone like mine. Whataya know, I said to myself, a high flying executive who's as cheap as me.

I climbed back down to where Philip and Blake were preparing dinner. Philip nodded toward the river. "We've got this under control, Cal. Go catch some fish. There's some good water downstream."

Part of the deal when I agreed to help my friend guide during the salmon fly hatch was that I'd get some personal time to fish. But I was in no mood for it. "Thanks, but I'll pass. Maybe I'll hit it tomorrow morning, early. Give me a job."

After listening to their messages and making their calls, our clients gathered around a long table that served as a bar.

Expensive Oregon and California wines, twelve-year-old scotch, and Portland micro-brews flowed along with raucous tales of the day's exploits.

During a lull in the fish stories, Hannon turned to Bruckner. "I saw you setting up a cot down by the bank. Looks like you're sleeping under the stars tonight, while Alexis gets the tent. This wouldn't have anything to do with your legendary snoring, would it?"

Daina took a sip of her drink, and Pitman and Streeter laughed nervously. They seemed wary of Hannon's cheeky comment, as if he were close to crossing some line.

"Snoring?" a deadpan Bruckner replied. "Actually, Alexis begged me to sleep in the tent in case something wild happens by during the night, but I love to sleep outside. How else am I to enjoy the stars and the sound of the river?"

At this point Alexis joined the group. The last to ring off up on the tracks, she'd been preening in her tent. She wore fresh makeup and tight, low-rider jeans, a scoop-neck turquoise sweater, and a pair of expensive camp slippers. "Begged?" she said with half a smile. "The only begging I did was for you not to drink too much tonight, dear. I'm afraid you'll fall in the river during the night."

The smile on Bruckner's face cracked, and an awkward silence fell over the group. The sound of the river suddenly seemed much louder. Finally Daina broke the silence. "Cal, why do they call those disgusting critters salmon flies, anyway?"

I looked up from peeling potatoes, swiped my knife clean, and held it up by the blade. A gift from Claire for my last birthday, the clear plastic knife handle had a full-size salmon fly encased in it, like a bug suspended in amber. "It's probably because salmon love them for dinner, but maybe it's for the two rings around the neck—they're bright salmon pink. You can see it here." I pointed to the handle.

The group gathered around for a closer look. "Oh, I see what you mean. Two perfect salmon colored necklaces," Daina said. "And look at those wings. They run the length of its body."

Even Alexis was impressed. "My God, those wings are beautiful. They look like stained glass in an old cathedral."

This broke the tension, and soon the group was back to fish stories.

After a dinner of pan-seared steaks, sautéed potatoes and mushrooms, stir-fried veggies, Caesar salad, and steaming homemade biscuits, Bruckner tapped his wineglass with his fork. Philip, Blake, and I were busy cleaning up, and my fellow guides were oblivious to what was playing out at the dinner table. I stayed alert to what was going on, curious to see what kind of team-building could possibly go on with this group.

"Folks," Bruckner said, "can I have your attention?"

Pitman sighed like he'd just been asked to give two pints of blood. Streeter shot a glance at Hannon, and they both rolled their eyes.

This should be interesting, I said to myself.

Chapter Seven

The sky had turned deep lavender, and a cool breeze sifted through the trees in the camp. The canyon rose above us, its western rim traced razor sharp by the sun's afterglow. The lower slopes, green with spring grass, led the eye up to a line of massive basalt outcroppings that reminded me of the abandoned dwellings of some long-forgotten cliff people. I was clearing the table as Bruckner began to speak to the group, which had gathered around a blazing fire in the ring.

Like servants everywhere, I'd become invisible to the group.

"You all know," Bruckner began, "that NanoTech has grown exponentially over the last couple of years. Revenues doubled in the last year alone. The impact of the Diamond Wire Project will sharply accelerate this trend. We're at a crossroads, folks. The high tech industry's cluttered with companies that have failed, because they didn't know how to manage their growth. I don't want this to happen to NanoTech. This company needs to transition from an entrepreneurial, seat-of-the-pants company to one that's well organized and well managed.

"Sorta like goin' from an oily machine to a well-oiled machine," Streeter said.

"You could put it that way, Andrew," Bruckner replied above a patter of laughter, attempting to hold the serious mood. "And you also know that I've asked Daina and her company, Accelerated Management Development, to come on board to help us make that transition. I'd like to turn it over to her now for a little after-dinner exercise. Daina?"

As Daina stood to address the group, Hannon crossed his arms, Streeter leaned back in his chair and looked up at the darkening sky, and Pitman stared impassively into the fire as if she weren't there. Alexis didn't move. I couldn't see her face since she'd moved her chair just outside the light thrown by the fire, in apparent recognition of the fact that she wasn't a part of the management team.

"Thank you, Hal. I like Andrew's metaphor. What we're after here is a well-oiled *management* machine." She paused as if searching for the right words, but I was sure she knew exactly where she was going. "A basic premise of the AMD approach is that development of management skills can be *accelerated* by identifying and proactively dealing with the issues that exist between management and employees at all levels in the organization. To this end, we've been interviewing people across your company. But tonight I'd like to focus on *this* group, the top management team."

"Gulp," said Streeter in mock horror, "I knew there was no such thing as a free fishin' trip."

"Uh oh," Pitman chimed in.

"Why us?" Hannon said, not bothering to hide his annoyance. "We know where the management problems are. All we need to do is clean out the deadwood."

"Stay with me," Daina said, raising her hand, palm out. "Remember, good management starts at the top." She smiled. "I'm sensing some tension in this group. So to get started, let's try to relax a bit."

I watched in the darkness as Daina led the group through an exercise consisting of tensing and then relaxing every major muscle group in their bodies. Daina's dark eyes glowed in the firelight. Her voice was soft and soothing, and above the river noise, almost hypnotic. Before I knew it, I had gone from being a covert observer to a participant. Given the situation with Claire, I needed some relaxation.

Daina gently brought the group back. "Okay, I think we're ready to proceed now. One of the keys to good management is getting the issues between people out in the open. Issues can't be dealt with until they're identified. The next exercise is designed to do just that. We call it speaking truth to power."

I listened with interest as she explained. Members of the management team were encouraged to raise any issue or complaint they had with the boss, Hal Bruckner. The only catch was that they had to mention something *positive* about him first. Bruckner's job was to listen and then repeat as closely as possible what he'd heard. That was it. Any follow-up as a result of the session, I assumed, was up to the individuals involved.

Daina had Bruckner move his seat to the center of the circle, and then she placed an empty chair in front of him. The group fell silent. Nobody moved.

After a long pause, Duane Pitman sighed, hauled his long frame out of his chair, and sat down in front of Bruckner.

Go ahead, Duane," Daina urged in a soft tone.

"Hal," he finally began, "you and me, we go way back—all the way to grad school at U-Dub. I've always admired your business savvy, your guts, really. You've never been afraid to make the tough calls. But, damn it, I'll say it—I'm *angry* that you and the rest of this so-called management team fail to recognize the value of my technical contributions to the business." By this time, Pitman was leaning forward, glaring at Bruckner. "I deserve the same treatment as anyone else in this group."

Bruckner's eyebrows lifted, and his body stiffened as if Pitman's words were striking blows. "That's not—"

Daina, who was standing behind Pitman, cut Bruckner off. "Remember the rules, Hal." She held up an index finger. "Just repeat what you heard Duane say, and shake hands. This is about *listening* to what people have to say to you, Hal."

Bruckner reluctantly responded, although it took him a couple of tries before he was able to accurately summarize Pitman's words. The tension in the circle was now palpable.

"Thank you, Duane," Daina said. "Who wants to go next?"

There was another long pause. Finally Mitch Hannon said, "What the hell," and took the seat in front of Bruckner.

"*Et tu, Brute?*" Bruckner said with a forced smile.

Hannon gave him a look that said he hadn't read much Shakespeare. "Hal," he began, "I'm frustrated by your lack—"

"Remember, Mitch," Daina interrupted, "you need to start off with something positive."

"Oh yeah," Hannon responded. "I forgot." Clearing his throat, he began again. "Hal, I, uh, think you've done a good job of starting up and bringing the company along, but I'm frustrated with the pace. We've talked about this before, and I know she's your baby, but I think you're holding us down. We're ready for the NASDAQ *right now*. We're sitting on a platinum mine."

Bruckner struggled to maintain a neutral expression as his face tightened. He obviously wasn't used to this level of honesty, particularly in front of his entire management team. He managed to roughly paraphrase what Hannon had said, they shook hands, and Hannon sat back down.

Andrew Streeter followed Hannon. Streeter pretty much echoed what Hannon had said, although he tried to be more diplomatic. When he'd finished I noticed he glanced over at Hannon, who gave him an approving look. *More data on the pecking order*, I thought to myself. Streeter is Hannon's yes man. By the time Streeter finished, Bruckner's expression had relaxed, but his eyes were hard and flat.

Seemingly unfazed, Daina picked up the empty chair and put it in front of Mitch Hannon, whose body recoiled involuntarily at the act. "Okay," she said cheerily, "who would like to speak truth to Mitch?"

The tension spiked again when Pitman immediately sat down in front of Hannon. He glanced over at Daina, who nodded encouragement. "Mitch, you, uh, do a good job of managing the sales and marketing group."

"Thank you," Mitch responded, a wary look on his face.

"But I resent very much your opposition to my last budget proposal. With all due respect, I think you simply don't understand the nature of technical work nor do you have a clue about the resources required to carry out world-class research and development in the high-tech arena."

Before Hannon could respond, Streeter said, "Hah," in a derisive tone.

Pitman shot him a withering glance, and Daina put up her hand. "Please, Andrew. Let them continue. Now, go ahead, Mitch. Just repeat what Duane said. Show him you heard what he said."

Hannon looked at Daina and said, "Why should I have to repeat something I don't agree with?"

Bruckner jumped in. "Mitch, knock it off. Everyone's playing by Daina's rules tonight, even you."

"Daina's rules are a load of touchy-feely crap," Hannon shot back.

Bruckner glared at him and repeated, "Play by the rules, Mitch."

Hannon expelled breath through pursed lips and managed to summarize Pitman's compliment, but he stumbled on the part about his lack of support on the budget. Daina intervened again, asking Pitman to repeat what he'd said. Finally Hannon got it right, and the two reluctantly shook hands.

It went on like this until most of the substantive issues and petty gripes between members of the management team had been flushed out. I had to hand it to Daina. The process was bold and innovative. On the other hand, it was apparent the fissures ran deep in this group. Maybe Daina hadn't realized just how deep.

Chapter Eight

As the group was breaking up to go to the tents, Philip stepped out of the shadows. "Folks, don't be surprised if you hear train noises tonight. We're about a hundred yards from a Barlow Northern switching area."

"What do they do way out here?" Alexis asked.

"Oh, they pull onto the siding to let other trains go by. They drop or add cars. It can get pretty noisy, I'm afraid."

"It's all part of the romance of the place," Bruckner said. "I'll find it as relaxing as the river sounds."

Pitman groaned, and Hannon said, "Right."

Good nights were said, and, flashlights in hand, the group wandered off in the direction of the tents. I went down to the river with a cup of water and my toothbrush. While I was brushing my teeth, I thought about the NanoTech top management team. No question, Bruckner and Daina had their work cut out for them. Greed, ambition, jealousy—just one big, happy family.

The camp had grown dark except for the soft yellow glow from the tents strung in an irregular row downstream of the cooking area. I could hear the soft murmur of voices above the river babble and smell the faint odor of sage on the breeze. Philip, Blake, and I opted to sleep under the stars like Bruckner, although we put our sleeping bags upriver of the campfire to afford our clients maximum privacy. I hadn't brought a flashlight, so I was moving slowly toward my sleeping bag when I heard voices in a near whisper off to my left. I recognized one of the voices. Curious, I stopped, stepped off the trail into the deep shadows, and listened.

"...Oh my, I can feel your enthusiasm already. Come to my tent tonight. I'll leave it unzipped. Just wait until you hear Hal snoring."

"Uh, not a good idea, Alexis. Let's cool it tonight."

Then I heard the heavy nasal breathing and soft groaning of a kiss in progress.

Through the tree branches I could just make out the shadowy outline of two people embracing. Then one broke free, and headed toward the tents. It was Alexis. The other shadow stood motionless until Alexis reached her tent and then started off. I lost the figure in the dark, then picked it up again just as it entered the tent this side of the Bruckner's. Mitch Hannon's tent.

I headed off down the path. I almost laughed out loud when I realized I was actually feeling a pang of, what, *jealousy*? I shook it off. Ah, the male ego, I thought—I don't want her, but you can't have her. I wasn't that surprised Mitch Hannon was sneaking around with his uncle's wife. Alexis and Hannon? A match made somewhere, but definitely not in heaven.

When I reached my cot I realized I'd left my fleece jacket on the chair back at the fire. It was getting cold, and I knew I'd need it in the morning. I groaned and retraced my steps. Only a few fading embers remained in the fire ring, and in the near darkness I couldn't find the jacket. Since Philip and Blake had moved the chairs after the evening session I didn't think much of it.

By the time I crawled into my sleeping bag, I could hear both Blake and Philip—who had set up their bunks down closer to the river—in a duet of soft snoring. I rummaged through my bag for a wool sweater, slipped it on and crawled into my sleeping bag. There was no moon and the stars hung in the soft glow of the Milky Way like luminous saucers. A meteor burned white hot across the sky, faded to red, and disappeared just as I fell into sleep.

It must have been three hours later when the train noises Philip had warned about woke me. I lay there listening to the sounds and wondering who else was awakened by the keening of steel on steel and the screech of hydraulic brakes. The noises finally subsided, and as I was spiraling back into an alpha state, I heard the snap of a single dry branch. I awoke instantly. I'm still not sure why. Maybe it was the sense I had that the branch had been crushed under someone's foot.

The sound seemed to come from the direction of the switching area, although I wasn't sure, and it seemed so vivid that I ruled out a dream. An animal? Maybe, but the critters that prowl campsites are known for their stealth.

I lay there listening but heard nothing else except the river noise and the breeze ruffling the cottonwood branches. As I drifted back into sleep I thought I could hear the sound of two trains receding into the distance in opposite directions.

Chapter Nine

I awoke the next morning feeling like I'd just surfaced from a deep dive in a dark ocean. I pressed the stem on my watch to illuminate the face. It was 5:08. The stars that burned so fiercely in the night sky had withered to faint points, and the sun cowered somewhere behind the rim of the canyon. It was shivery cold, and I was groggy from a night of fitful sleep from the noise of the passing freights. For the first time in my life I considered going back to sleep rather than getting up to fish. But I'd had worse nights and fished in colder weather. This is the salmon fly hatch, I reminded myself, as I groaned and crawled out of my sleeping bag.

I sat down on a stump, pulled on my waders and boots, and put my fishing vest on over the thick wool sweater I'd slept in. My fly rod leaned against the mesquite bush with a fly already tied to the leader, ready to go. Everything in camp seemed in order, and as I started out I felt better. It looked like a morning of good fishing.

I followed a narrow path that ran through the saw grass, mock orange, and water hemlock along the river. I planned to go downstream and fish my way back in order to be in time for breakfast. A thin gauze of clouds had formed, promising to diminish the morning sunlight. I shivered at the thought of entering the frigid water and envied our clients, who would awaken to the smell of fresh-brewed coffee and sizzling bacon.

I cut over to the bank and, using my wading stick for balance, entered the river next to a jagged, bleached out snag. The air was still and laced with the smell of wet vegetation and dank earth. I turned to face the current and surveyed it silently for break-fasting fish. A low alder leaned out over the water, its exposed roots clutching the bank like bony fingers. The light was low, the water dark, but under the branches I spotted a spreading set of rings. I moved closer, and the trout rolled again in the center of the rings. I heard the flick of its tail and saw the faint flash of its underbelly. I felt better instantly. This is what I got up for.

My pulse quickened as I let my line trail out in the current behind me. Worried about snagging my fly in the alder branches, I side-armed my first cast. It had the right distance but went wide of the spot where the trout had rolled. My second cast put the fly in under the branches and directly upriver of the feed-ing fish by about ten feet. It gently settled on the water among several coils of leader and began to drift toward me without the slightest wake, mimicking a salmon fly that had surrendered to the river. Philip would be proud. It was what he liked to call a dead float, and it was a perfect one. I tensed, knowing a drift like that promised action.

I saw a flash of silver first, then the arc of its back as the big redside ripped the fly from the surface and then dove back toward the bottom like a submarine. My rod wrenched double, and line stripped off my reel at a furious rate. I turned to face the fish and nearly lost my balance on the slick rocks as I brought my pole tip up and pulled back hard on the line. Violently shak-ing its head to throw the hook, the fish came up in a geyser of spray and iridescent color, up, up until it was completely out of the water. Then it ran toward the center of the river where the swifter current magnified its considerable strength. Fearing the leader would snap, I let the fish take more line.

As I waited for the trout to make its next move, I heard the first scream. It was just audible over the river noise and seemed to come from the direction of camp. The sound was high-pitched. My first thought was a cougar. I froze in the current, straining to hear. Then I heard a second, louder scream. That was no cougar, that was a woman! Then a man's voice cried out, "Oh, my God! Oh, my God!"

My line went slack, and the trout slipped the hook in an instant. I hardly noticed as I waded to the bank and took off up the trail as fast as my wading boots would allow. Approaching camp, I saw Philip trotting toward our clients, who'd gathered in a tight knot near the riverbank. They had their backs to me, staring at something.

"Philip," I called out, "what's wrong?"

He stopped, spun around, and cried, "Cal, it's Bruckner. For Christ's sake, get over here!"

Chapter Ten

I joined Philip, and together we moved around the others. What I saw next will stay with me as long as I live. Hal Bruckner lay on his back, snuggly zipped into his sleeping bag, his arms dangling on either side and his head tilted back, as if he were gazing at the sky. I stepped up for a closer look as flies buzzed excitedly around his face. His eyes, vacant and opaque, were frozen in a look of terror, and his mouth raged in a silent scream. His throat was gone, utterly, slashed through to the vertebra and open like a bloody mouth. The visage staggered me like a blow to the body, and as I reeled backward my boots squished in the blood, quarts of it, surrounding his body.

I steadied myself and fought back a gush of bile in my throat and an overwhelming sense of disbelief. Someone needed to take charge, and I guessed it would have to be me. "Uh, folks, you need to get back. This is a crime scene. Please get back, and for God's sake don't touch anything in camp. Philip, we need to get the sheriff in here right away."

Philip was already headed for the tracks on a trot. "Right," he called back over his shoulder.

I moved the group over to the breakfast area. Daina was tending to Alexis, who by this time had gone from wailing to sobbing and repeating, "No, no, no." Daina, ashen-faced but dry-eyed, was speaking softly to Alexis and stroking her hair. Hannon, Streeter, and Pitman stood in a circle talking in hushed tones. Blake stood off by himself studying his boots.

It would take some time for the sheriff to arrive, so I decided to have a look around. I went back to the body first. Flies swarmed, and the coppery smell of blood hung in the air. I moved around the cot carefully, looking for anything, but most particularly a murder weapon. Nothing. The campsite was bounded on the east by the river and on the west by the railroad tracks. I walked from the cot over to the solar toilet located below the tracks on the south boundary of the camp without noting anything unusual. I opened the door to the toilet, and although the smell turned my already queasy stomach, nothing was out of place. I headed from the toilet toward the riverbank, scanning the brush and stony terrain. I stopped at a narrow path on my left that cut through the shin-high thistle grass toward the railroad switching area, located a hundred yards upstream around a sharp curve. The path began about halfway between the toilet and the riverbank.

I stood there for a moment thinking about the sound of snapping wood that awakened me the night before. Then I continued over to the riverbank where our two float boats and the raft were moored. As far as I could see, nothing had been disturbed. I walked another sixty feet upriver to where Philip, Blake, and I had slept. Our cots were probably ten feet apart, and mine was separated from theirs by a large mesquite bush.

I sat down on my cot and held my head in my hands. I craved a cup of coffee, and the lack of caffeine was giving me a headache. I tried to recall details from the night before. After brushing my teeth, I had overheard the exchange between Alexis and Hannon. By that time the rest of the party had retired. Streeter was in the tent closest to the campfire. I remember seeing his light through the tent wall. Pitman was in the second tent, Daina in the third. Hannon was next, with Alexis in the final tent. Bruckner was sleeping on the riverbank about fifty feet directly across from Alexis' tent. When I finally turned in, the camp was dark and, except for the snoring of Blake and Philip, silent.

The train noise began around 1:30—I remember checking my watch—and lasted until around two or so.

I started up the path toward the campfire. Philip was spooning ground coffee into the top of a big, soot-stained pot that was heating on a propane burner.

"Figured we could use some coffee," he said without looking up.

"You figured right, my friend. How are Alexis and the rest of the crew holding up?"

"Okay, I guess. I don't think reality has sunk in yet."

"You guys hear or see anything last night?"

"Nothin' at all, not even the trains," Philip replied, looking up for the first time.

Blake nodded in agreement.

"You sure?" I persisted. "*Anything.*"

Blake shifted in his seat. "Well, I did see somebody go back up to the tracks after we turned in. Saw the flashlight. Figured somebody making a last phone call."

"Did you see which tent the person came from?"

"No. I really couldn't tell."

"What about the kitchen knives?" I continued, pointing in the direction of the table where I'd left them to dry with all the other utensils the night before.

"All present and accounted for," Philip answered. "So, what do you make of this, Cal? Some maniac passing through, or do we have a slasher in our happy little group?"

"Well, most people are murdered by people they know, but who knows what happened here? In any case, whoever did it didn't leave the murder weapon lying around."

"Probably in the river," Philip replied, glancing out at the water. He scratched the side of his face and flicked a salmon fly off his forearm. "You know, if somebody tossed the weapon out there it would be fairly easy to find."

"How's that?"

"The gravel bar. The knife would be sitting out there. Easy to spot by a diver."

"Good thinking, Sherlock. Hold that thought for the sheriff. You're an expert tracker, right?"

"Yep. Learned from the best. My granddad."

"You know the path leading over to the switching area?"

"Yeah."

"Do me a favor. Go over there and check it out. Tell me if anyone was on it last night."

"Why?"

"I thought I heard something last night is all. Could've been a dream. I'm not sure."

"Heard what?"

"A twig or a branch snapping. It woke me right up."

"Hmm," Philip said as he finished loading the coffee, "I'll have a look."

Philip was heading off in the direction of the path when Mitch Hannon called me over to where he, Streeter, and Pitman were huddled. As I approached them, Hannon said, "Where the hell's the sheriff, Claxton?"

"On the way." I glanced at my watch. "Another thirty minutes, maybe. They're coming from Madras."

"You see anything in your little walkabout?" Hannon continued.

"Nope. Not a thing. Did you guys hear or see anything unusual last night?"

"We've already compared notes," Hannon replied.

"Nothing but the trains," Pitman said.

"What about you, the chief, and boat boy?" Hannon asked.

Hannon's tone was getting on my nerves, but I ignored it. "Same with us." Then I added, "Which one of you made a call last night after everyone had turned in?"

All three of them looked up at me, but no one said a word.

"Blake saw someone with a flashlight go up the hill after we turned in. Thought maybe it was one of you. Guess not." I excused myself and walked over to Alexis and Daina. I knelt down on one knee in front of them.

Daina was still comforting Alexis, who continued to sob with her head down. Before I could speak, Daina said, "Calvin, who could have done something so horrible?"

"I don't know. Did you hear or see anything unusual last night?"

"No. Not a thing. Not even the trains. I'm a sound sleeper."

"You make a call after we all turned in?"

"No."

"How about you, Alexis?" I said as gently as I could. Her eyes were red and swollen. I was struck by the fact that she looked older, much older in the morning light. I realized it was the wrinkles around her eyes, revealed by a lack of makeup.

"I didn't make any calls, and I didn't hear anything except the train noises," she answered. Then she looked up at me. "His bracelet's gone."

"What bracelet?"

"The gold one. The one I gave him in Maui."

"I see. Be sure to tell the investigators about that."

I went back over to the campfire to check the coffee. Blake had already taken it off the burner and poured himself a cup. He was sitting there cradling it in his hands. I did the same and sat down next to him. The coffee was warm and familiar in my hands, and the first sip soothed every cell in my body. The second sip was even better. We sat there drinking without talking until Philip came back. He poured himself a cup and sat down with a heavy sigh.

I waited for him to speak and finally said, "So?"

"You were right. Someone walked that trail last night. Matter of fact, halfway in he stepped off the trail and took a leak."

Chapter Eleven

I set my coffee down and stood up to face Philip. "You're sure?"

"Yep. The spring grass where he stepped hasn't recovered yet. And the pissed-on area was still damp. Had to have been last night."

After another maddening pause, I asked, "Anything else?" I kept my tone patient. I knew better than to rush my laconic friend.

"Uh, yeah. The tracks go both ways."

"Meaning?"

"Meaning someone walked in here from the switching area and then walked back. Or vice versa, I suppose."

"Did you see anything at the other end, at the switching area?"

"No. The area's all gravel and rocks. Lost the trail immediately. But I didn't have time to really give it a careful going-over."

"Any idea what the train was doing over there last night?"

"I think it was two trains coming in opposite directions."

"That happens?" I said, a little surprised.

"Sure. One pulls off on the siding while the other goes by. Last night it sounded to me like they both stopped, so maybe they switched some cars as well. That would explain why it took so long."

"You may be right, Philip. I remember thinking I heard trains going in opposite directions just before I fell back to sleep."

I looked up in the direction of the dirt road on the other side of the railroad tracks. A patrol car, an ambulance, a van, and an unmarked sedan came around the bend. The patrol car had its emergency lights on but wasn't using its siren.

"Looks like they brought half of Madras," Blake said.

We all gathered at the base of the hill and watched them work their way down to the campground. There were two uniformed officers, two detectives in shirts and ties, two crime-scene technicians in white smocks, and a man in a rumpled suit who got out of the ambulance with the driver. I assumed he was the medical examiner.

The lead detective quickly introduced himself and his team. His name was Vincent Escalante. Strikingly well-groomed, with short-cropped black hair and a neatly trimmed mustache, the guy looked like he just stepped out of the shower. His brown eyes were deep set and moved quickly as he talked. His partner, William Dorn, looked more like an ex-linebacker for the Green Bay Packers. With slabs for shoulders, a barrel neck, and huge, gnarled hands, he probably had ten years on Escalante. Dorn didn't say much, seeming to prefer grunts to words.

The ME and the forensic technicians quickly set to work on the blood-soaked area near the body. The two detectives spent fifteen minutes or so checking out the immediate crime scene and then dispatched the two uniformed deputies to begin searching the campground, much as I had done. They then announced they were going to interview each one of us separately. Setting up three camp chairs in the shade, they began the questioning with Philip. The rest of us were requested to remain at the table near the campfire.

It was then I began to wonder about the whereabouts of two items—my knife and my jacket. I can't tell you what triggered the thoughts. They just popped into my head. I'd left my jacket on the back of a chair, and I'd used my fishing knife to peel potatoes. I was pretty sure I'd left the knife on the fold-out table where the utensils were stored. Philip had told me none of the knives were missing. But would he have missed mine? Probably not. I got up and casually walked over to where the kitchen utensils had been left the night before. My knife wasn't there.

I still hadn't seen my jacket, either. "You see my North Face jacket, the blue one? I asked Blake. "I left it on one of these chairs last night."

"No, Cal, I haven't."

I was in an unsettled state when Escalante called my name. I sat down and faced the two detectives, telling myself I had nothing to hide and nothing to worry about.

"So, Mr. Claxton, I understand you were the take-charge guy this morning? Do you have a background in law enforcement?" His smile was affable, but his eyes were like brown lasers.

"I was a Deputy DA for the city of Los Angeles. I did mainly prosecution of felony cases."

"I see," Escalante answered as he glanced at his partner.

Dorn grunted. "Well, don't be surprised if we do things a little differently out here."

Escalante did most of the talking, and his questions were more or less what I expected. It took only about fifteen minutes for me to lay out everything I knew. I mentioned the tracks that Philip had picked up on the trail to the switching area. Escalante seemed mildly interested and said they would follow up after they finished the preliminary interviews. I could understand his lack of enthusiasm. He knew that the odds were high that someone in our group had done the deed. He didn't want any distractions.

Since Escalante didn't ask if I actually knew any of the clients, I decided not to reveal that I'd had an affair with the victim's wife. However, I knew that I'd have to own up to that uncomfortable fact, probably in the next round of questioning. After all, there were plenty of phone records that would link Alexis and me. What would she decide to say, I wondered? It wouldn't look good if she told them about the affair, and I had neglected to mention it at this juncture. The thought caused my already sour stomach to ball into a tight fist.

By this time, the entire campground had been cordoned off with yellow crime-scene tape. Everyone averted their eyes when Bruckner was zipped into a body bag. I was encouraged to see that after Philip's interview, Dorn, Escalante, and the forensics team followed him over to the path leading to the switching area. The group periodically knelt down as Philip pointed out the tracking evidence. Photos were taken as well. A sample of the soil where Philip noticed the urine was also put in an evidence bag.

When the group returned to the campground, Dorn and Escalante walked over to the spot where Bruckner had been killed and stood looking out at the river. Dorn lit up a cigarette while they talked with their backs to us. A couple of salmon flies darted through the smoke as it drifted downriver. Then Escalante placed a call on his cell. I caught just enough of the conversation to know he'd requested a team of divers to search the gravel bar for the murder weapon.

I stood there listening to the blood pounding in my ears. I reminded myself I was an innocent man. And then I reminded myself again. But I couldn't shake this feeling—like watching a big, silent thunderhead boil up just before the hail cuts loose.

Chapter Twelve

When the interviews were finished, Philip laid out some fruit and crackers for the group to nibble on, but nobody touched the food. Alexis was calmer now and managed to take a few sips of bottled water. But as soon as she saw her husband's body being carried up the slope to the ambulance, she broke down again in deep, rhythmic sobs.

Perhaps she'd loved her husband more than I realized, or more likely she was simply reacting to the shock of the murder. Frankly, I felt a sense of relief that I think the others shared when the body was finally out of sight in the ambulance. The bled-out corpse seemed to have no connection to the man we had been with the night before. An assemblage of bones and flesh, its lifeless presence had hung like a huge weight on our psyches.

Our sleeping bags and most of our personal belongings had been placed in evidence bags for screening at the county crime lab. I had nothing left except the clothes on my back and my fly rod. They even impounded my fishing vest. I imagined some fly fisherman in the sheriff's department helping himself to my fly collection.

Around 3:30 Escalante called us together and said we were free to leave the site but warned us not to the leave the Portland area without notifying him or his partner. He also told us we could expect further interviews as the case progressed. As Escalante talked I stood off to the side with my hands propped in the back pockets of my jeans, watching the group. The afternoon was hot and still. The only background noises came from the random slosh of the river and an occasional bird call. Alexis had recovered her composure and was standing between Mitch Hannon and Daina. I thought it likely she would come into a sizeable amount of insurance money. How much? I also wondered about NanoTech. Would she get that too, or had Bruckner made other arrangements in the event of his death?

Hannon stood very close to Alexis, his open hand pressed lightly on the center of her back in a gesture of support. He'd been sleeping with his boss' wife. He also wanted his boss to give up private ownership of the company or, as he called it, the "platinum mine." How much would that enrich him personally?

Standing next to Hannon was Andrew Streeter—a brooding, unpleasant man anxious to please, especially Hannon. Why had he acted so erratically on the river the day before?

Duane Pitman stood apart from the group. Slightly stooped, he looked thin and gaunt, as if the events of the day had weakened him physically. Pitman seemed to admire Bruckner, but at the same time he was mad as hell about not being recognized for his technical contributions to NanoTech. How deep did that anger go?

Then there was the consultant, Daina Zakaris. Bruckner had brought her in to help him smooth out the relationships within his management team—a tough task given the deep divisions that existed between them. She had sensed me watching the group at the restaurant and had figured out I wasn't a full-time guide. And she had instantly concluded Alexis and I had been lovers. I was sure of it. The latter made me nervous, and I wondered what else she might know or suspect.

Since our cars had all been ferried down to the take-out point below Maupin, we had to wait for them to be brought back. Fortunately, Philip had had the foresight to call the ferrying service around midday, and they arrived a little after four. I kept expecting—dreading would be a better word—that the press corps would rear its ugly head, but it never happened. Philip, Blake, and I stood watching as our clients headed off for Portland. Pitman was with Streeter in his Hummer. The behemoth spanned most of the width of the road. Alexis, Daina, and Hannon vanished behind the heavily tinted windows of Hannon's Lexus and sped off into Streeter's dust.

As they rounded the bend, Philip kicked the dirt and sighed. "Shit, this isn't going to be good for business."

Blake nodded his head in agreement, exhaling sharply through his nose.

I said, "Well, there's no need to panic. Just make sure they spell Northwest Experience correctly in the paper, and you'll be fine."

They both chuckled at that.

Philip sighed again and turned to Blake. "Escalante told me we can come back tomorrow afternoon and pick up the boats and the raft, after the divers do their thing. So how about driving my rig back to Madras? You can stay at my place and we can get the boats tomorrow."

As Blake was pulling out in the extended cab, Philip said, "Figured we needed to talk. Did your jacket turn up?"

I shook my head. "Nope. I left it on one of the chairs last night after dinner. I went back to get it, but it was gone.

"That's weird."

I nodded. "There's also a problem with my knife. You know, the one Claire gave me with the salmon fly in the handle."

"Problem?"

"I'm not sure where it is. Thought I left it drying with the other utensils last night. But it wasn't there this morning. I'm hoping I put it back in the boat instead."

"Probably in the boat," Philip responded.

"Uh, and one more thing." I needed to get this behind me. "What's that?"

"I, uh, started seeing Alexis Bruckner after your birthday dinner at the Lyle last fall. It only lasted eight weeks or so, but there it is."

Philip looked at me with an incredulous half smile. "You *what?*

Chapter Thirteen

Philip's half smile crumbled as my confession about Alexis Bruckner sunk in. He exhaled loudly and locked onto my eyes. "Damn it, Cal! I guess I neglected to tell you the first rule in river-guiding—Don't fuck the clients!" He looked away as color rose in his neck. He was pissed. I didn't blame him.

"I wasn't working for you then."

"Well, yeah. I guess you weren't, but who the hell knows that except you and me? No, this isn't going to look good for either one of us. Shit, Cal, she came on to me, too. She's that type."

I looked at him quizzically.

"The type that marries up and fucks down. You know, Lady Chatterley."

I looked away and felt my checks burn as I resisted an urge to swallow.

"So who knows about this affair?"

"Just Alexis and me and now you. Problem is we exchanged several phone calls last fall. When they check, they'll find them."

Philip shook his head, kicked at the dirt with his boot, and said, "What'd you tell 'em this morning?"

"They didn't ask, I didn't tell. But I'll have to come clean next time they interview me."

He shook his head again. "That won't look so good, will it?"

I shrugged. "It is what it is. Look, Philip, I had no business screwing around with one of your clients. It was stupid, and I apologize."

"Accepted," my friend answered in a tone that let me know the beef was over.

Then he added with a sly grin, "Truth is I remember the way she looked at you that night at the Lyle, man. It was lust at first sight."

After a good chuckle, our first of the day, I said, "You know, the best thing that could happen for both of us is for Bruckner's murder to get solved in a hurry. Otherwise, both our livelihoods could take a pounding when this hits in the press. Frankly I don't have a lot of confidence in that Jefferson County team, particularly the big guy, Dorn."

"It's Bull," Philip replied with a wry grin.

"What?"

"Bull. That's his nickname. I heard Escalante call him that."

"That fits."

We sat for a few minutes gazing down at the river in silence. I pulled out my cell phone and redialed Chad Harrelson. He didn't answer, and I left a message for him to call me. I sighed and flipped the phone shut.

Philip read my look and didn't say anything. We both watched as a bald eagle dropped like a dive bomber and took a squirming trout from the river. Finally, Philip said, "So, what do you want to do, partner?"

"For starters, I'd like to go to the switching area and go over it with a fine tooth comb. I'm convinced that's where the killer came from."

"Let's do it."

We drove around the bend in the dirt road and parked adjacent to the switching area. A sign on a tall metal pole next to the tracks said simply, *Kaskela*. We fanned out on either side of the tracks and started working our way back toward the campground.

"What are we looking for?" Philip asked.

"Anything unusual, anything that shouldn't be there."

As we inched our way along, oil and diesel fumes bloomed off the hot gravel, causing my eyes to water. The ground was littered with the usual railroad detritus, rusty spikes and bits of braided cable, spent flares, and the occasional untarnished aluminum beer can. I became discouraged almost immediately but didn't let on. Thirty minutes later, Philip had finished his half of the search. I was nearly done. Neither one of us had found a thing.

Philip had worked his way over to where the trail led off to the campground and with his eyes to the ground started moving down it one more time. Suddenly he bent down and pointed at something in the grass. "Looks like I missed something this morning."

"What?"

"A cigarette butt. Can I pick it up?"

I hesitated for a moment. It was physical evidence, but the area had already been searched and cleared. "Yeah, go ahead. They can get a DNA profile from the urine sample."

Philip picked it up and put his nose to it. "Jeez, smells like camel dung, but it's fresh, probably less than twenty-four hours old. He took several more steps and said, "Here's where he took a leak. Looks like he flicked the butt away while he was peeing."

"Nice work!" I said as I came over to have a look. The filter was still intact and some unburned tobacco was packed in against a ridge of remaining paper. I brought the butt to my nose and smelled it. My head kicked back reflexively. "Camel dung's putting it mildly. People actually smoke this crap? Can't be American tobacco."

We went back to the car, and I carefully wrapped the butt in a tissue and put it in the glove compartment. "So, you think our guy dropped it?"

"My gut says yes. The trailhead's at the northwest corner of the switching area, a good fifteen yards from the tracks, and the urine spot another twenty yards down the trail. It's unlikely the butt was dropped by a railroad worker, but I guess I can't say for sure." He paused again and nodded toward the glove compartment. "You sure we shouldn't give it to Escalante?"

"Nah. We've compromised the chain of possession. Besides, I don't want him to get the impression we're trying to lead him. After all, you already showed him the tracks and all."

"Yeah, and he wasn't very impressed. I think he likes one of our party for the killer. He won't want to hear any phantom of the railway theories."

"You're right. I shudder to think what a good prosecutor would do to your description of how the spring grass was bent but not broken. Good Paiute tracking work but not strong physical evidence in a court of law."

"Figures," Philip answered.

"But we know someone came down that path last night. That's the important thing. And we know he was probably a smoker. That's more than I could have hoped for an hour ago."

We sat in my car for a while, not saying anything. It suddenly occurred to me that my friend had never once questioned my innocence. He'd taken my explanation at face value and had thrown himself into the task of helping me without a word of complaint.

A cool breeze sprang up. Across the river a pinto mare and her colt grazed languidly on the grass that carpeted the slopes running down from the basalt formations. Below, the surface of the Deschutes glittered in the sun's angled rays like a strand of braided gold.

We didn't need to say it. It was a given that we both longed to be down there, wading in that cold, green water, waiting expectantly for the next strike. But the events of the day had pushed that possibility away. It looked like we had a lot of work to do before we would be fishing together again.

Chapter Fourteen

I asked Philip to drive my car as we headed back to Madras so I'd be free to phone Harrelson at Well Spring. He'd left a message for me to call, but no details. The extraordinary events of the day had managed to neutralize my anxiety about Claire, but it was now coming back with a vengeance. I caught him on his commute home.

"Mr. Claxton, thank you for getting back to me. We, uh, still haven't been able to reach your daughter's group. But, again, there's no need to worry. We—"

"No need to worry?" I interrupted. "She's *five* days overdue for our call."

"I understand your concern, Mr. Claxton. We've consulted with the AU, and as a precaution, we're sending a security team in to locate them."

"Who's the AU?"

"The African Union. Actually, our security team is being escorted by Nigerian troops. They're part of the AU's peacekeeping contingent."

"I see. How long will it take for them to get up to northern Darfur?"

"They'll be there tomorrow. Meanwhile, I want to assure you we're doing everything we can to locate your daughter. We have no reason to believe there's anything amiss here. I'll call you tomorrow with any news. Okay?"

No reason, my ass. If there's no issue, why send in a security team? But I held my tongue and instead made him stay on the line as I asked a dozen other questions about the situation. To Harrelson's credit he answered them with more patience than one would expect from someone commuting home in L.A. traffic.

I dropped Philip off at his place, a two-acre spread north of town off Route 97. Although I felt tired and a little light-headed from lack of food, I begged off a dinner invitation from his wife, Lanie. I needed some alone time as well as something to get my mind off Claire. The answer was simple. I'd see what I could learn about the Barlow Northern Railroad's comings and goings, and do it now before the trail, if there was one, went cold.

I stopped at a gas station, filled my tank, then bought a cup of coffee and the last turkey sandwich in the case. I forced the sandwich down, knowing I needed food. The coffee was freshly brewed and was called, appropriately enough, "Fog Cutter." I had two cups.

I got directions to the B-N freight yard, located northwest of town off Route 26. Of course, I had no way of knowing whether the intruder had boarded a northbound train at this point. Nor did I know what in the world I would look for out there. But Route 26 was the most direct route in from Portland, so if the bad guy came in from that direction, the freight yard would be a logical point for him to hop a train for the short ride to the Kaskela switching area. Besides, checking it out would give me something to do in my restless state.

The food and the coffee began to kick in, and as I headed out of town I noticed my surroundings for the first time that day. The air was sparkling with that late, gold-tinged light photographers dream about. The volcanoes dwarfed everything on the horizon. Mount Hood was dead ahead, Jefferson at ten o'clock, Three-Fingers Jack at nine, and the Three Sisters at four.

When I arrived at the freight yard I sat in the small public parking lot for a couple of minutes trying to remember why I had driven all the way out here. The yard went on for what looked like acres. Freight cars and tankers were scattered around, singly and in combinations of various lengths, waiting to be hooked up and hauled off. The place seemed deserted except for someone in a small guard shack that stood next to the main entrance gate.

I finally got out of my car and approached the guard shack. A young man with dirty blond hair and a scraggly mustache sat inside reading beneath a dim bulb. Out in the yard, a crane suddenly sprang to life and began swinging one of the truck trailers onto a flatbed railroad car.

"Hi," I said cheerfully through the open window.

After a long pause, the young man raised his eyes, but not his head, from a wrinkled paperback. "What can I do for you?"

I noticed that he was reading *The Hitch Hiker's Guide to the Galaxy*. "Doug Adams fan, huh?" I nodded in the direction of the paperback.

The man's head came up, and his eyes met mine. "Yeah, man."

"Name's Cal." I extended my hand and smiled. "What's yours?"

"Billy," he replied, shaking my hand indifferently.

"Billy, I'm investigating a death that happened out on the Deschutes last night. Wonder if I could ask you a few questions?"

"Sure. Another drowning?"

"No. A man was murdered."

"Far out. You a cop?"

"No. A lawyer. Were you working here last night, Billy?"

"Sure. I'm here Monday through Friday, four to twelve."

"I see," I replied, trying not to show my disappointment. The intruder could have boarded the train *after* Billy left work. "What time did you leave last night?"

"Three. I covered for Franny Halstead at the last minute."

Relieved, I continued. "A northbound freight came through here last night at 12:30 or so. Right?"

"Right. That would be the 504 heading for The Dalles." His eyes quickly scanned the screen in front of him. "Twelve thirty-two, to be exact."

"Hang on a sec," I said as I took a pen and small notebook from my shirt pocket and jotted the information down. "You see or hear anything unusual around that time? Like maybe someone hopping it?"

"No," he said as he scratched his temple with his index finger. "I wouldn't see anything from in here, and I didn't hear about any hoppers. Usually only hear when somebody gets hurt. It was quiet last night."

"Who would have told you about hoppers?"

"You know, security," he answered.

"Can you give me a name of someone in security I can talk to?"

"Sure." He pulled up another screen and obligingly read off a name and a number that I jotted down.

"How about a second train? I continued. "Was there one coming south on the same tracks?"

"Sure was. That would be the 1520 from Spokane. The 504 lets her pass at Kaskela."

Bingo, I said to myself. "How about that crew in there?" I nodded in the direction of the crane. "Any chance *they* saw something?"

"Nah, they get off at eight. They would've been long gone last night."

I thanked Billy and left. As I was driving back to the highway I noticed some kids skateboarding under the lights in the parking lot of a large warehouse. The loading dock with all its ramps, stairs, and railings provided a challenging set of obstacles. I pulled over and watched for a few minutes, wincing at some of their maneuvers. Then on a whim, I turned into the lot. When they saw me they took off around the building.

I stopped, got out of the car, and yelled, "Hey, guys. It's cool. I'm not a cop! I just want to talk to you about something that happened last night."

They didn't answer, so I followed the four of them around to the side of the warehouse. I guessed they came from the Warm Springs Reservation, which was only a couple of miles up Route 26. I found them sitting under the only light on the side of the building, their skateboards propped next to a row of low-slung dirt bikes. Insects were spiraling in the light, and the air was heavy with the pungent smell of cedar. The warehouse must have been full of raw lumber.

"I saw some pretty awesome moves out there. You guys skate here often?" I began.

No answer.

"Look guys, I'm looking for information about something that happened last night. I was wondering if any of you noticed someone coming down this road last night between, say, ten and twelve? Were you here then?"

After a pause that was so long I was ready to give up, the boy sitting closest to me looked up and said, "So what if we did?" His dark eyes shone in the harsh yellow light, his cheeks were flecked with acne, and the hair on his upper lip looked more like a shadow than a mustache.

"Well, it could be really important. I'm trying to find out who killed someone last night on the river."

The boy who'd spoken up eyed me. "No shit? Someone got murdered?"

"Yes. Did you see someone around here last night?"

Their spokesman said something under his breath that I didn't catch. The others laughed. "What's it worth to you?"

I sensed they knew something, so I didn't hesitate. "Ten bucks a piece, but I don't want any bullshit." To prove good faith, I pulled my wallet from my back pocket, took out two twenty-dollar bills and placed them in my shirt pocket. Then I took out my pen and notebook and knelt down in front of them. "So what'd you see last night?"

"We was sittin' right here havin' a brew." The other boys chuckled at this. "This dude pulls up and parks under those trees across the street, way back where you can't see his car. We're quiet, thinkin' maybe he's a cop or something. He locks up and heads up the road toward the tracks."

"What time was it?"

"About ten-thirty."

"What did he look like?"

"Couldn't see much, man. The dude was pretty tall. Dressed in jeans and a black hoodie."

"Taller than me?"

"Maybe."

"What else did you notice about him?"

"Uh, he had his hood up and was carrying some kind of backpack."

"White guy?"

"Yeah, I think so."

"What kind of car?"

"F-150 pickup, man. Nice ride," he said with a sly smile. The other boys started giggling at this. The boy who was speaking shushed them and dropped the smile.

I probed with several more questions, trying to squeeze out more details. But it was clear that was about all I was going to get, so I handed over the two twenties. I was also pretty sure that the boys had taken the Ford F-150 for a joy ride, but I didn't go down that path for fear of scaring them off. Their spokesman willingly gave me his name, Oliver Dan. I was right, they lived on the rez. My first witnesses.

The impact of the day's events had finally caught up with me. It was all I could do to keep my eyes open and my car on the road. I decided to head back to the motel in Madras rather than press on to Dundee. I was exhausted, but at the same time I felt a flicker of excitement. I was pretty sure I'd figured out how the killer had come and gone at Whiskey Dick, and I had a sketchy description of him. Not a bad evening's work. I would tell Escalante and Dorn about what I'd learned, but I didn't hold out much hope that they'd buy it. I'd worked with a lot of investigators, and I knew they usually took the path of least resistance. I had no reason to think these detectives would be any different.

I thought about that bled-out corpse with the slashed neck and vacant eyes that had been Hal Bruckner. A cold shadow passed over my heart. At the same time, I had a sense of anticipation. It was a little like the feeling I get after a good cast. The fly settles into a dead float, and I wait with the knowledge that something is about to play out.

Chapter Fifteen

The only act I managed to perform before falling into bed back at the motel was to set my alarm for six a.m. I wanted to get an early start back to Dundee. The next morning broke cloudy and decidedly cooler, and when I arrived at Pritchard's Animal Care Center to pick up Archie, a light mist was falling. Pritchard's Saab 900T convertible was parked around back. The classic Saab was in mint condition—the only conspicuous concession to consumerism my friend allowed himself.

Hiram Pritchard was an intellectual, a vegan, and a passionate champion of animal rights. He told me once he'd been thrown out of Johns Hopkins Medical School in his fourth year for an incident involving the "liberation" of some rhesus monkeys being used for medical research, but I never got the whole story. He was tall and lanky with pale, freckled skin, and a receding hairline that served to magnify an already large forehead. He had a long, thin nose and gray eyes that usually twinkled above a crooked, affable smile.

"So, the great white fisherman returns," he said as he opened the door and looked at me above his granny glasses.

I had phoned him that I was picking up Archie early, but I hadn't told him why.

"I trust you didn't torture too many *mykiss iridus* on this trip?"

"If by that mouthful of Latin you're referring to desert red band trout, I'm pleading not guilty. Catch and release, yes. Torture, no."

"Actually," he continued, warming to the task, for my friend loved to argue, "I chose the term *torture* with some care. Did you know that it's been shown *scientifically* that fish feel pain when they're hooked?"

I was thinking about how to respond to this without getting trapped when Archie burst into the room. He was wagging his entire back end, his high pitched yelps reaching the pain threshold. I dropped to one knee and grabbed him in a bear hug while he scrubbed the side of my face with his tongue.

I used Archie's sudden arrival as an excuse to change the subject. I wasn't up to a debate on the cruelties of fishing with my sharp-witted friend. Instead, I filled him in on what had happened on the Deschutes. I left out the parts about the affair with Alexis and my missing knife and jacket. Hiram was shocked by the story and full of questions. I didn't start home with Arch for another hour.

With Arch in the backseat I headed into the Dundee Hills, whose volcanic soils and southern exposures underpinned the local wine industry. After passing several rows of houses with excellent views of the northern valley, I drove through the vineyards that hugged the rolling hills with geometric precision. As I rounded a curve, I caught a glimpse of the ridge where my house stood behind a line of Douglas firs. A glint of white through the trees told me my sanctuary was still standing.

The 1917 farmhouse stood on the south edge of five acres of sloping, tillable land atop the ridge. It was a "Four Square"—four rooms built over four rooms—and was clad with the original shiplap siding and a weather beaten, shingle roof of old-growth cedar. A wide, wraparound porch surrounded the structure like a moat. The only outbuildings were a two-car garage and a small barn housing my twenty-two-horse John Deere and a multitude of gardening tools. A sign with letters deeply carved into a block of red cedar greeted visitors at the gate:

Claxton's Aerie
Welcome

The word *aerie* is Gaelic for fortress on a hill.

◇◇◇

The following Saturday morning Archie and I worked our way down to the mailbox while playing a leisurely game of fetch the tennis ball. News of Hal Bruckner's murder was on the front page of *The Oregonian*. There was a photo of Bruckner and an inset showing a map of the river with an arrow pointing to the Whiskey Dick camping area. The story was sketchy, although the reporter had managed to get all the names of the NanoTech employees on the trip. Detective Escalante was quoted as saying they had no suspects, but several leads were being aggressively followed. If anything had been found in the river, it wasn't mentioned. The story did mention Philip's guide service, Northwest Experience, although no names, including mine, were given.

Like most Australian shepherds, Archie showed no signs whatsoever of tiring of our game, nor was he the least bit concerned that the tennis ball had acquired a thick coating of slobber, dirt, and fir needles. We had just worked our way back up the long drive and through the gate when my cell rang. I gave the ball a final heave and accepted the call.

"Mr. Claxton? This is detective Escalante from the Jefferson County Sheriff's Department."

"Yes, Detective. What can I do for you?"

"We'd, uh, like to talk to you again. There're some loose ends we'd like to clear up."

Chapter Sixteen

Escalante's voice was even, businesslike, and even though I knew the call would come, my gut still tightened at the sound of it.

"Your place or mine?"

"Well, we're conducting some interviews over at Government Camp, the Clackamas County sheriff's substation. Maybe you could meet us there? It's halfway, give or take."

"What time?"

The small village of Government Camp sits at four thousand feet on the southern slope of Mount Hood. I'd passed it countless times on my way to Timberline Lodge to ski. I wished I were headed for a ski trip this time rather than the third degree from a couple of hard-nosed detectives who'd love nothing better than to nail my butt for first-degree murder. I turned the situation over and over again in my mind as I drove toward the mountain. Escalante had been noncommittal, but I was worried that he and Dorn had found something. My knife? The phone calls to Alexis? Both? In any case, they were still treating me like a witness instead of a suspect. For how long?

The sheriff's substation was a low, wood frame building painted institutional green, trimmed in white. A large American flag mounted on a silver pole in front of the building snapped loudly in the afternoon breeze. I arrived ten minutes early for my four o'clock meeting and parked in the designated lot. I opened the back door of my car and let Archie out to stretch his legs. I had no idea how long the interview would take, but I thought the ride out there would be a treat for him. After a quick walk on the edge of the lot, I put him back in the car, cracked the windows, and went into the substation.

Needless to say, I wasn't brimming with confidence when I presented myself at the front desk. The desk officer had me escorted to an office on the second floor, third door on the right. "The Jefferson County detectives are in there," my escort told me, and then waited while I rapped twice and entered.

"Well, well," Dorn said as he looked up, stubbed out his cigarette, and showed a thin, reptilian smile. "If it isn't the hot-shot L.A. lawyer."

I met his eyes for a moment but didn't speak. Escalante gave his partner an annoyed look, then motioned for me to sit. "Hello, Mr. Claxton. Thanks for taking the time to meet with us." After a modicum of small talk, Escalante turned on a small tape recorder and stated the location, date, and time of our discussion. He didn't waste any time. "Mr. Claxton, do you know anything about a fishing knife with a salmon fly in the handle and the initials CCIII on it?"

"Uh, that sounds like my knife."

"Is it in your possession now?"

"No."

"What happened to it?"

"Either you folks impounded it with my fishing gear or it's missing. I used it to peel potatoes the first night of the trip, washed it with other utensils after dinner. I thought I left it to dry there. When I noticed it wasn't there the next morning I assumed I'd put it back in my fishing vest in the boat without thinking about it. I've been known to do that."

I realized now with sparkling clarity that I should have told them at the first interview that my knife might be missing. But it was too late now. The explanation I offered sounded lame, but at least it was the truth.

"When did you first miss your knife?"

"Like I said, I didn't think it was missing at the time. I noticed it wasn't with the other knives sometime that morning after the body was discovered."

"Why didn't you tell us about this?" Escalante asked.

"At the risk of repeating myself, I didn't think my knife was missing at the time."

Leaning forward on the desk with both hands, Dorn said, "But you *did* notice it was missin' from the other knives. So you must've been lookin' for it. You want us to believe you didn't think that was important? Come on, hotshot, you can do better than that."

I ate a sarcastic comeback. "I wasn't *looking* for it, Detective. I just noticed it wasn't where I thought I'd left it."

Dorn snorted. "Would this be your knife?" He reached in his briefcase and slid a couple of photos across the table at me.

I studied the photographs carefully. "Yes, these appear to be photographs of my knife."

"Our diver found it in the river, about thirty feet from shore. Straight out from where Bruckner's body was found. Any idea how it got there?" Escalante again.

"No, sorry, can't help you." I knew that as we spoke the Jefferson County ME was busy trying to match the wounds in Bruckner's neck to the blade of my knife. I wondered if it could be done with scientific certainty. I didn't think so, but wasn't sure. "If you're trying to show that knife killed Bruckner, I think you're going to be disappointed."

Dorn leaned back in his chair. Escalante said, "Why is that, Mr. Claxton?"

"Because the person who killed him was a professional, and pros use their *own* knives, not some fishing knife lying around on a table, which, incidentally, everyone in that camp had access to."

The two detectives exchanged a glance, and Dorn snorted again. Escalante said, "Is there anything else you'd like to tell us about the death of Mr. Bruckner, now that you've had some more time to think?"

"Yes." I proceeded to remind them what Philip had shown them on the footpath from Kaskela to Whiskey Dick and also to tell them about my visit to the freight yard, the timing of the freight trains through the Kaskela switching station, and the tall male the skateboarders had seen heading toward the yard after he'd parked his Ford pickup. I didn't bother to mention the cigarette butt, since there would be no way of using it as evidence in any case. I also gave them the address of Oliver Dan, the boy who had spoken for the skateboarders.

As I related what I'd found out, I felt the conviction drain out of me. The story sounded weak. Escalante listened politely and even made a few notes, but Dorn's body language made it clear he wasn't buying any of it. And I still had the damn affair with Alexis to get off my chest. It was the last thing I wanted to talk about at the moment, but I knew it was better that I tell now than to have them discover it later.

"Uh, there's one other thing I need to advise you of," I began. Their eyes swung to me like a couple of searchlights. "I had a brief fling with Mrs. Bruckner last fall. It lasted six weeks, maybe. I broke it off in early December."

Dorn leaned in and Escalante's eyes narrowed, like he was taking aim. He said, "I see, Mr. Claxton. Why didn't you tell us about this earlier?"

"You didn't ask me. And let's face it, it's not exactly something I was anxious to let the world know. It was just a fling. Nothing more."

Dorn leaned back, crossed his arms across his chest, and smirked. *"Right."*

"Tell us about it," Escalante said.

"Not much to tell." I went on to describe our dinner at the Hotel Lyle, the subsequent meetings with Alexis, and the fact that I'd been the one to break it off.

"Did you have sexual relations with Mrs. Bruckner during these meetings?" Escalante continued.

"Yes."

"I see. Did Mr. Bruckner find out about these liaisons?"

"Not that I know of."

"Did you and the little missus have any discussions about the upcoming fishing trip on the Deschutes?" Dorn this time.

"No. I haven't spoken to Mrs. Bruckner since last December. I had no idea who the clients were for this trip. As I told you earlier, I was just filling in for one of Philip's guides who hurt his back." I liked that. It was something I knew they would cross-check with Philip.

"And you waited this long to tell us?" Dorn pressed.

I expelled a long breath. "Like I said, I was trying to save Mrs. Bruckner and myself the embarrassment that such a disclosure would've caused. I'm sorry now that I didn't own up to it sooner."

"Such a gentleman," Dorn said with a smirk I was learning to hate.

The interview veered into the timing and other details of Alexis' and my trysts. At this point Dorn seemed to come alive, his face drawn up in a leering smile as he peppered me with insults. I was responding to a question from Escalante when he interrupted and said, "Yes, sir, Mrs. Bruckner's, uh, intelligently built. A real beauty, but kind of pushy, you know? She ever let you on top, hotshot?"

At another point he took a deep drag on his cigarette, and as smoke sputtered out of his mouth said—"Bet it was hard to share that nice body with Bruckner. Yeah, I'll bet that was real hard. A man wants a woman with a body like that all to himself, right?"

I'd finally had enough. I shook my head and smiled, maybe even chuckled. *What's up with this guy?* I remember thinking. I stood up abruptly and looked at Escalante. "You've got to be kidding me. I'm trying to cooperate with this investigation, and this is what I get? Unless you're going to charge me with something, I'm outta here, gentlemen." I saw Dorn shift in his seat out of the corner of my eye, but didn't give him a glance. Escalante said, "I'm reminding you, Mr. Claxton, don't leave the Portland area without contacting us."

As I was closing the door to the interview room, I heard Dorn say, "You did him ear-to-ear, didn't you, hotshot?"

As I was walking to my car, a bright yellow Hummer H3 swung into the lot and parked a couple of slots down from my old BMW. Andrew Streeter got out on the driver's side. Mitch Hannon followed from the passenger's side. I stopped in front of them and forced a smile. "Afternoon, gentlemen. More interviews for you, too, huh?"

Streeter folded his arms across his chest, cocked his head, and smirked. His eyes lay hidden behind dark glasses, his polo shirt stretched taut by a protruding belly. Hannon looked trim in an open neck Oxford, chinos, and tasseled loafers. I caught myself wondering what the attraction was between these two. Hannon said, "They wanted us back in Madras and we told them no friggin' way. We got too many issues at work to deal with. Our attorney worked this deal out."

"I'm in your debt, then."

"Yeah, well, are they making any headway on the case?"

I shrugged. "Nothing they were willing to tell me about." I knew Escalante and Dorn would show them the knife to get their comments. That stir things up for sure. I wondered what else they'd choose to tell them about my interview.

Hannon shook his head. "Doesn't surprise me. I mean what a dynamic duo. A wetback and a Madras good old boy. Shit, we'd be better off with the Keystone Kops."

Streeter snorted a laugh, removed his shades and eyed me like I was a bug under glass. "Way I figure it, someone in that camp killed Hal." His eyes narrowed. "Doesn't leave a whole lot of suspects for those boys, I'd say." His eyes lingered on me for several beats, then he looked at Hannon.

Hannon tipped his head toward the building. "Come on, Andy, let's get this over with." With that, the two of them sauntered off.

I took stock of the situation on the way back to Dundee. I was already Escalante and Dorn's favorite for the murder, and I'm sure my disclosure about the affair just made their day. I wondered what Alexis would tell them in her second interview. The thought of Alexis brought me to another point—I'd been focusing on the intruder from the train, but my guess was that someone at the campsite had helped him. I'd assumed Alexis' silence after our breakup was a sign she bore me no ill will. Had I been naive to assume that?

As I drove north on I-26, I called Chad Harrelson at Well Spring but was told he was tied up. I left him a voice mail. When I turned onto Route 212 heading toward Boring, I called Philip and filled him in about my knife, what I'd learned about the freight trains, and what the skateboarders had seen. He told me Oliver Dan's great-grandfather and namesake was one of the founding elders on the first tribal council at Warm Springs. He assured me he would find out about the Ford F-150 without causing a stir.

The news at his end wasn't good either. His next clients had read about the murder and canceled their trip. I apologized profusely when I heard this. He assured me that he didn't consider it my fault, and I believed him. One thing I admired about my friend—when he said something you knew he meant it. We finished up the conversation by joking about how much free time we were going to have to fish as a result of all this.

When I pulled through my gate later that afternoon, I saw a lime green VW bug parked close to the house. A feeling of annoyance came over me. I didn't appreciate people barging into my sanctuary unannounced. As I approached the front porch, a woman stood up and waved.

"I'll be damned," I said to Archie. "What's Daina Zakaris doing here?"

Chapter Seventeen

I parked in the garage and let Archie out. He headed straight for the front porch. Standing at the foot of the steps, he squared his shoulders and barked up at Daina. Not his deepest, most threatening bark, but one with more of a scold to it. He didn't appreciate her unannounced presence on our property any more than I did.

Daina wore a pair of baggy cargo pants, scuffed-up Nikes, and a black t-shirt that said *Subvert the Dominant Paradigm* in white letters on the front. Her hair was swept back in a massive ponytail. Her pants were authentically faded and cinched by a woven belt, the end of which dangled carelessly on her thigh.

She dropped to one knee and made a couple of sharp clicking sounds with her tongue. "Come here, boy." Archie climbed the steps without hesitation, and a moment later his tail was wagging furiously while Daina stroked his broad back and cooed in his ear.

She smiled as I approached. "Hello, Cal. Hope you don't mind my barging in like this."

"Uh, not at all, Daina." I was wary but managed a weak smile. "What can I do for you?"

Reading my discomfort like a book, her smile faded. She looked back at my dog, his head between her hands. "What's his name?"

"Archie."

"So it's Archie the Aussie, huh? He's huge."

I chuckled. "Seventy-eight pounds. He's big for his breed. People often take him for a Bernese Mountain Dog."

"Well, Aussies are great dogs, and tricolors have the best markings." Then she looked at him more closely. "Oh, look, his eyes are the same copper color as the trim on his coat. How cool is that?" She flashed another smile, brilliant against flawless olive skin. "I've got a mutt I found at the pound. Not as big as this guy."

"Is the dog here or in Seattle?"

"Oh, Dylan's here with me. I never travel without him."

"Dylan as in the poet or the singer?"

She laughed at this, a pure note that reminded me of when she caught that first fish out on the Deschutes. "Both, I guess. The singer took his name from the poet, you know."

But I was tired and had a limited appetite for small talk. "What's on your mind, Daina?"

Our eyes met. Hers were huge dark pools, but friendly. She started to tear up and looked away. "I…I'm still upset about what happened on the river, Cal. I need someone to talk to. I guess I figured you might be going through the same thing. I called first, but you didn't answer. So I came over anyway. Pretty cheeky, huh?"

I shook my head. "Nah, I don't blame you for being upset. That was a bad scene out there." I was skeptical about why she was here. On the other hand, it seemed to make sense. After all, I couldn't see her going to someone in the NanoTech group, and she probably didn't know anyone else in the area. Besides, her take on the murder would be interesting. I said, "It's a nice afternoon. Why don't we sit out on the porch?"

I was starving, so after I showed her around the corner to the side porch, I excused myself and went to the kitchen. I loaded up a big tray with a half-full bottle of Sancere from the fridge, two wineglasses, a chunk of Gruyere, a bowl full of hazelnuts, a ripe mango, an apple, and a half a baguette. When I came back with the tray, Daina was standing at the railing taking in the view of the valley.

"Love your view," she said wistfully over her shoulder. "And this property, it's really beautiful. The Aerie. The name fits."

"It's a work in progress. The farmhouse is nearly a hundred years old. I love the view, too, but sitting on a ridge with a southern exposure in the Willamette Valley is not without its challenges."

"Horizontal rain, huh?"

I laughed and started pouring the wine. "Tons. I should own stock in a caulk factory."

She sat down, accepted a glass of wine and eyed the food with a decided lack of enthusiasm.

"I was hungry," I said, a little defensively. "Help yourself."

"I, uh, haven't had much of an appetite." Her face clouded over. "I just can't seem to get that scene out of my head. I mean, I ran over to see what Alexis was screaming about. I thought Hal had had a heart attack or something. My God, when I saw him!" Her eyes filled, but she managed to stave off the tears.

I nodded. "Yeah, I know. It jolted *me*, and I've seen my share of murder victims."

"Not as a small-town lawyer, surely?"

"I was a prosecutor for the city of Los Angeles in another life."

She raised her eyebrows, nodded, and to my relief let the subject drop. "Anyway, talking's good therapy, at least for me. I mean, that's how people worked out their problems before shrinks were invented, right?"

"You've got a point."

Her face grew dark again. "So, how *do* you get a grisly scene out of your head?"

My mind involuntarily flashed back to my wife, her pale arm hanging limply over the side of our bed, her blank eyes staring at me, unseeing. I grimaced. "There's no cure-all. Time. It takes time. Things begin to fade."

We fell into silence for a few moments. A crow cawed noisily high up in a Doug fir on the fence line. Daina managed a smile. "You know, I've worked with a lot of dysfunctional management teams. That's what I do. But this NanoTech crowd, I mean, I got this unbelievably bad vibe the first time I met with them. Now this. I should be getting combat pay."

"Are you going to stay on as a consultant?"

"As far as I know. I have a contract. We'll see how it plays out."

"You think one of them could have killed Bruckner?" I said, cutting to the chase.

She looked a little surprised at my directness. "Oh, I don't see how, but there's something about that group that doesn't feel right."

"What might that be?"

She paused to sip her wine, then eyed me with curiosity. "You sound like you're investigating this crime."

I took stock for a moment—how much should I tell her? Sensing her insights might be valuable, I decided to abandon my lawyerly caution and open up a bit. "Well, I am, sort of. See, I'm, uh, concerned that someone's trying to blame the killing on me."

"You're kidding."

"Afraid not. If you haven't already, you'll be contacted soon by Escalante and Dorn to talk about the knife they found in the river—"

"Knife?" she interrupted. "So that's what they want. I'm talking to them tomorrow."

"Yeah, *my* knife. A police diver found it on the gravel bar out in front of where Bruckner was killed."

Her hand went involuntarily to her mouth. "Oh, dear."

"Bruckner was killed with a knife. So, that makes me suspect number one."

"That's absurd! You didn't kill Hal Bruckner."

She said it with such conviction that I asked, "How do you know that?"

She looked at me with those big eyes and smiled. "Fly fishermen are a peaceful lot, right?"

"Right. Strictly catch and release for me." I went on to tell her about how I'd left my knife out on the table to dry the night of the murder, and about the hostile interview at Government Camp. But I didn't tell her that I suspected the actual killer had come in on a freight train.

When I finished, Daina said, "Do the detectives know that you and Alexis were lovers?"

Her matter-of-fact comment caught me by surprise, even though I was pretty sure Daina had guessed there was something between Alexis and me. "What affair?" No way I was giving her that. She was going to be questioned again the next day.

Daina took another sip of Sancere and smiled. "Didn't mean to pry. Your secret's safe with me."

I met her eyes and held them. "Why would you keep my secrets? Let's face it, you don't even know me."

She sighed, looked down at her scuffed sneakers. "I've learned to go with my instincts, even if it means breaking a few rules." She brought her eyes back up, and there was a look of defiance in them.

Encouraged by the comment, I said, "I know you're bound by confidentiality, but what can you tell me about NanoTech and the management team? I gathered from your little bloodletting session around the campfire they have a few issues."

She laughed. "Well, you already know too much. I saw you listening in the other night."

I shrugged. "I was just curious to see how you were going to handle that unruly crew. I was impressed. That truth-speaking session was powerful."

"Thanks. I call that draining the swamp. The irony is that the company's poised to cash in on a tremendous breakthrough. You'd think this would be a good problem to have, but it seems to have brought out the worst in everyone."

"How so?"

"Well, you heard them grousing, right? Mitch Hannon and Andrew Streeter want to take the company public, but Hal stood in the way. Hannon and Streeter are down on Pitman, who's complaining about not being recognized. Poor Hal, caught in the middle."

I nodded. "Yeah, Pitman was not a happy camper."

"For sure. Hannon and Streeter don't think Pitman's pulling his weight. To them, he's just a technical geek who doesn't know anything about running a business."

"But didn't Pitman come up with some important new technology, diamond something?"

"Yes, he did. Diamond Wire. His name's on the patent, and it came out of his lab, but others were involved, too, particularly Pitman's lab manager." Daina paused, met my eyes for a moment, as if gauging how much to reveal. "The issue seems to be whether Pitman deserves to be an officer of the company."

"Oh, I get it. If Pitman's not an officer, there are fewer people to divide the pie with."

"Exactly."

"So they want to get rid of him?"

Daina leaned back, sipped her wine, and changed the subject. "This wine's great. What is it?"

I turned the bottle so she could see the label. "Sancere, from the Loire Valley."

She smiled a bit teasingly. "French? No loyalty to the local wines?"

I chuckled. "I'm a Dundee Hills pinot noir fan through and through. The local whites are fine, but you just can't beat a good Sancere, in my opinion." Then I tried to bring her back. "So, Bruckner brought you and your company in to grease the skids for growth?"

"Yes. We're training people and putting management systems in place. He also asked us to take a look at their security systems." She shook her head. "They're really behind the curve—no locked-door policies, no security cams, no accounting for electronic keys, the list goes on and on." She reached in her purse and pulled out a gray plastic rectangle and waved it. "Hal gave me this master key. He doesn't even know how many of these he's given out."

I took a sip of wine and put a knife to the Gruyere and the apple. I placed the cheese on a slice of apple and offered it to her.

"Thanks," she said, taking a bite and closing her eyes. "This is *delicious*. I haven't eaten anything all day."

"What about Mitch Hannon?" I persisted. "What's his relationship with Bruckner?"

"Mitch is Hal's nephew, his sister's only child. He went to Georgia Tech, then picked up an MBA at Stanford several years later. I think Hal picked up the tab."

I rolled my eyes.

Daina smiled. "*What?* You have something against MBAs that cost a quarter of a million?"

I chuckled. "Yeah, I'm a state school kind of guy. Berkeley."

She raised her eyebrows and laughed. "Berkeley. Oh, that explains a lot. Anyway, Hal brought him into the company. He's brash, but damn sharp."

"So why's he sleeping with his uncle's wife? I doubt if they teach that at Stanford."

I thought the question might surprise her, but I should have known better. Daina tipped her chin up and laughed. "Oh, *that*. I'd say that was more Mitch being used by Alexis." Then she met my eyes and added playfully, "I don't need to tell you the woman has a healthy sexual appetite."

I tried to hold a neutral expression as I busied myself peeling the mango, pitting it, and laying out long slices on the plate. "What about NanoTech? Who gets the company?"

She shrugged. "Alexis, I assume. I'm sure there's a boatload of insurance, too. Hal adored her"

Her eyes shifted to the view, as if she were suddenly tired of talking. The valley was a hazy patchwork, the mountains soft lavender. Some distance out, a bald eagle drifted on a late afternoon thermal. We both sat there for a long time without saying a word. There was no discomfort in the silence.

Finally Daina said, "I've been doing all the talking, Cal. I know you're upset about the murder, but I sense there's something else. Do you want to talk about it?"

The question caught me off guard. I hadn't heard from Claire, nor had I any word from Well Spring that day. I said, finally, "It's my daughter, Claire. I'm worried sick about her."

I poured out the story of Claire's disappearance and what Well Spring was doing to find her and her team. Daina listened quietly. When I had finished she stood up, walked around behind me, and gently laid her hands on my shoulders.

"You're carrying all this worry right here, Cal. She gently squeezed my shoulder muscles. "Try to relax. Let your shoulders down."

When she said that, I became aware of just how high I was carrying those muscles. I exhaled deeply and let them find their natural resting place.

"Good," she said. "Now, trust that Claire's alright tonight. Know it." She gently massaged my shoulders and then moved to my neck, expertly kneading out the knots and kinks in my muscles with gentle yet surprisingly strong hands. A warm heat radiated out from her touch. At one point I moaned involuntarily, and when she finished I placed a hand on hers in a gesture of profound thanks. She said, "I've got to go now. Thanks for listening to me, Cal."

As I walked her to her car I said, "You have a faint accent. Where are you from?"

She laughed dismissively. "Lithuania. I came here when I was a teenager."

"What brought you here?"

She got in her car and started it up. "You know, the American dream." She pulled away, waved, and said, "*Sudie*," which I took to be Lithuanian for good-bye.

As Archie and I watched her go I had the distinct feeling her background was a topic she avoided—a feeling I could relate to.

Later that evening I thawed a slab of Chinook salmon and grilled it on a cedar plank, and that, together with a roasted sweet potato and some steamed broccoli, made a decent meal. I left the dishes stacked in the sink and started up the stairs to my bedroom, which felt like a climb up Mount Hood.

My head was buzzing with the new information I'd gotten from Daina. But when I finally fell into bed that night, I could think only of Claire, and as I drifted into a shallow, fitful sleep, Daina's words echoed in my head—*Trust that Claire's safe. Know it.*

Chapter Eighteen

I awoke the next morning to the sound of water dripping onto my windowsill, a steady plok, plok, plok. Rain had blown in during the night at the precise angle required to set the window leaking. I got up, mopped the sill with a towel, and set out a small pot I kept behind my armoire for just such emergencies. I worried about black mold growing in the wall cavity and resolved to re-caulk the window for the umpteenth time.

I made toast and a double cappuccino and headed for the study where I logged on to my laptop and checked my e-mail. After perusing the online *New York Times* I leaned back in my swivel chair, put the heels of my hands on my forehead and pushed hard, as if the physical pressure would relieve the anxiety I felt about Claire. No luck. It was too early to call Harrelson at Well Spring, and my head felt like it was going to explode.

Archie was in the corner watching me like a hawk for signs of a morning run or at least a trip down to get the paper. I stood up and stretched, whereupon he shot to his feet. Aussies need a job, and it was Arch's job to run me. He took his work seriously.

"Okay, big boy, you win." I patted his broad back. "Let's go for a run."

We headed down Eagle Nest and turned right at the highway toward the old cemetery, where many of the pioneers who had settled this area were buried. I had my cell phone with me in case Claire or someone from Well Spring called.

I was breathing hard as we crested the hill at the cemetery. I'd kept my thoughts at bay to clear my head. Archie looked back at me to see if we were going to stop. I said, "Home, big boy," and without breaking stride, turned around. He immediately shot in front of me and let out two sharp yelps of pure delight.

I began thinking about my discussion with Daina Zakaris. I'd let my guard down a bit with her last night, but the risk seemed worth it. After all, I'd gained more insight into the cast of characters that surrounded Hal Bruckner—all viable suspects. And, in truth, my skeptical side hadn't completely ruled Daina out either. So, the question that dogged me all the way back was—what the hell do I do next?

By the time we got back to the Aerie, I had the answer. I would focus on the one person I *knew* was involved, the train-hopping intruder.

I was hungry and dying for another cup of coffee, but the first thing I did was call Harrelson at Well Spring. I got a recording that gave me another recording and, cursing under my breath, decided that the worst invention of the twentieth century was the answering machine.

My thoughts turned to Oliver Dan and the young skateboard-ers I'd talked to at the warehouse. Their remarks and body language led me to believe they had probably taken the pickup truck for a joyride. But what if the truck had actually been stolen by the killer in the first place? It was worth a look. I logged on and pulled up the online version of *The Madras Pioneer.* In a couple of minutes I had last Tuesday's edition in front of me. I checked the police reports. Some petty crime, a couple of DUIs, but no F-150s reported stolen. Ditto for Wednesday, our first day on the river.

No stolen vehicles reported on Thursday either, but the lead article in that edition jumped out at me. A Madras man had been murdered in an apparent carjacking that took place early Friday morning. The man, Henry Barnes, had been stabbed once in the chest and left to die in a ditch on I-26, near the Horse Creek Road intersection. Time of death was believed to be around five a.m. His Grand Cherokee was missing.

My pulse rate ticked up as I brought a map of Madras onto my screen. Horse Creek Road intersected I-26 about half a mile past the turnoff leading to the Barlow Northern freight yard. What if the intruder, finding his F-150 missing, had waited until daybreak, walked out to the highway, flagged Barnes down, stabbed him, and took his Jeep? It could have gone down that way.

I called Philip immediately, and when he answered I blurted out, "Did you hear about the carjacking in Madras out on 26?

"Yeah. Everyone in town's talking about it. Why?"

"I think our train ghost killed him because he needed a getaway car."

There was a pause while Philip processed this. "That son of a bitch," he said finally, half to himself. "What'd Barnes ever do to him?"

"So I was right. Oliver Dan and his boys stole that F-150, didn't they?"

Another pause. "Look, Cal. The only way I could get Oliver to open up was to give my word there'd be no blowback on him or his buddies. I can't go back on that."

"Understood," I said impatiently. "No problem. What'd he tell you?"

"The kids stole the truck alright. But they were going to put it back. Trouble is they happened to run into an older cousin. The cousin took the truck from them. It's probably stripped clean by now."

Another maddening pause. "Did they look at the registration? Can they tell us who owns the damn thing?"

"I'm coming to that, man," Philip answered with a measure of irritation in his voice. "I talked Oliver into going back to ask the cousin."

"Good move."

Another pause.

"And? What did you find out?"

"No registration—"

"*Shit.*"

"But he did give me the VIN."

I exhaled. "Great. I know someone who'll run the number for me. Nice work, Philip." Before we signed off, I asked Philip one last question. "Did you tell Bruckner or anyone else at NanoTech that I was going to guide on your trip?"

"Uh, yeah, I did mention it to Bruckner when we were negotiating. You two seemed to hit it off that night at the Lyle Hotel, so I figured it might help sell the trip."

I called Nando Mendoza next. He agreed to chase down the VIN for me. As an afterthought I asked him for a second favor. Any chance he could find out if a stolen Jeep Grand Cherokee registered to Henry Barnes of Madras had turned up anywhere, like the Portland area? What the hell, I just might get lucky.

I was starving by then, so I fixed myself a huge bowl of granola, added frozen blueberries from a bag I kept in the freezer, and took it out onto the side porch. I was halfway through the cereal when my cell rang.

"Mr. Claxton? This is Chad Harrelson from Well Spring."

My heart froze. "Yes, Chad. Have you heard something?"

"We have, Mr. Claxton. We've located your daughter and the rest of her team. They're in a remote village above Miski, near the Chad border."

"Thank God. Is she okay?"

"As far as we know, but we haven't spoken to her or anyone else from Well Spring directly."

"What's the problem?" I asked, struggling to stay calm.

"Uh, the village they're in has been taken by the Arab militia, the Janjaweed. They're denying all access in, and unfortunately, all access out as well.

"Where's your security team?"

"They're outside the village now. We think this is just a temporary setback. The Janjaweed have no reason to hold our people. We're in contact with the State Department, and we're negotiating with the militia as we speak."

"Negotiating! My God! Surely they won't hold noncombatants!"

"Well, that's what we think, too." Harrelson droned on, but I had gotten the message. Claire had been found safe, but it wasn't over yet. Not by a long shot.

When I hung up, a crippling sense of impotence came over me. I sat down and stared out over the valley as the frustration ate at me like an acid. Archie came up and put his head on my knee. A squall blew in, but we didn't go into the house until the rain had soaked through my shirt, and I'd begun to shiver in the stiffening breeze.

That night I lay in my bed playing tag with sleep. My nerves had just begun to ease their grip at about midnight when my phone rang. I answered it with a sense of foreboding. A woman sobbed, and my body went rigid.

"Who is this?"

"Cal? It's Daina. Someone's broken into my house."

"What? Are you all right?"

"Yes, I think so. I came home and surprised the bastard. He pushed me, and I hit my head."

"Where are you now?"

"I'm locked in the house. The police are on the way. The prowler took off, I think. Can you come over, Cal? I'm a little freaked out."

Chapter Nineteen

The winding road along the Willamette River into Wilsonville was wet, and I nearly spun out on the second hairpin turn. It wasn't easy, but I found the place Daina was renting—a low, wood and stone structure on a big lot that sat behind a massive forsythia hedge in full bloom. She was on the front porch talking to two Wilsonville cops, who were taking notes. A small dog sat next to her—Dylan, no doubt. They all turned when I pulled in, and she waved to me and said something to the officers.

These were lean times for law enforcement, so Daina's call had only managed to muster a single patrol car. Deciding to have a look around, I went back to my car, got a flashlight out of the trunk and wandered down the driveway toward the back of the house. A side window was ajar and crisscrossed with yellow crime tape. I assumed it was the suspected point of entry and would be dusted for prints at some point, probably in the morning, if they ever got around to it at all. I could see that the plants below the window had been trampled. I drew closer, but I was no Philip Lone Deer. I couldn't see anything resembling footprints in the tangle of stems and leaves.

I made a complete circuit around the house without noticing anything out of the ordinary. I stopped again at the window the prowler used to enter and tried to imagine his approach. He probably drove past the house, parked well down the street, and doubled back through the vacant lot next door to Daina's yard.

As I strained to see in that direction, a shape loomed out of the shadows. The flashlight beam revealed a children's wooden play set, which would provide good cover for someone watching Daina's place, I decided. I walked over and looked around, hoping to find something of interest, like a smelly cigarette butt. But I found nothing except a half-empty bottle of Crystal Geyser water standing on one of the cross braces of the structure. The bottle might have been slightly cooler than the air, but I wasn't sure.

By this time, the officers had finished with Daina and were writing up a report in their squad car. I wandered back to the porch, and she came over and hugged me. "Thanks for coming, Cal. I feel so embarrassed about bothering you. I was terrified when I called. I didn't know how long it would take the police to get here."

"Hey, it's okay." I pulled back and looked at her in the porch light. She had a small, ripening bruise on the side of her face, and her ear was nicked and bloody. "My God, are you sure you're all right?"

She dabbed at her ear with a tissue. "Yeah. I'm just a little sore." Then she massaged her left shoulder and grimaced. "The officers wanted to call an ambulance, but I wouldn't let them. I'm more pissed off than hurt."

"Maybe you should go to the emergency room to have that shoulder looked at?"

"No. I'm okay," she answered with a finality that hinted at a certain stubbornness at her core—a trait I understood instinctively. Then, changing the subject, she looked down at the dog at her feet and smiled. "This is Dylan. He risked his life for me tonight."

I looked down at the dog, whose muzzle was graying with age. "He did? Tell me about it. What the hell happened?"

She sighed, dropped her head, and combed her fingers through her hair. "Well, I spent the evening at NanoTech catching up on paperwork. Took Dylan with me. I have a small office there. Anyway, I came home about 11:45. Dylan had wandered into the yard to pee. I unlocked the back door and was fumbling for the wall switch when all of a sudden someone burst out of the laundry room and slammed me against the wall. He was big with strong hands. I must have surprised him."

"Did you get a look at him?"

"No. It was pitch black. All I know is that he was tall, about your height, maybe, or taller. Anyway, he pushes past me toward the door, and suddenly Dylan appears, yapping like crazy and biting at this guy's ankles." She bent down and picked up the small dog. "He kicked Dylan and made him yelp, but he's okay." She hugged the dog. "Aren't you, fellah? Then he was gone. I locked the door behind him."

I scratched the top of Dylan's head. "Good work, boy. You're a hero," then to Daina, "What's the house look like? Anything disturbed?"

"He took some petty cash and jewelry, a Timex I wear when I work out. Stuff you could put in your pocket. Pretty much trashed my bedroom and the other bedroom I use as a study."

"Expensive jewelry?"

"You're kidding, right? Beads and minerals, a little turquoise, that's all I wear. He must have been desperate to take the stuff."

"What about the study?

"Oh, he went through everything."

"Anything missing?"

"Well, at first I didn't think so. But then I remembered two NanoTech files I was working on here. Looks like they're gone. Everything else was just tossed around."

"Anything sensitive in the files?"

"No, not in the grand scheme of things. The files contained some personnel interviews, reports by my teams in the field, that sort of thing. Heaps of paper, but nothing very sensitive."

I nodded toward her computer. "What about that?"

"No access, unless he hacked his way in. It wouldn't have mattered anyway. I learned a long time ago to keep confidential information off my computer."

"What did the cops say?"

"They think it was drug-related. There's been a rash of break-ins in Wilsonville over the past several months. Meth epidemic."

"What do you think?"

"I'm not sure what I think at this point," she answered and then added, "I saw you out in the yard. Did you find anything?"

I shrugged. "No. Not really. Just a half-empty water bottle that might have belonged to the intruder. Not much to go on, I'm afraid."

"Oh. So the creep was out there watching me?"

I nodded. "Looks like it. Why are you renting a house? I would've thought you'd be staying at a motel around here."

She chuckled and shook her head. "Not a chance. I *hate* motels. Never stay in them unless I absolutely have to. I like to have my dog with me, cook my own meals, that sort of thing."

At this point, one of the officers joined us on the porch. He told Daina an evidence team would come in the morning to dust for prints. I followed him out to his car and told him about the water bottle. He gave me a weary look and told me about his caseload. I didn't argue, because I knew a burglary didn't justify trying to isolate the DNA on the mouth of the water bottle, and I wasn't about to tell him that I believed the crime was connected to two recent murders, one of which I was involved in.

It was clear Daina was too spooked to stay in the house, so I offered my spare bedroom. She shot me an anxious glance. "Can Dylan come?"

"Sure. Archie likes small meals."

She rolled her eyes and laughed, the tension draining from her face.

I was glad to help out, and besides, it would give me a chance to better assess whether she had an ulterior motive for befriending me.

Chapter Twenty

Neither Daina nor I felt sleepy, so we sat out on my porch, bundled in sweatshirts with a bottle of Rémy Martin to keep us warm. Archie and Dylan got on immediately and were both lying at Daina's feet, as if they knew it would be a comfort to her. The valley appeared as a black hole beneath a dim chunk of moon shaped like a lopsided football. Coyotes yipped now and then down in the quarry, causing Dylan to spring to his feet and bark into the darkness. Archie's only response was to lift his head off the cedar planks in mute irritation.

We didn't speak for a long time. Finally Daina said, "What happened tonight is connected to the murder of Hal Bruckner, isn't it?"

"That's my guess. Looks like someone wanted those Nano-Tech files and tried to cover it up by staging a garden-variety burglary. A clumsy attempt but good enough for the local cops. Do you really think the prowler was trying to hurt you or just trying to get out of there?"

She paused for a moment. "I really don't know."

"Suppose the break-in *was* connected to the murder. Any idea what this guy might've been looking for?"

She sighed heavily and sat up a little straighter. "Well, like I said, the particular files he took don't seem valuable in any way I can see. But I'm constantly bringing confidential stuff back and forth from work—project reports, financial spreadsheets, personnel evaluations—you name it. Lots of sensitive stuff."

"What's the *most* sensitive?"

"That's a no-brainer—anything relating to Diamond Wire."

"What the hell's Diamond Wire all about, anyway? What can you tell me?"

Daina gave me a look, and I added, "I know, I know, you'll have to kill me once you do."

She laughed. "Well, I'm sure you've heard of quantum computing, which is an area of exploding importance across the globe. Quantum computers will make our current computers look like adding machines."

"Oh, great. Can't wait to see what the NSA does with that."

She laughed. "Well, they're more theoretical than practical at the moment."

"What makes them so fast?"

"They'll use *photons* instead of clunky old electrons to move the data around."

"Like replacing a tortoise with a hare?"

"More like replacing a tortoise with a *rocket*. It's the quantum properties of the photons of light that make the difference. See, current computers work by manipulating bits that exist in either one of two states, zero or one, which limits them to one calculation at a time."

"The binary system."

"Right, but because of the weird quantum properties of photons, a quantum computer can use multiple zero and one states *simultaneously*. This gives it the potential to be millions of times more powerful than today's supercomputers."

I wrinkled my forehead. "I don't—"

Daina laughed and raised a hand like a traffic cop. "It has something to do with the wave-particle duality of photons, but don't ask me to explain it. I'm no quantum physicist."

"Okay, I concede. So, how does the Diamond Wire project fit into this?"

"Well, it turns out one of the biggest stumbling blocks to making a practical quantum computer is the lack of a reliable device to generate single photons and deliver them to a processor. Pitman claims his Diamond Wire invention solves that problem."

"How does he do it?"

She smiled. "That's the confidential part. Actually, I couldn't explain that either, but I can tell you it involves forming nanotubes in a diamond substrate and then generating the photons with a laser. The nanotubes act like guides for the photons, sort of like what copper wires do for electrons. But these tubes are 50,000 times *smaller* than a human hair. Pitman told me comparing a nanotube to a human hair's like comparing that hair to the Eiffel Tower."

"How do you know these nanotubes really work?"

"I have a good technical man on the inside. He's looked over the patent applications, the experimental setup, and the data. Rusty tells me Diamond Wire's the real deal."

Who'd be interested in the project?"

"*Everyone* actively working in quantum computing—private companies, top universities, even national governments. A working quantum computer would be an awesome cyber weapon. It could smash every encryption algorithm ever invented. No state secrets would be safe."

"Any thoughts on who might pose the biggest security threat to NanoTech?"

"Hal was worried about a French firm called TM-E, and a Chinese company, Guangzhou Micro Tech. They're both known to have no scruples and to be willing to pay handsomely for trade secrets. Nothing confidential about that."

"Was he worried about Pitman going over to the dark side?"

She hesitated for a moment, as if considering what to say next. A satellite crossed the night sky like an errant star, and the frogs holding forth down in the quarry went mute as if to listen in. "Actually, he did have some concerns."

"Isn't Pitman legally prevented from working for a direct competitor?"

She paused again, meeting my eyes for a moment. "We're getting close to the line here, Cal. I'm bound by confidentiality. You're a lawyer, you know the drill."

I smiled. "Yeah, I understand. It's just that this seems pretty relevant to my, uh, I should say *our* situation." I pointed to her face. "Judging from that bruise I'd say you've got some skin in this game, too."

She laughed, and her hand went to her cheek. I guess I can tell you that Pitman's legally bound to NanoTech *only* if he signed a security agreement to that effect."

"Did he?"

"Good question. Hal claimed he had, but the trouble is he apparently misplaced the agreement." She chuckled and shook her head. "When I asked him about it, he said, 'I'm an entrepreneur, not a goddamn file clerk.'"

"Does Pitman know the document's missing?"

"I'm not sure. I do know Hal had a lot of people in the company looking for it. Pitman could have easily heard about the search. One thing's for sure, if Pitman's planning to bolt, he needs to know if the document's still around."

We fell silent again as I topped up our glasses. A breeze stirred, carrying the faint scent of the lilac bushes along the fence line. Daina swirled the brandy in her glass, breathed in the aroma, took a sip. "You know, Pitman loves his bottled water. He's never without one at work, in his office, at meetings. It's like an extension of his hand. Maybe that was his water you found out in the yard."

I set my glass down. "Huh. Interesting thought. We're all creatures of habit, you know. The water was Crystal Geyser, I think. Ring a bell?"

Daina shrugged. "No, but I guess I could check out what kind of water he drinks."

"Wouldn't hurt." In the weak light, I could see that the bruise on the side of her face had darkened, but the bandage I'd put on her ear had stopped the bleeding. "How's your shoulder feel?"

She gingerly rotated her arm. "Better, thanks."

"Your inside guy, what's his name again?

"Rusty. Rusty Musik."

"Right. Sounds like he has a pretty free run of Pitman's operation. Has he seen anything suspicious?"

Daina got up abruptly and walked to the porch railing. Dylan followed. A couple of coyotes cut loose, raising a ridge of fur along Dylan's back. "I've already told you more than I should've about NanoTech, Cal."

"I appreciate that. I just thought, you know, maybe Bruckner wanted Rusty to snoop a little…e-mail, correspondence, that sort of thing. See what Pitman was up to."

"That's *not* the kind of consulting I do."

She spoke with such finality I knew the subject was closed. I was also pretty damn sure she knew more than she was telling me.

Chapter Twenty-one

It must have been close to three when I showed Daina and Dylan to the guest bedroom at the end of the hall on the second floor. We had gotten around to discussing Claire, and wishing to avoid another emotional meltdown, I'd put a positive spin on her situation. I could tell Daina didn't buy it, but to her credit she didn't press it. She and her dog came down the next morning as I was making coffee. Suddenly her presence felt awkward. Maybe having a woman in my kitchen in the morning was too intimate or an invasion of my space. The Aerie was my refuge, and I wanted to keep it that way.

I offered Daina breakfast, but to my relief she turned me down. As she and Dylan pulled out in her Bug, I had the distinct feeling she understood where I was coming from, although not a word passed between us about it. The last thing she did was squeeze my hand and say, "I feel like Claire's safe, Cal."

I checked in with Harrelson at eight o'clock. He wasn't so upbeat this time. Apparently, the Janjaweed militia was demanding weapons as well as safe passage out of the village. He also told me the story had been picked up by the wire services. They were describing it as a "tense standoff" between the militia and African Union forces. The only good news, at least as far as I was concerned, was that in addition to Claire's team, the rebel militia was holding several UN and Red Cross workers hostage. Surely this would put more pressure on them to release everyone.

I thought about flying to Khartoum and vowed I would if the situation threatened to drag out. I had to smile at one point, picturing myself on a camel like Lawrence of Arabia. I went online and found a Lufthansa flight with two stops for $1,644. I was sure my presence in Sudan would just thrill the State Department, but I felt better knowing I had a course of action, no matter how crazy it might be. I'd give Harrelson and Well Spring one more day, I decided, and dismissed the thought that Escalante and Dorn could veto my travel plans.

Dwelling on the past was something I fought against every day. But thoughts of Claire had a way of breaching my defenses. I found myself drifting back to my old life and the events that had nearly broken me.

It should never have happened. It was that simple and, of course, that complex. My wife, Nancy, had been an artist who also taught art history at Occidental College. She had a beautiful, spirited daughter and a husband who was rising fast in the city of Los Angeles' criminal justice system. By all accounts, ours was a happy family. Sure, she was taking anti-depressants, but so were a lot of other people.

On a rainy Tuesday morning after Claire and I had hurried off to school and work, Nan swallowed an entire bottle of prescription sleeping pills, crawled back into bed, and slowly and enigmatically slipped away from us.

A tragic result of a depressive personality, Claire and I were told. An act that could not be foreseen. We must not blame ourselves. Claire, of course, was as without blame as any loving daughter could be. But I wasn't. I should have seen the warning signs, the dark, unapproachable moods, the Cimmerian turn her paintings had taken, the medications she'd stopped taking. And I would have if I hadn't been so all-consumed with my job and so puffed up by my career. I missed the warning signs, and now she was gone. Like I said, it was that simple.

Back from the funeral service, Claire sat across from me at our kitchen table. The house, packed with friends and relatives earlier that day, had fallen silent except for the ticking of the old kitchen clock that had belonged to Nan's grandmother. I'd held up pretty well at the funeral, but now, sitting alone with Claire, guilt and despair settled on me like a wet fog that penetrated every pore of my body. Claire had cried most of the day, but now her eyes were dry. I remembered her eyes. They were Nan's—perfect replicas, cut jewels of the finest sapphire—and they shone with something I hadn't seen before, a strength that had been quietly growing within her, a strength that was now fully realized in our time of desperate need.

"Dad, she said, "Mom was sick. She didn't know what she was doing. She would never have done this otherwise. I *know* that, Dad, and I know that it wasn't your fault. It wasn't."

The memory of my daughter's words that day felt like a lifeline. Not because they absolved me—they didn't—but because she had the courage to speak them when I was speechless and defeated. I could just hear her scolding me the same way now. I pushed away the negative thoughts and focused my mind on Claire. I could see her face like she was standing next to me, her lips curling at the corners with that smile, those sparkling eyes, her laugh, the sound of it so much like her mother's. I held my head in my hands, closed my eyes, and willed thoughts of strength and safety to her. It was as close to prayer as I was able to get.

Despite the lack of sleep, I wasn't tired so I drove to my law office in Dundee. I'd cleared my schedule to go fishing, but I'd also left a pile of delinquent paperwork. The office had once been the site of the town's only barber shop, and I had the original barber pole in a closet to prove it. It was a simple frame building with a large window in front and six parking spaces in back. Inside, I'd re-exposed a set of muscular Douglas fir beams by removing a drop ceiling and, by ripping up some butt-ugly linoleum, a handsomely worn oak floor. A wood stove provided adequate heat, and the walls were decorated with local art and pictures of the Oregon outdoors.

In L.A. my office had been on the twenty-second floor of the Parker Center, looking west across the city toward the Pacific.

My office in Dundee sat at sea level looking out on the always busy 99W. That was fine with me.

When we arrived, Archie settled on his mat in the corner and began his ritual of snoozing with one eye and watching me out of the other for a sign we were going out to stretch our legs or go to lunch. I sat down, put my feet up on my desk, and opened the day's issue of *The Oregonian*. There was no mention of the "tense standoff" in Darfur, but when I read the headline on the front page of the Metro section I could hardly believe it.

Dundee Lawyer Implicated
in Deschutes River Murder

By Tom Richardson

A source within the Jefferson County Sheriff's Department has disclosed to *The Oregonian* that Calvin Claxton III, a lawyer in Dundee, has become a "person of interest" in the brutal slaying of Hal Bruckner, a prominent businessman from Wilsonville.

Bruckner, who was president and CEO of the technology firm NanoTech, was stabbed to death while on a fishing trip on the Deschutes River on June 1. The trip was being led by Northwest Experience, a popular guide service out of Madras, Oregon. Mr. Claxton was one of three guides and six guests on the trip. The guests consisted of three members of the management team at the high-tech firm along with a consultant, Bruckner, and his wife. The trip was planned as a team-building exercise for the company.

According to the source, Mr. Claxton's fishing knife was found in the river, adjacent to the murder scene. Forensic experts believe the knife is consistent with the weapon used to kill Bruckner. Other physical evidence as well as the accounts of members of the fishing party are being carefully examined to determine the next steps in the investigation, the source revealed.

Mr. Claxton could not be reached for comment.

"Oh, that's just great!" I said out loud. Archie, not catching the sarcasm, came over to my desk, tail wagging, an expectant look on his face. I should have anticipated something like this, but I was stung by it nevertheless.

"'Could not be reached for comment'?" I continued in an even louder voice. "My phone number's in the book, Richardson. All you have to do is call. I'll give you a *comment*." By this time, Arch had lowered his ears and stopped wagging his tail.

I finally calmed down enough to think the situation through. Aside from embarrassing me, I suppose Escalante and Dorn wanted to use the press to put the heat on, make me squirm. I wasn't sure Escalante would stoop to that, but I could easily see Dorn making the call to Richardson. I doubted they would've done this on the basis of the knife alone. I'm sure my disclosure of the affair with Alexis had been a swing factor.

I wondered about Alexis. Would she help them incriminate me? Of course, she could be the one behind the frame, I supposed. Even if she weren't, she wouldn't want to jeopardize a fat insurance-payoff by looking like a coconspirator in her husband's murder. Thinking about that made me angry all over again, and I shuddered to think what she might say about me under pressure of an indictment—insane jealousy, threatening comments, God knows what. Sure, it would be her word against mine, but there'd be a built-in bias to believe the suffering widow over the former lover.

Calm down, I told myself. How do I know what she told them? Maybe she has more integrity than I give her credit for. If I could talk to her face-to-face, I'd have a chance of reading her. Besides, I owed her an explanation as to why I revealed the affair to Escalante and Dorn—an act of courtesy, if nothing else. And that might ensure she'd back me up rather than try to hide the affair or, worse yet, give her own version.

I wondered if I should chance it.

I tossed the bulging file of paperwork I'd come to work on back in the drawer and slammed it shut. I called Philip Lone Deer and then Nando Mendoza but didn't reach either of them.

I was particularly anxious to talk to Nando. I left him a voice message with my cell phone number.

I pulled the paperwork back out of my desk and forced myself to begin working. After all, life goes on, and I had a business to run. I struggled through to midafternoon without thinking of lunch and then left for the Aerie, but not before checking the street for TV trucks. I wouldn't have put it past one of the networks to send a reporter out there to confront me, but the coast was clear.

When I arrived home I changed into my running gear and took Archie for a four-mile jog. The sky was gray and oppressively low, and a light rain had raised the smell of wet earth. I felt winded going out and never found my second wind. At the end, I felt bone-tired, but I'd managed to make a decision about Alexis Bruckner. I would pay her a visit, and the sooner the better.

It wasn't a task I looked forward to.

Chapter Twenty-two

Alexis Bruckner lived in an upscale development set on a wooded hillside at the southern edge of the Stafford area. The developer called it Valley View Estates. The longtime residents of the rural area had another name for it—McMansion Hill. The individual houses sat on five-acre plots with trendy names like Pheasant Run and Fox Watch Manor, but of course the pheasants and foxes that once roamed there had been forced out by the intensive development. Cut into the hillside and outlined by a few interior lights, Alexis' house reminded me of a docked ocean liner. I wasn't about to park right in front, so I looped around to the street above her place.

I sat in my car overlooking the rear of the mansion, reviewing the wisdom of my decision. The area was dead silent, and nothing moved except the ragged, fast-moving clouds screening the lopsided moon. The back windows of Alexis' house were dark except for two lights at either end of the first floor and a single light on the second. Maybe she's not home, I told myself, feeling a sense of relief. After all, talking to her had plenty of potential downside. But I was still shaken by that damn article, so I got out of the car and headed down the side street toward the house.

A grove of mature cedars and Doug firs that had miraculously escaped the developer's chainsaw stood behind the house. The trees loomed out of the deep shadows like ramparts and stopped at a fence that bordered the back of her property. The moon broke free for a moment, and I saw something move up near the fence line. I was sure of it. I stopped and stood there staring into the shadows below me. The shape took form—the silhouette of a man standing at the fence looking into the back of Alexis' house. Or was he looking at me?

The moonlight dimmed, and the shape dissolved back into the darkness. My pulse ramped up. Could that be the man who broke into Daina's place and roughed her up? I slipped my cell phone out of my shirt pocket but stopped short of punching in 9-1-1. Calling from my phone would put me at the scene and raise a lot of questions. Did I really want that?

That argument was cut short when the moon reappeared. The person at the fence line got a clear look at me and took off running. They say never run from a cougar, because you'll trigger its chase response. Well, apparently, you shouldn't run from me either, because without a second thought I began to chase the guy. He disappeared into the cedar grove, but when I got to the edge, I put the brakes on. I wasn't armed, but the man I was pursuing sure as hell could be. I stood there trying to hear which way he might've gone, either back toward my car or around Alexis' house and down the hill. A thick carpet of fir needles in the grove apparently dampened his footfalls, because I didn't hear a thing until a car started up down below and tore out of the development.

My first impression was that I'd caught the intruder while he was casing the back of Alexis' house, but I quickly realized he could have just as well been coming out rather than preparing to go in. I decided I'd better check to see if Alexis was okay.

I moved along the fence line and let myself into the backyard through a side gate. The yard was dark except for a light beneath the surface of a large swimming pool, giving the water an eerie, radioactive glow. I took the steps up to the massive deck that ran the width of the house and moved across to the back door. I tried the knob. It was locked. A good sign.

At the other end of the house, more light shone from a large window and an adjacent sliding glass door that opened out onto the pool. The blinds on both were drawn. The slider was closed, but it gave when I nudged the handle. I eased it open, stuck my head in, and called out. "Alexis? Are you in there, Alexis? It's Cal Claxton." Nothing. I called again and got no response.

One wall of the room was lined with floor-to-ceiling book-shelves, the other with an assortment of framed photographs. At the far end of the room, a laptop with its screen up sat on a back bar behind a humongous teak desk. At my end, a low glass and chrome coffee table sat in front of a black leather couch and between two matching chairs. This had to be Bruckner's study. The door leading into the room was shut. I walked across the room, opened the door, and stood listening. Not a sound. I called out again and got no response.

I had no appetite to check the rest of place, a dozen rooms, at least, but what if Alexis was hurt or dead somewhere in the house? Against my better judgment, I made a quick sweep of the house and found nothing. As I was leaving through Bruck-ner's study, I noticed a packing box on the edge of the teak desk; not the box so much, but what was written on the side of it with a Sharpie marker—*Hal's NanoTech Files.* I thought I recognized Alexis' handwriting. My guess was she had bundled up Bruckner's files, the material he brought home to work on. The management team at NanoTech had probably requested the files. After all, they still had a business to run.

I hesitated, but not for long. Using a ballpoint pen, I quickly leafed through the box, a series of folders that were upright like contents of a filing cabinet. Most of the files had typed headings that didn't interest me, but three had handwritten headings that did. One was labeled *Security,* a second, *Diamond Wire,* and a third, *Streeter.* All were thin files, labeled in a strong, slanted cursive I took to be Bruckner's handwriting.

Before my lawyerly conscience could come up with a good counterargument, I removed the files, stuck them under my arm, and replaced the lid on the box. For my eyes only, I told myself to salve my conscience. And I promised myself I'd find a way to give them back. I closed the sliding door and headed for my car, stashed the files under the passenger seat, and got the hell out of there. The whole episode had an air of unreality. Someone had planned to break into Alexis' house, and I'd stumbled right into the middle of it. I tried hard to picture the details of the intruder as he sprinted away, but all I could pull up was a shadowy figure who'd run like a bat out of hell.

Was it worth taking those files? Would the intruder have taken the same ones? What the hell was he looking for, anyway?

Chapter Twenty-three

I was anxious to get back to the Aerie to have a look at Bruckner's files. At the same time, I was wired and needed someone to talk to. I knew just the person. When I got back to Dundee, I swung by the Pritchard Animal Care Center, knowing my chances of catching Hiram there were pretty good. An avowed workaholic, my friend spent more time with his animals than at home. Sure enough, his Saab was parked behind the building, and the light in his office was on. Hiram must have seen my headlights because he was waiting for me at the back door of the building. When I stepped into the light, he looked at me over his granny glasses and smiled. "Cal, come in."

I shrugged. "I was in the neighborhood. Felt like talking."

I followed him down the hall to his office. A white lab coat draped loosely on his lanky frame, and his battered boat-sized sneakers slapped the tile floor. I thought of a scarecrow, but make no mistake, this scarecrow had found his brains. He took a Mirror Pond pale ale from a mini-fridge behind his desk, opened it, and handed it to me. Then he opened a cabinet on the wall and extracted a bottle of Macallan 12 single-malt Scotch and a glass. After blowing dust from the glass, he poured himself three fingers. When I clinked the neck of my bottle on the rim of his glass, he looked at me, his gray eyes tinged with concern. "So, what is it that needs discussing at this late hour? Does it have to do with that murder on the Deschutes? I read that disgusting article in *The Oregonian*. I called you about it, but you didn't return my call."

I opened my hands in mock surrender. "I know. I know. Things have been hectic, Hiram." I took a long pull on my beer and settled back in my chair. "You know, when I was a prosecutor down in L.A., I had this crystal-clear picture of the law. Sure, life could be murky, but the law—that was different. You were either on one side or the other. Good guys. Bad guys. Nothing in between." I expelled a breath and shook my head.

Hiram nodded. "It's never black and white. And sometimes laws need breaking."

"I'm not talking about what you did with those rhesus monkeys at Johns Hopkins. That was civil disobedience. Your hero is Gandhi, and I get that. I'm talking about laws and ethical codes that should be obeyed. You know, the righteous path. Trouble is, when you come under pressure, see your future on the line, things get a little less clear-cut. Maybe Machiavelli was right about the ends justifying the means."

Hiram chuckled. "Machiavelli didn't actually say that, but your point's taken. Absolutes are hard to come by in this world." He drank some Scotch and eyed me carefully. "What happened tonight?"

"I, uh, got in a situation and crossed a line. Not a bright one, but a line, nonetheless. That's new territory for me. It got me thinking about all those folks I prosecuted down in L.A. I can only imagine the kind of circumstances some of them were up against."

"You had a job to do down there."

"Yeah, I know that. I know how the law works. I guess it was my *attitude* back then. I was quick to judge, didn't give a damn what choices people were up against. That never even entered my mind."

My friend smiled. "I trust that you had good reasons for whatever you did tonight."

I had to laugh. "Oh, yeah. Which brings me to the Bruckner murder. I'm worried they're going to charge me with it, Hiram.

You know what that would mean? I could be held without bail, awaiting a trail that could take eighteen months just to get started. I couldn't be there for my daughter, and defending myself would break me financially. Even if I'm acquitted, it's a freaking disaster. Yeah, I had good reasons."

Hiram drank some more Scotch, nodded slowly, and pursed his lips. "So, where does the case stand?"

I took my friend through what I knew at this point, and when I'd answered all his questions he said, "I'll grant you that fellow Pitman's acting rather suspiciously. Perhaps his desire to leave the company was strong enough to drive him to murder the CEO. Maybe it was just pure rage at being disrespected by the CEO and his colleagues." Hiram leaned forward and propped his elbows on the desk. "But I'm more inclined to suspect the wife and her boy toy. For my money, they hired somebody to do it, and they're trying to blame it on you."

I nodded. "Yeah, it's a pretty sweet deal for both of them. She gets rid of an alcoholic husband, collects insurance, and probably inherits a company worth millions. He gets her and a shot at taking the company public. Pretty compelling motives."

But there was a loose end I was reluctant to share with my friend, because I didn't want to disclose where I'd been earlier that night. If Alexis was in on the murder, then why was someone watching her house? And if she wasn't involved, then her life could be in danger, and I still needed to warn her.

The whole thing was a shotgun blast of dots, and I didn't have the first clue how to connect them.

On his final glass of Scotch, I brought my friend up to date on Claire's situation. Hiram listened with intense interest, because he was very fond of my daughter. When I finished, he removed his glasses, massaged his eyes, and when he looked at me again, a couple of vertical wrinkles had formed above the bridge of his nose. "This is insanity. Well Spring had no business exposing their volunteers if they couldn't ensure their safety."

"I knew the risks. I mean, Darfur? Are you kidding me? But I was trying to be supportive. You know, not get in the way with all the baggage I'm hauling around." I puffed out a breath and shook my head. "I should have dug my—"

"No, Calvin, don't blame yourself. Claire's a grown woman and knowing her as I do, I doubt very much that you could have persuaded her to stay."

I forced a smile. "You got that right. But if anything happens to her I'll—"

Hiram waved his hand dismissively. "That's not going to happen. Claire's a remarkably resourceful young woman. She's going to be fine, Cal."

A voice screamed in me. *She's being held by the Janjaweed, a bunch of blood-thirsty rapists.* But I held my tongue. The spoken words would only reinforce my fear and sense of helplessness. And besides, that's no way to respond to a friend who's trying to be supportive.

I nodded as if Hiram had reminded me of some truth I'd lost sight of. "You're right," I said, "Claire's going to be fine."

I wanted to believe that with every fiber in my being.

Chapter Twenty-four

I got back to the Aerie around midnight. When my headlights illuminated Archie he began barking and raced away. He did this to show he'd been patrolling the acreage, not spending the night waiting at the gate. Working dogs have their pride, you know. After I opened the gate he raced back, squealing and whimpering with delight when I knelt down to hug him. As if to join in, a barred owl from up in one of the Doug firs began hooting its eight-note refrain, *who-cooks-for-you, who-cooks-for-youuu?* I was home.

I let us both in, wiped the mud from his paws with a towel I kept by the front door, and went to the kitchen, where I downed a glass of cold well water. The house had a musty fish smell from last night's dinner, so I opened the side door to a blast of fresh air. I settled into my old roller chair in the study and spread the folders I'd taken from the Bruckner house on the desk in front of me. I opened the thinnest folder first. It was marked *Security* and contained mostly handwritten notes. I quickly realized they were almost certainly Bruckner's notes from the security meetings Daina had told me about. The bulk of the file dealt with more-or-less routine items relating to improvements at NanoTech, such as beefed-up computer firewalls, employee lock-up procedures, and the installation of a security camera system. I was getting tired and had to concentrate hard to keep the words from squirming off the page. However, when I came to the last page, I snapped to attention. It was dated May 29, just one day before the Deschutes trip. In a strong, firm hand Bruckner had written:

Rusty Musik findings - - -

Upcoming tech conference, San Francisco—Duane has meetings Aug. 18 with TM-E rep Clivas & Aug. 19 with Y. P. Chang from Guangzhou Micro Tech

What the fuck??

"*I knew it,*" I said out loud. Rusty Musik *had* done some snooping. TM-E and Guangzhou Micro Tech were the two competitors Daina had told me about the other night, the ones Bruckner was worried about. He had learned about these meetings right before the Deschutes trip, and judging from the fact that the last line he wrote was nearly punched through the page, he'd become furious. Had he confronted Pitman?

I opened the Diamond Wire file next. It was crammed with handwritten notes, memos, tables of data, and press releases, all relating to the technical breakthrough that Duane Pitman had made. The file made for interesting reading. In an e-mail message to Bruckner dated thirteen months ago, Pitman wrote:

Hal,

Hope you and your lovely wife are enjoying your cruise in Alaska.

I have the best of news for you. The U.S. patent office has just advised us that our Diamond Wire application has been allowed! All claims were accepted with the exception of the alternate plasma conditions. (We didn't expect to get those anyway.) I think we can be commercial on a small scale in 36 months. We did it!

Regards, Duane

But following the euphoria of the breakthrough and the allowed patent, tensions developed in a hurry between the two. Pitman laid out his complaints about lack of recognition and having his budget squeezed in a series of e-mails, the first of which was dated about nine months ago. It was essentially the litany I'd heard that night on the Deschutes during the speaking-truth session.

I opened the file marked *Andrew Streeter* next. On top was a six-month-old, formal letter to Streeter from Bruckner stating in no uncertain terms that Streeter's performance was unacceptable and demanding that he improve it "over the next period." Mitch Hannon was blind-copied on the letter. On the bottom margin of the memo Bruckner had penned a handwritten note to Hannon dated May 26:

> *Mitch,*
>
> *This is fyi. It's just not working out with Andrew. He's had more than enough time to straighten himself out since I put him on probation last March. I think it's best to go ahead and terminate him when we get back from the fishing trip. Since I don't have all my ducks in a row, I decided to let him attend the fishing trip. Otherwise, it gets too awkward.*
>
> *Hal*

Mitch had scrawled the following at the bottom of the note and sent it back to Bruckner:

> *Hal – I don't agree! Let's talk after the trip, before you do anything irreversible!*
>
> *M.H.*

Whoa, enter another suspect. Getting fired right before the big payday would cost Streeter a bundle, but with Bruckner out of the way and Hannon at the reins of the company, problem solved.

It was one-fifteen when I finally dragged myself upstairs, collapsed on my bed, and fell into a deep sleep. I awoke a little after six. In the midst of shaving, I became aware of my reflection in the mirror. I slowly lowered the razor and looked at my face as if for the first time. The image startled me. My eyes stared wearily back at me, the pupils like bugs caught in red spider webs, the fine creases at their corners like cracks in a windshield. I could swear my hair seemed flecked with more gray than before this whole mess started, and my mustache, although holding its own against the gray, traced a ragged, untrimmed line across my upper lip. I turned sideways and put my hand on my gut and stretched out my six-two frame. A thickening around my waist threatened to become a paunch if left unattended. I pinched the flesh on my hip between my thumb and forefinger. "Shit. Where did this come from?" I said out loud.

Archie, who'd been dozing on his mat in the corner, got up and followed me down the back staircase. I gathered up Bruckner's files in the study and took them out to the garage, emptied out the thick plastic envelope that held the owner's manual to my John Deere tractor and put the files in it. Then I taped the flap shut with duct tape and stashed the envelope in an underground irrigation box at the top of my property. The files weren't earth-shattering, but I sure as hell didn't want to get caught with them. I was expecting Dorn and Escalante to show up with a search warrant any time now.

When we got back to the kitchen, the phone rang. I held my breath as I picked up the receiver.

"Dad? It's Claire, Dad. I'm okay, Dad. I'm okay."

"Claire!" I shouted into the phone, "Claire! Where are you?"

We're on our way to Khartoum in a convoy. We were released forty minutes ago."

"Thank God. Are you sure you're all right, sweetheart?"

"Yes, except for my leg, Dad."

"Your leg? What's the matter with your leg?"

"I, uh, sort of broke it. But no worries," she added hastily. "There's a doctor with us, and he has it all splinted. It's not a bad break. Doesn't even hurt that much."

"What happened? How did it happen?" I replied, struggling to stay calm.

"We wrecked our jeep trying to get away from those jerks. I was the only one seriously hurt. But there's no need to fuss. They're telling me I need to go back to the States. I want to come to the Aerie, Dad."

"Sure. Right. Of course. Come to Oregon."

"Listen, Dad. I have to get off now. I'll be flying into L.A. Uh, I know you're busy, but do you think you could meet me there?"

I wanted to tell her I'd be there no matter what, but I knew there'd be no going to L.A. with Bruckner's murder hanging over me. "I'll check with Well Spring and let you know, sweetheart. Call me when you get to Khartoum, okay?" I said good-bye, knowing I'd sounded more like a damn lawyer than a parent, but it was the best I could do. I had, what, maybe a week to clear up the Bruckner matter? Fat chance.

After I'd hung up, I thought for a moment, about how both Daina and Hiram had predicted this outcome. "Archie, you hear that!" I shouted. "She's okay. Claire's okay!"

Archie's ears came forward, his backside began to wag, and he yelped a high-pitched note that told me he knew exactly what I was talking about. Claire was coming home.

Chapter Twenty-five

I stood at the kitchen window, the espresso maker churning at my elbow. Two dark, viscous streams slowly filled my chipped mug. I breathed in the aroma, rich, like black earth, and full of promise for the day. The sun had seared the thin haze, and the fields in the valley rippled with spring color. Goldfinches and black-capped chickadees nibbled at the feeder, crows cawed in the firs, and hawks drifted at a thousand feet. Life was good again, or at least a helluva lot better.

After a second cappuccino and a bowl of oatmeal, I turned on my cell and scrolled down to Philip Lone Deer. "Philip? It's Cal. Didn't wake you, did I?" I asked, knowing full well he'd been up for hours.

"Are you kidding? I've already made love to my wife, tied half a dozen flies, and washed my truck. What's up?"

"Claire's okay," I blurted out. "She's on her way to Khartoum in a convoy, and then on to the States."

Philip let out a war whoop. In the background I heard his wife Lanie shout, "Philip, what is it?" Philip called back to her, "Claire's okay! She's on her way home!" Then he added to me, "That's a load off. What a great piece of news!"

I went on to tell him about her broken leg, the need to arrange her transportation home, and my legal complication. Without hesitating, Philip said, "Look, Cal. Don't worry about L.A. If you can't go, I'm there. Just buy me the ticket." I also wanted to tell him what had happened to me the night before but decided against doing that on the phone. Toward the end of our conversation he said, "Things are still slow for me. I'm going over to Hood River on Friday to look at a used drift boat. Why don't you meet me there, and we can get caught up? We could even get in a few casts. "

"What did you have in mind?"

"I don't know. I hear there's a nice steelhead run in the Hood River right now. We could fish below the dam, then have lunch in town."

A fishing break was just what I needed. "Let's do that."

"Okay," Philip responded. "And let's make it interesting. Whoever hooks the fewest fish buys lunch."

"Gee, I don't know. That would require an honor system. Hardly seems fair."

"You question my honor, paleface? You're the ones who break all the treaties."

"Okay. Okay. It's a deal. Where should we meet?"

"There's a parking lot below the dam. We can walk in from there. Need to get there no later than six-thirty."

I groaned. *"Six-thirty?* It's gotta be an hour and half drive for me."

"Me, too. You want to beat the crowds or what?"

"Okay, sounds like a plan. Uh, better e-mail me directions. I'm not sure I can find the place."

It was just after eight, so I dialed Well Spring next. An ebullient Chad Harrelson came on the line. He told me that Claire would be briefly hospitalized in Khartoum to make sure she was fit to travel. The trip home would be grueling with stops in Cairo, Amsterdam, and finally L.A., but she'd have someone from Well Spring with her all the way. I told him either I or a family friend would fly down to L.A. to accompany her up to Portland. She would be on her way back to the States by early next week.

After calling Hiram with the good news, I left for Alexis Bruckner's place. I parked at the same spot I had the night before. I ducked into the trees to see if I could pick up any clues about the prowler I'd seen the night before but didn't see anything. I was planning to ring the front bell, but when I reached Alexis' side gate I heard the rhythmical splash of someone swimming laps in the pool. I knew Alexis was fond of swimming, so I let myself in and closed the gate behind me. I watched her swim for a while, surprised at the strength and smoothness of her stroke. Finally I walked to the edge of the pool. She pulled up abruptly when she saw me.

"Oh. Cal. You scared me. What are you doing here?" Her eyes lingered on me as she removed her swim cap and shook her hair free. Rivulets of water streamed down the curves of her body.

"Hello, Alexis. Sorry to interrupt your morning swim, but I need to talk to you about a couple of things. It's important."

Her one-piece looked like it had been sprayed on, and she came out of the pool languorously, inviting me to watch. I felt relieved when she put on a terry bathrobe. Before I could say another word the back door swung open, and a man backed out with a tray of steaming cups and covered dishes. He turned around and stopped dead when he saw me.

"Claxton? What in hell are you doing here?" It was Mitch Hannon.

"Maybe I should ask you the same thing," I responded much too quickly. It wasn't really my place to say anything.

"I came by to have breakfast with, uh, Mrs. Bruckner. We've got business to discuss."

"Fine. I won't keep her very long."

"I'm stepping in as CEO at her request. We have a lot to go over." Hannon continued in what was now an annoyingly self-righteous tone. He put the tray down on a wrought-iron table and stepped toward me.

Alexis moved between us. "Sit down, please. Both of you." She turned to Hannon. "Cal said he has something important to tell me." Then she turned to me. "Do you mind if Mitch sits in?"

"No. I suppose not," I answered unenthusiastically. No way I was going to mention the affair in front of Hannon. "I came by last night to talk to you, Alexis." It was about nine-thirty."

Alexis raised her eyebrows but let me continue. Hannon shifted in his seat. "I, uh, wanted to discuss a couple of things."

"Oh, that's rich. Sounds to me like you were stalking her, Claxton," Hannon said. "Did you bring your fishing knife?"

I ignored Hannon. He'd obviously heard about my knife being found at the scene. "I parked up behind your place, and as I was coming down the lane I saw someone in the trees there, watching your house. I spooked him, and he took off."

Alexis' eyes registered surprise. "Watching the house?"

"Yeah." I pointed in the direction of the grove of trees. "From back there. You need to be careful, Alexis. I think someone's watching you."

She started to speak, but Hannon beat her to it. "You've got a lot of goddamn nerve coming here. And your bullshit story isn't going to wash. Not with me, not with anybody. You better stay away from Mrs. Bruckner."

I forced a smile and shook my head. I didn't want any trouble with Hannon. "You're entitled to your opinion."

"*Opinion?* Are you kidding me?" Hannon pointed a finger at me, his face filling with color. "The evidence points to you, Claxton. You killed my uncle, you bastard." Alexis tried to speak again, but he waved her off. "I'm warning—"

"That's enough," I broke in. "You want to talk evidence? Okay. You're obviously sleeping with your uncle's wife, you had full access to the murder weapon on the Deschutes, and now you're stepping in to take over the company. That's motive, opportunity, and means."

"*You son of a bitch.*" Hannon jumped up, toppling his chair behind him. Seeing rage build in his face, and not liking the angle he had on me, I got up, too.

Alexis leaped up as well. "Mitch, stop it, plea—"

Before she could finish, Hannon pushed me hard in the chest with both hands. I almost fell over. When I righted myself, I took a step back to try to de-escalate the situation.

Alexis said, "Damn it, Mitch. Stop!" She grabbed his wrist, but he shook his hand free.

I took another step back, only to find myself at the edge of the pool. "You heard her, Hannon. Back off."

Eyes narrowed to slits, he closed the distance between us. I saw the first punch coming and rocked back on my heels. His fist just missed my jaw, and I nearly fell into the pool. He swung again. I ducked the punch, grabbed his arm with both hands, and used his forward momentum to throw him into the pool. He came up sputtering and swearing but made no effort to climb out.

Alexis screamed, then turned her wrath on me, pointing toward the gate. "Get out of here, Cal. Just get out."

I turned to face her. "What I just told you is true, Alexis. Be careful."

"Well, that didn't go very well," I said out loud as I got back into my car. On the way back to Dundee I kicked myself for letting the situation get out of hand. Should've shut up and left when it was clear where the thing was heading. The last thing I needed was a fistfight with the nephew of the man I was suspected of murdering. Suppose he accuses me of assault? If Alexis backed him, I would be in an awkward position, to say the least. But as I thought about it, I decided they were very unlikely to do anything that would call attention to their cozy arrangement.

I felt like my warning to Alexis had gotten through, but I was disappointed that I wasn't able to talk to her alone. I wanted to see her reaction to my revealing the affair. Would she back me up? And what about her demeanor? Would I see anything to lead me to believe she was mixed up in Bruckner's murder? The only thing I did observe was that old come-hither look that had gotten me into trouble in the first place.

As for Hannon, I wondered if his anger was genuine or just for show. I wasn't sure.

I took some solace in the fact that I'd tried to defuse the situation. I hadn't always shown that kind of forbearance. As I wound along the Willamette River toward Dundee, my mind drifted back to the events that unfolded after Nancy's suicide. My boss had told me to take some time off, but I was afraid to. Work had been my primary focus. The thought of time to myself was terrifying—what would I do?

Three weeks or so after Nancy's funeral I was interviewing a key witness to a double homicide I was about to take to trial. My witness had heard three shots and seen the shooter leave a liquor store with a gun in his hand. The elderly couple who ran the store lay bleeding to death inside. But as I was preparing my star witness to take the stand, he suddenly claimed he wasn't sure about anything. "What the hell," I asked, "somebody get to you?"

He shrugged and smiled nervously. "Hey, man, I like breathin', you know what I'm sayin'?"

It had a lot to do with the casual way he tossed the comment off, or maybe it was the fact that I'd just finished a tear-soaked meeting with the victims' daughter, or that I'd spent better than a hundred hours in preparation for the trial. Whatever it was, it caused me to go off like an IED. The next thing I knew, I had the witness by the throat, pinned against the wall with both feet off the ground. "You can't do this. We'll lose the case," I screamed in his face.

That got me a leave of absence. When I told my boss I was ready to come back to work, he advised me to seriously consider the early retirement package the city was offering at the time. I took the hint and the package. Three months later I sold my house and moved to Dundee, Oregon.

I popped out of my reverie when a big pickup ran a light in front of me in Newberg. When I arrived at my law office, I put the blinds down on the front window and slumped down in my chair. Despite the good news about Claire, I worried about the pressure I was under and what it would do to me. The truth was, I'd come very close to doing a lot more to Hannon than just tossing him in the pool. The realization chilled me. Pressure or no pressure I needed to control my temper, I reminded myself.

As I brooded over the issue, my cell chirped. It was Daina Zakaris checking in. I gave her the good news about Claire and invited her to lunch. No sooner had I put the phone down than it rang again.

"Cal? This is Nando. I've got some information for you."

Chapter Twenty-six

I gave Nando a quick run-down on my "person of interest" status as well as Claire's situation before asking him what he had on the Ford F-150. "It was reported stolen last Wednesday night. It's registered to a student named Lawrence Cantwell. He's a freshman at Portland State. It was stolen in the Park Blocks and is still missing."

Wednesday night, I said to myself. The timing fits perfectly. "Useful. Thanks, Nando. Uh, any luck on the Grand Cherokee from Madras?"

"Actually, I do have something on the Jeep. It was found abandoned at the northwest corner of Milwaukie and Knapp in southeast Portland. The PPB has it impounded until Jefferson County can pick it up."

That would be Escalante and Dorn. "Nando, you never disappoint,"

"Thank you, my friend. This affair on the Deschutes is troubling. Do you need any additional help?"

"Nothing I can think of at the moment, but stay tuned."

"Whatever you need, Calvin."

I was anxious to check out the area in Portland where Barnes' Grand Cherokee had been abandoned. But that was going to have to wait. For the next hour I focused on getting some work done—the kind that actually pays the bills. At noon I headed off to meet Daina for lunch.

I got to the restaurant first, a great little Thai joint a block off the 99W in Newberg, took an outdoor table and ordered a Singha. Halfway into my beer, I saw the lime green VW flash by and park across the street. I watched Daina through a potted hydrangea as she approached. She wore clogs, black slacks, and a white cotton tunic cinched at her waist, set off with a squash blossom necklace of silver and jade. Her hair, thick and lustrous, bounced to the rhythm of her rapid gait. Her eyes were shielded by a large pair of dark glasses, but her face showed…what, a look of anticipation?

I stood up and waved, and when she joined me, got a big hug. "I'm glad your daughter's okay, Cal. You must feel so relieved."

I nodded, holding her for a moment at arm's length. The bruise on her cheek had lightened some against her olive skin. "How's the shoulder?"

"Oh, still a bit stiff, but fine." I must have held my gaze a beat too long because she smiled and wrinkled her brow. "*What?* I'm overdressed for Newberg?"

"No, no, you look great." Then, trying to recover, I added, "The burglar must've missed that necklace."

She tucked her chin and looked down. "Oh, this. Right. He took the cheap stuff and left this, not that it's any treasure." After I answered her questions about Claire's situation, she grew serious. "I was horrified by that hatchet-job article in *The Oregonian*. How did that happen?"

I shrugged. "Most likely my buddy, Dorn, but I don't know for sure who leaked the story. Not exactly a confidence-builder for my clientele in Dundee."

She shook her head. "Have there been any repercussions?"

"Not yet."

After we ordered our food—a massaman curry for me, tom yum soup for her—Daina said, "So, anything new with your investigation?"

"Calling it an investigation might be overstating it." I went on to describe surprising the prowler at Alexis' house, leaving out the part about the files I'd come across and what I'd learned from

them. I also left out my return visit the next day and my alter-
cation with Mitch Hannon. That was just plain embarrassing.

When I finished, she said, "Do you think it was the same
person who broke into my house?"

I nodded. "Same M.O. He was watching Alexis' place before
breaking in, just like with you."

Her face lost some color. "Do you think he'll come back to
my place?"

"Hard to say. He's bungled two break-ins so far. My gut says
he won't risk another."

The muscles in her face tightened, and her eyes narrowed.
"Well, I'm staying put, that's for sure." That bozo wouldn't dare
risk another run-in with Dylan." We both laughed at that. She
continued, "I bought some Mace, just in case."

Mace might make her feel better but would offer little protection. I pictured her rental house, isolated on all sides with a big
hedge obscuring the view from the road. I didn't like it, but her
defiant look reminded me a lot of Claire. I knew it would be
fruitless to advise her to move. "Keep your doors and windows
locked."

The food arrived, and after tasting her soup Daina said, "The
best test of a Thai restaurant is the tom yum. This is first rate."

I had tears in my eyes from the curry, which I'd ordered extra
hot. "The massaman's good, too. Serious heat." I took a sip of
Singha. "So, what's new that you can tell me about at NanoTech?"

She took a sip of tom yum and sat back. "We had our first staff
meeting without Hal Bruckner. It was tense. The emotions are
still pretty raw. I gave a status report on the management systems
and the security of their technical information. I told them if
they wanted the IPO to go well they needed to up their game,
that the investment banks would be all over them demanding
to see their game plan."

"How'd they take it?"

"Oh, I think I got Hannon's attention, for sure. But the meeting pretty quickly devolved into another bitch session between

Hannon and Streeter on one side and Pitman on the other. But now, there's no Hal Bruckner to referee."

I had to chuckle. "Did they say something nice first, like you taught them on the river?"

She shook her head and gave me a pained look. "I'm afraid it's crossed over to outright incivility. And Hannon's ambivalent. He knows he needs Pitman, but he doesn't know how much. Streeter's coming on more aggressively, too. At one point he made this pronouncement, you know, wrapped in that sugary Southern drawl of his, that the Diamond Wire scale-up would pose no problems, inferring that they didn't need Pitman."

"How did Pitman take that?"

"Not well. He got right in Streeter's face. The man was shaking with anger, said something like, 'This is above your intellectual pay grade, Andy. You aren't intelligent enough to even ask the right questions.'"

"Whoa. What happened next?"

"Streeter's neck turned the color of a fire hydrant, and I thought he was going to pop a blood vessel. He stood up, shook a finger at Pitman, and said, 'Bring it on, Duane.'"

I had to laugh this time. "Took a page right out of W's playbook, huh?"

Daina laughed, despite herself. "I'm not making this up, Cal. Honest."

"So, still one big, happy family."

"Right. I'm afraid any hope I had that Hal's death would pull them together is sadly misplaced. Hannon did finally get between them, but Hal was more of a peacemaker than I gave him credit for. Anyway, now Pitman's twisting in the wind even more, and he's not taking it well. He's the kind of personality who needs order and predictability, and I'm afraid he's not going to get that from Hannon. Pitman's scary, Cal—you know, the kind of guy who might show up at work one day with an assault rifle under his raincoat."

"Did you check his bottled water supply?"

"Yeah, I peeked in the staff kitchen fridge where he keeps his stash. No designer brands, just what's on sale, apparently—Poland Springs, Arrowhead. Three of each. No Crystal Geyser. But there could have been earlier. No way of telling."

I nodded. "Has Rusty Musik turned up anything new on him?"

She gave me her best impression of a blank look. "Nothing more than I told you last time."

"No trysts with TM-E or Guangzhou?"

She held her blank expression, but her eyes registered surprise. "Trysts? What do you mean?"

I smiled. "Come on, Daina. Your secret's safe with me," I said, echoing what she'd said about my affair with Alexis. "I have a feeling you might have access to information that could help break this case, but you've got to trust me. I have no interest in NanoTech's proprietary secrets or their IPO."

She broke eye contact, took a sip of soup, then looked back at me. "Jesus, Cal, where did you get that information?"

I returned her blank look. "I'm just interested in finding a lead. Being a person of interest in a murder investigation is not my favorite thing. "

She laid her spoon down absently and let out a long breath. "I want to help, Cal, believe me. My confidentiality agreement is with Hal Bruckner, since he was the sole owner of NanoTech. He's gone, so I suppose that, technically, I have some leeway." She took another sip of soup, giving herself a moment. "I, uh, did agree to have Rusty take a look at Pitman at Hal's request. See, Rusty's not just a good physicist. He's also a damn good hacker. He can crack just about anyone's system. Hal wanted to scan Pitman's e-mail. He owns the computers, so I wasn't breaking any laws. Okay, it was borderline ethical, for sure, but I thought Hal had some justification, so I went along with it."

"Why didn't Bruckner have his own IT people do the snooping?"

"Oh, word would have gotten back to Pitman in a heartbeat. You know how the rumor mill works."

I nodded. "Why would Pitman be so cavalier about his e-mail?"

"Oh, he had a layer of protection, but not enough. You'd be surprised how careless people are, even techies like Pitman. Or maybe he just doesn't give a damn?"

"Did Musik find any hanky-panky?"

"She glanced around the room before speaking. "Yes. Pitman was going to attend a big tech conference in San Francisco and had made arrangements with TM-E and Guangzhou—the meetings you alluded to."

I laughed. "Lucky guess on my part."

She gave me a look. "Yeah, right. Anyway, he had to cancel because of Hal's death. But, get this—a representative from TM-E, the French firm, is coming to Portland to meet with him. A guy named Clivas. A cozy dinner is planned."

"What about the Chinese company?"

"They pulled back when Pitman cancelled the San Francisco trip."

"When's the dinner?" She gave me the details, and I jotted them down. "What about the run-up to the fishing trip? Would you know if he communicated with anyone about that outside the company?"

"I read all the e-mails carefully, Cal. There was nothing about the fishing trip at all."

"My name. Any mention of my name?"

"Nope."

I decided to show my final hold card. "Uh, was there any mention of railroad schedules, the Kaskela switching station, the Barlow Northern Railroad, anything like that in conjunction with the trip?"

The blank look, again. Genuine this time. "No, not that I recall. Nothing about railroads. Why do you ask *that*?"

I waved a hand dismissively. "Oh, just one of my wild-ass theories. Not worth your time." She wrinkled her brow and studied me for a moment but to my relief didn't press it.

I felt let down. All I'd learned was that Pitman planned a brazen meeting with one of NanoTech's direct competitors, but that didn't make him a killer. I said, "I gather you know that Hannon's the new CEO of NanoTech?"

"Right. It'll be announced to the company tomorrow." She shook her head. "I'm not even going to ask how you heard about that."

I shrugged. "Looks like sleeping with the boss' wife paid off for Hannon."

She laughed. "Actually, I think Alexis made the right business move. Hannon may be an arrogant SOB, but he's pretty damn competent. The IPO could go well north of a half billion."

I almost choked on a bite of my curry. "*Wow*. Big stakes make for strong motives." I shook my head, thinking about how Bruckner's death hadn't benefitted Pitman, at least in any way I could see at the moment. And with Hannon in charge, he would almost certainly be cut out of a major block of shares when the company goes public. "What about Streeter?" I asked. "Will he be cut in as an officer of the company?"

Daina gave me a knowing smile. "I'm not privy to that, but my guess is, yeah, he'll come out smelling like a rose."

"Never hurts to kiss a little ass, right?"

"Oh, he's a master."

I decided to press my luck. I leaned forward and met her eyes again. "I've got too many suspects here, Daina. Uh, your inside man, Rusty, could he take a look at Hannon's and Streeter's e-mail, too? You know, anything related to the fishing trip or railroad schedules. I know it's a long shot, and the cops will probably get around to it eventually, but I'd sure like to stay a step ahead of them."

She rolled her eyes. "I'll see what I can do. Obviously, I expect you to protect me as a source at all costs."

"I'm a lawyer. That's what I do."

"There's one glitch—some of Streeter's e-mail's encrypted."

"Rusty can't beat it?"

"Afraid not. Streeter uses a sophisticated system that scrambles messages he wants protected. He can reassemble them using special software only he has access to. We'd have to know his pass code to get in, and it would take Rusty the next millennium to break it."

I wrinkled my brow. "Is this unusual?"

"Not at all. Lots of NanoTech employees use encryption. They know how easily their mail can be hacked. Pitman's system was no problem for Rusty. Mitch doesn't bother."

I nodded. "What about Streeter—anything else you know about him?"

"Not that much. "He's from South Carolina. Played soldier at the Citadel, then took a masters at Georgia Tech, where he met Hal. His daddy's some kind of player in state politics, I think. Andrew's a very private guy. Bachelor. Hard worker. Fancies himself a bit of a ladies' man, but the women at NanoTech would dispute that. That's about all I know."

A smiling young waitress topped up our nearly full water glasses, causing a lull in the conversation. After a couple of silent bites, Daina said, "So, when exactly is Claire coming home?"

"I'm waiting to hear the details of her itinerary, but she's stopping in L.A. I'm hoping to fly down there to meet her so I can travel back with her."

"Hoping?"

"I've been told to stay local by Escalante and Dorn. I'll have to get their okay, unless something breaks in the case."

Daina winced. "Forgot about that. I hope it works out. She'll appreciate it, I'm sure." She smiled and met my eyes. "You're wearing the good news, Cal. You have this glow."

I nodded. "Right. That explains why I never win at poker."

We shared a laugh, and just like that I felt something shift between us, a sort of acknowledgment, unspoken, of our mutual attraction.

We both carried on like nothing had happened, and after we wrapped up and she'd left, it didn't take me long to start questioning. Face it, I told myself. Your track record's not good. I pushed down feelings of anticipation tinged with curiosity and even a nub of excitement. After all, a relationship was the last thing I needed, something I'd promised myself to avoid.

Keep your head in the game, I told myself.

Chapter Twenty-seven

When I got back from lunch, I googled "Streeter, South Carolina politics" and learned that Streeter's father, Paxton K., had been a prominent state senator for over thirty years before forming a foundation that supplies disadvantaged kids with laptops and tablets. The only other thing I learned was that Andrew had been a standout linebacker on the Citadel gridiron. Nefarious family ties or interest in railroads? No such luck.

I had just wrapped up a short appointment with a woman facing her second DUI charge when I heard the sound of car doors opening and then snapping shut out front. I rotated in my chair and pushed the blinds to the side just in time to see Bull Dorn in mirrored sunglasses pull up his trousers, scratch his crotch, and nod to someone outside my field of view, presumably Escalante. A portable blue light pulsed on the roof of the unmarked sedan.

I opened the door and stepped out into the afternoon glare. Behind the unmarked sedan, two uniformed officers were getting out of a blue-and-white with the Yamhill County Sheriff's seal on the door. It was their jurisdiction, after all. Further back, the same evidence van used at the river was pulling in along with a cherry red Miata. Deb Fitzhugh, a lawyer from McMinnville whom I knew professionally, got out of the Miata. Cars slowed on 99W to rubberneck, and two customers came out of the bakery across the street to watch. I could see my friends Tim and Aurora, the owners, watching from inside.

"Welcome to Dundee, officers," I said with a smile I hoped didn't look forced. My palms were already sweaty, but I wasn't going to give them an ounce of satisfaction. "Is this an official visit, or should I put on coffee?"

Dorn fell a step behind Escalante, who, ignoring my question, took off his Ray-Bans and said, "Mr. Claxton, I have a warrant here to search these premises along with your residence." This is in connection with the murder of Harold Bruckner." He handed me a sheaf of papers on a clipboard and turned to acknowledge Fitzhugh, who was walking up to join us. "This is—"

"I know her," I interrupted. "Hi, Deborah, I assume you're the special master for this deal." She nodded and forced an awkward smile. When a lawyer's office is searched in Oregon, the judge signing the search warrant appoints a so-called "special master" to ensure client confidentiality is not violated. The job had fallen to Deb Fitzhugh, although it was clear she wasn't relishing the task. No lawyer likes to see one of their own in trouble.

By this time, a small crowd—make that a large crowd for Dundee—had gathered across the street. I recognized all of them, but I tried not to let it bother me. I knew the drill. The public spectacle and the embarrassment were all part of a play to rattle me. I invited the entourage into my office and read over the documents carefully. They were looking for physical evidence and any correspondence between me and the persons who were present at the murder scene. I could live with all of that.

When I'd finished reading, Dorn put his face up to mine. "When we finish up, we'd like to have another chat with you, hotshot." I could see myself in his glasses and turned my head slightly to avoid his breath, which was flavored by stale cigarette smoke and something less pleasant in his nasal passages.

I was anxious to get this over with. "Fine. Tell you what. We can save time if you get started on my house now, too. I'll stay here, but I can probably arrange to have someone meet you there to represent me. Although I didn't want to impose this on my friend, I knew Hiram Pritchard would be a good stand-in. No lawyer but a damn quick study and a stickler for detail, he could hold his own after I briefed him on the warrant. I speed-dialed his direct line, and he picked up on the third ring.

After I briefed him on the situation, he said, "So, the Visigoths are at the gate."

"You might say that, although the Visigoths were a sensitive lot compared to these guys."

He chuckled. "I'll have to rearrange some things. I'll be there shortly."

Twenty minutes later he pulled up with the top down in his vintage Saab. By this time, the crowd across the street had nearly doubled. They were obviously waiting for some sort of resolution, like them cuffing me and stuffing me into a patrol car.

I went over the key points of the search warrant with Hiram. Summing up, I told him, "Just remember, they aren't allowed to even browse through anything that's not within the scope we just discussed. If you have *any* questions, call me." I thought about Bruckner's files—the ones I'd hidden up by the garden—and little spiders of fear began crawling down my back. Why didn't I just burn the damn things?

Dorn and Escalante had divided the chores, with Escalante opting to supervise the search team at my office. He maintained a poker face, but I could see the enthusiasm drain from him as the search droned on without any payoff.

The group that searched my office finished at about six that night. I worried they would confiscate my computer, which would have shut down my law practice. But they simply copied my hard drive and made photocopies of some of my written files pertaining to the fishing trip. Other than that, they hadn't put a thing into evidence.

The search team at the Aerie hadn't finished, and they were having no better luck. They knocked off at the same time, locked up my house, posted a guard, and left. I spent the night on Hiram's futon with Archie sleeping on the floor next to me. The next morning I had a cup of coffee with my host and headed for my place. I got there just before Dorn and the three-member search team arrived. Escalante wasn't with them.

I was sitting on the rocker on the front porch talking to the guard when they drove up. They climbed the front steps, stone-faced. "Top of the morning, gentlemen," I said. "Has anybody calculated what this is costing the taxpayers in Jefferson County?"

Dorn shot me a withering look that caused Archie to growl, but no one said a word.

The search ended around ten-thirty. I didn't have to sign for anything except some useless computer records and another fishing knife—the one I used for years before Claire gave me the one now in their possession. I figured the knife was a means of saving face, allowing them to claim they hadn't come back completely empty-handed. I was still on the rocker when Dorn came up and said, "We're taking you in for questioning now. Would you come with me, please?"

Instantly wary of his formality, I said, "Where's the interview?"

"We'll use the facilities in Newberg. My partner's waiting for us."

He descended the stairs and walked toward his car. I followed him, speaking to his back. "I need to feed my dog and give him some water before we go."

Dorn turned, looked down at Arch then back at me. "Fuck the mutt. We need to get on the road, Claxton."

A small flame of anger flared in my gut and threatened to fill my chest. I scrambled to contain it, swallowing an urge to invite the detective to try an impossible biological act. "It'll just take a moment. The food's right inside the kitchen door."

Dorn paused for a moment, as if considering my request, his eyes hiding behind the mirrored glasses, a muscle twitching along his right jawline. "He said, "We're moving out, hotshot. The mutt's not my concern."

I folded my arms across my chest. Archie moved in front of me and issued a low, guttural warning. "Hush, big boy," I told Arch, then to Dorn, "I'm not going anywhere until my dog's taken care of."

Dorn smiled, took a step back and unbuttoned his blazer to show the service revolver on his hip. "Turn around, put your hands on the car and spread 'em."

"Are you kidding me?" I shot back, my voice rising. Archie growled again, with more feeling this time.

"I said, turn around and spread 'em." He put his hand on the grip of his gun. "And if you don't back your dog off, I'll put a bullet in his head."

I stood there for a moment in disbelieving silence, shaking my head. The reality that the guy was a wacko was sinking in, and I sure as hell didn't want anything to start between him and my dog. I snapped my fingers and pointed at the ground. "Archie, lie down, boy, and *stay*." Then I turned around, placed my hands on the hood of the car and submitted to the search.

When he finished, Dorn slipped a pair of plastic handcuffs on my wrists and ratcheted them down, pinching skin against bone and said, "Standard procedure for taking in a murder suspect, hotshot. Can't be too careful, you know." Then he recited my Miranda rights. Even though I was not being formally arrested, Dorn knew that if he didn't read me my rights I would be able to challenge the admissibility of the interview down the road.

As we rolled down the driveway I craned my neck and caught a glimpse of Archie, who was still where I'd commanded him to lay, an anxious look on his face.

I was feeling anxious myself. Not only was I murder suspect number one, but now I was in a full-on conflict with a sociopath masquerading as a sheriff's detective. What else could go wrong?

Chapter Twenty-eight

I cooled my heels for better than forty minutes in the interview room at the Yamhill County Sheriff's Station in Newberg. I considered simply refusing to talk. That's certainly what a lawyer would have advised me to do. But I wanted to see what they had, and I also wanted to apprise them of what I'd learned. Maybe I had a shot at convincing them that Henry Barnes' death on the highway outside Madras was tied to the killing of Hal Bruckner. Maybe I could get them to see how perfectly it fit with my theory of the Bruckner murder. *Maybe.*

I was standing when they came in, each carrying full cups of hot coffee. The aroma hit me like a brick in the head, but I wasn't about to ask for any. The day was half-shot, but Escalante still looked fresh as a daisy in a starched white shirt, creased slacks, and maroon paisley tie. His glistening black hair was sharply parted and his mustache neatly trimmed. Dorn, on the other hand, looked like he had spent the night in his car. The rim of his shirt collar was frayed and discolored, and there was a coffee stain on his right sleeve and a small, black-edged hole above his pocket from a cigarette ember. His face was flushed, his cheeks pocked like the surface of the moon.

"Have a seat, Claxton," Dorn said as our eyes met. He nimbly retrieved a cigarette out of a nearly empty package, lit up, and blew smoke in my direction. The smoke settled on me, and I stifled an urge to come across the table and slap the cigarette out of his mouth. While this was playing out in my head, Escalante was reciting the date, time, and place of the interview for the small tape recorder that was perched on the table between us like a referee.

"We'd like to go back over portions of your statement, Mr. Claxton," Escalante began. But instead of going back over "portions" of my statement, Escalante started back at the beginning. For the next two hours I found myself explaining, once again, what had happened out there on the Deschutes in mind-numbing detail. Finally, Escalante got around to my relationship with Alexis. "Mr. Claxton," he began, "during your, ah, liaisons with Mrs. Bruckner did you ever threaten Mr. Bruckner or indicate you would like to do him bodily harm?"

"Absolutely not." I stiffened involuntarily in my chair.

Dorn eyed me. "Come on, Claxton, Bruckner was no angel, was he? A mean drunk, right? You all jealous and wanting to protect the little missus."

"I said I never threatened Hal Bruckner."

"Okay," Escalante continued in a tone that had turned irritatingly dulcet, "but Mrs. Bruckner is suggesting otherwise."

I remained silent.

"She said your feelings for her were intense, that you were probably jealous of her husband," Escalante continued. "You know, Mr. Claxton, it would be a shame for you to take all the heat on this. Maybe there was more to your relationship than you're currently telling us? We can understand how hard it must be."

I laughed out loud. "You're off base, Escalante. We had a brief, physical fling. That was it. No jealousy, no intensity, no nothing. Look, gentlemen, if you're trying to play Mrs. Bruckner and me off against each other, it won't work. I'm a busy man. Either let's get on to something substantive or let's call it a day. This is a waste of everybody's time."

Escalante paused, and Dorn leaned back in his chair. I saw my opening and kept talking. "Look, I know you're investigating the murder of Henry Barnes, which occurred after the Bruckner's murder on the same morning. I'm certain the two killings were committed by the same person." Dorn came forward in his chair, but Escalante waved him off before he could cut in. "That person came in on the northbound Barlow Northern freight train— number 504—from the Madras yard, got off at the Kaskela switching yard, killed Bruckner, hopped on the southbound 1520 and got back off at the Madras yard. Check the schedules like I did. It fits like a glove. He'd left a stolen car near the Madras yard, but when he returned, *it* had been stolen, so he carjacked Barnes, left him dead on the side of the road, and drove Barnes' car back to Portland, where he abandoned it at the corner of Milwaukie and Knapp in Westmoreland."

Dorn came out of his chair. "How do you know where Barnes' car was left?" he shot back with more surprise than I'm sure he meant to show.

"I have my sources in Portland, too." Dorn started to say something else, but apparently thought better of it. I went on to remind them about the physical evidence of an intruder on the path between Whiskey Dick and Kaskela and the fact that I'd supplied them with the name of my skateboarder witness. It felt a little sketchy as I laid it all out, but it was all I had—at least all I was willing to share. I sold it as hard as I could.

Escalante actually made a couple of notes while I talked, but Dorn looked more and more like a hypertension poster child. Finally he switched off the tape recorder. "We're done here. Listen, Claxton, the only reason your sorry ass isn't in the Jeff County jail *right now* is that our DA doesn't have the balls to arrest you. So get the hell out of my sight."

Looking directly at Escalante, I said, "It hangs together, detective. Think about it."

Chapter Twenty-nine

I called Hiram to get a ride home and waited outside the sheriff's station, gulping in the fresh afternoon air to dilute Dorn's secondhand smoke. Hiram rolled up in his Saab with Archie sitting upright in the backseat like he was being chauffeured. I hopped in, tousled the fur on Archie's head, and said, "Want to show off your car in Portland?"

"Portland?"

"Right. Southeast. I've got some things to check out, and I could use some company."

A squall blew in, and rain began to spatter us as we approached the I-5. We pulled over and put the top up. We'd been talking about my interrogation. As we got underway again, Hiram said, "So, they're trying to cast you as the jealous lover. Can they make it stick?"

I thought for a moment. "I don't think so. What I heard today was mainly Escalante's spin on what Alexis allegedly told them about me. She didn't really give them anything incriminating, at least not yet. They were just fishing around to see if I would rise to the bait and make some kind of stupid mistake."

"Cunning bastards."

"Oh yeah. What I'm worried about now is how they might spin *my* interview to try to put the heat back on her. It's pretty easy to escalate the mistrust in a situation like this." I shook my head. "Been there, done that."

Hiram chuckled. "Ah, yes, I'm sure you used similar tactics down in Los Angeles. The irony is rich. But, at least one of the detectives let you lay out your theory of the crime. That's a good sign, isn't it?"

"Yeah, I think so. I mean I thought I saw a flicker in Escalante's eyes when I asked him to think about it. But it was probably just wishful thinking. Dorn's never going to agree to their looking seriously at anyone else but me. The guy's a real head case."

My friend shook his head. "I hope you're not letting him provoke you. That's exactly what he wants."

"I know. You're right. But the man has no right to carry a badge. Hell, he was ready to shoot Archie this morning. Arch had him pegged in a heartbeat. He knows an idiot when he sees one."

"Indeed."

We took the Sellwood Bridge across the Willamette. The river was high from the spring rains, a broad gray-green sheet ruffled by a stiff northerly breeze that buffeted the Saab. We took a left on Milwaukie, and parked a half block beyond the Knapp Street intersection. This put us in the middle of the Westmoreland neighborhood, a mostly blue-collar area in the early stages of gentrification, meaning there was at least one Starbucks and an artisanal pizza shop.

I left Hiram and Archie in the car to take a quick look around. A small market and a Thai carryout shared the northeast corner of the intersection where Barnes' car had been abandoned. A used bookstore stood on the northwest corner. I tried the market first, then the carryout, but got nothing but blank looks to my questions. As I exited the carryout, I saw a young man with a heavy beard dressed in jeans, sandals, and gray socks locking up the bookstore for the day.

I hurried across the street. "Excuse me. Can I ask you something?"

"You just did." He turned his back on me to set the lock.

Unfazed, I waited for him to turn back around. "I'm investigating a crime and was wondering if you saw the person who parked a dark green Jeep Grand Cherokee over there last Friday morning?" I pointed across the street.

"What kind of crime?"

"Uh, a murder, actually." His eyes widened just a little. I knew I had him.

"When did you say?"

"Last Friday. Probably mid-morning or later."

"The Jeep? Oh, yeah. The cops towed it yesterday. I saw this dude park it on Friday around, oh, eleven, I guess. I was sitting at my desk having a coffee when he pulled up. Thought maybe he was a customer."

"Could you describe him?"

He scratched his cheek through his beard and scowled in concentration. "Didn't get much of a look at him. Let's see. He was wearing a black hoodie and dark glasses. Tall and thin, maybe carrying a backpack."

The description matched the one Oliver Dan had given me. "How tall?"

"Your height, maybe a little taller."

"Race?"

"Uh, looked like a white guy to me, maybe Hispanic.

"Anything else? The backpack—anything unusual about it?"

He scratched his other cheek and grimaced. "No. That's all I can tell you."

"You see which direction he headed?"

He pointed north. "Up Milwaukie. Toward Bybee."

"Thanks. This has been helpful. Oh, one more thing. Did you notice if he was smoking?"

"Smoking? Uh, yeah, as a matter of fact. He flicked a cigarette on the sidewalk when he got out. Cretin."

I got the man's name and phone number and gave him a card. I scanned the wet sidewalk for cigarette butts with no success before heading back to the car. The sky had cleared, and Hiram had taken the top back down on the Saab.

"That guy at the bookstore actually saw the perp park the stolen Jeep last Friday," I said, trying to contain my excitement. "Bring Arch. Let's go for a walk."

We walked up Milwaukie toward Bybee, pausing at the Starbucks. "So, he pops in for a coffee after a long drive from Madras. That's what I'd do." I went inside. One of the servers had been on duty last Friday morning, but she didn't recall seeing anyone fitting the description.

I came back out and shrugged. Hiram pointed to a neighborhood bar across the street. "If it were *me*, and I'd just driven two hundred miles in a stolen car after murdering a couple of people, I think I would indulge myself with an adult beverage, a strong one."

"Good point." We crossed the street, and I went in to check it out while Hiram and Archie window-shopped an antique store. The bartender explained she hadn't been working the previous Friday, and the three customers in the place didn't know anything. It was the same story with a cafe and a bakery—nothing.

When I came out of the bakery, Hiram and Archie had turned back in the direction of the car. "Wait a minute. Our guy didn't just drop the Jeep here arbitrarily. He must've had a reason." That's when I spotted a sign up on the next block that read Moreland Mixed Martial Arts. Looking back, I think I subconsciously associated the man I was looking for with, fairly or not, the sport of MMA, which struck me as needlessly violent. In any case, I headed for the studio, saying over my shoulder, "Come on. Maybe he needed a workout rather than a drink."

The martial arts studio had been carved out of a large retail space, a pharmacy, maybe, or a mom-and-pop grocery. I hesitated out front until Arch and Hiram caught up to me. "This could cut either way. If they know him in there, I might get a name. On the other hand, if I go in there asking questions, I run the risk of tipping him off."

Hiram stroked his chin. "*Audentes Fortuna Iuvat*."

I shot him a puzzled look.

"Fortune favors the bold. One of Virgil's better quotes."

How could I argue with Virgil? The studio was warm inside, and the humid air carried the smell of sweat, wet leather, and something medicinal—liniment, probably. The lobby had racks of sparring gear and clothing—not just workout attire but casual wear for the MMW fan, as well. A cooler offered energy drinks, and posters on the wall captured the essence of the sport. One poster in the style of LeRoy Neiman depicted a fighter dispatching his opponent with a vicious knee to the face. Another pictured a fighter with his fist raised in triumph, blood streaming down his gap-toothed face. Between the posters, a sign said, Ask About Our Family Plan.

There was nobody behind the counter, and I began to feel silly. I mean, what were the chances I'd learn anything at this place? I was about to walk out when a voice called to me from the back of the studio. "Hello out there. We're back here." I worked my way through the exercise machines and racks of free weights to a large matted area. To my left two tattooed fighters were thumping heavy bags with punches and high kicks, their bodies glistening in the overhead lights. A third was on his back, grunting through a set of crunches.

In front of me, two men were sparring. They stopped when I approached. The man catching the punches said, "What can I do for you?" He appraised me through small, reptilian eyes, his chin dimpled like a crack in a block of cement, his dirty blond hair spiked up in front like he'd been electrocuted. Even in loose-fitting sweats, it was clear he had a powerful body.

"Uh, sorry to interrupt you folks. I'm trying to get in touch with someone. Thought maybe you could help me."

Spiky Hair gave me a blank look and didn't respond. The two hammering the bags stopped to listen. I rattled off the description, adding he might have dropped in the previous Friday around midday, and scanned the group for their reactions. I thought the eyes of one of the two working the bags, a woman, might have enlarged slightly, as if she might speak, but Spiky Hair cut her off. "Nobody like that workin' out here," he said, shooting me a smile draped with icicles. "Sorry. We can't help you." The tone rang with finality.

I smiled affably, watching the woman. "No biggie. Might have been the first time he'd come in. He smokes really foul-smelling cigarettes." The woman had a body sculpted by hard workouts and a head-turning face framed in jet-black hair. Her eyes flicked from me to Spiky and back before she lowered them to study her bare feet.

Resisting an urge to push it, I swung my gaze back to Spiky, and we looked at each for a moment. His arctic smile dissolved into a thin, straight line. He said, "You can go out the way you came in." As I turned to leave, I could feel his beady eyes boring into my back.

Joining Hiram and Archie down the street, I said, "They know him in there—at least a woman in there does. But she wasn't about to talk in front of the others." I shook my head and frowned. "Man, I didn't like the way that went down."

Hiram arched his brows. "You didn't use your name, did you?"

"Not on your life."

Chapter Thirty

The next day Claire called from Khartoum. Her leg was doing splendidly, she told me, and she would be arriving in L.A. the following Wednesday. "Look Claire," I said, "I'm, uh, afraid I can't make it down to meet you, but Philip Lone Deer will be there in my stead."

"Oh. Why can't you come, Dad?" Her voice had gone from enthusiastic to guarded.

"I've got a legal situation I can't duck." I sighed, long and deep. "God, Claire, there's nothing I'd rather do than meet you next week, but I can't do it."

"What's the problem?"

I laughed, trying to keep it light. "It's a long story. I'll fill you in when you get here."

I was hoping she would drop it, and she did. I listened for traces of disappointment in her voice but heard none. My little girl was all grown up now. After Claire signed off, I sat in front of the computer thinking about our lives since her mother's death. I looked over at the one picture of Nancy I had left out. The rest were in a box in the attic. Why that particular picture? I'd asked myself that many times and still didn't know the answer.

Certainly it had to do with the fact that Claire was in the photo, too. I couldn't look at any image of my wife without seeing my daughter, who was still with me, young, strong, and vibrant. They were standing together at Newport Beach framed against the Pacific, a brilliant blue gashed white by breaking waves. Claire was thirteen, wearing her first bikini and looking straight at the camera, unflinching. Nancy had a hand on Claire's shoulder with her head turned slightly toward her face. Her expression was carefree yet full of pride for her daughter, whose womanhood was blooming like a rose. Nancy had just beaten a three-month bout of depression. Things were on the upswing, or so it seemed at the time. We're all hopeless founts of optimism, aren't we?

I pushed away from the desk and went into the kitchen to scare up some lunch. I watched a big Northern flicker jackhammering a chunk of suet I'd hung in a wire basket next to the feeder, scattering the chickadees and goldfinches. For no particular reason, my mind flashed on the scene of the campsite on the Deschutes the night of the murder, the group socializing around the fire, the frenetic cell phone calls before dinner, the confrontation over the direction of the company. There was something about that scene that bothered me, some little detail that didn't seem to fit. But I couldn't for the life of me put my finger on what it was.

The news at my law office that day wasn't cheery. Two prospective clients phoned in and abruptly cancelled their appointments, and another left a voice mail saying he no longer required my services. The *Oregonian* article was extracting a toll already. On top of that, Daina called with bad news. The illicit scan of Hannon's and Streeter's e-mail correspondence over the last three months hadn't turned up anything suspicious.

On the bright side, I was forced to knock off early, which was fine with Archie. He'd been lobbying hard for a jog, but he had to settle for a walk through the grocery store where I did a week's worth of shopping in just under ten minutes. I love to cook, and I love to eat, but shopping doesn't rise above the level of necessary evil.

When we got back home, Arch surprised me by heading straight down the hall to the study, rather than checking out his food dish for a steak bone the dog fairy might have left him in our absence.

"What is it, big guy?" I asked when I caught up with him. He was standing in front of the sliding glass door that opened onto the back porch. His ears were up, and he was sniffing the floor and whimpering softly. The latch securing the door was in the unlocked position. I usually kept the door locked, but I wasn't religious about it. Arch looked at me, then back at the door, and took the whimper to a whine.

I slid the door open, and like a bloodhound he worked his way across the porch and down the steps. But when he reached the patchy, weed-infested grass, he moved first to the left, then right, then left again before turning to me and barking twice, sharp notes of frustration.

I joined him, and we walked together down to a narrow gap in the fence separating my property from an abandoned rock quarry. I stood surveying the strip-mined rubble and stunted misshapen cedars below me. Nothing moved. I patted Arch on the head. "So, big guy, what got you so upset? You think someone paid us a visit?"

We went back to the house, and I went through each room carefully. I'm not the greatest housekeeper, but everything looked more or less like I'd left it until I got to the study. The wastebasket seemed slightly out of place. I noticed this because I kept it positioned to catch my three-pointers. In fact, two of my basketballs—in the form of wadded-up paper—lay on the floor beside the basket. But the basket was now tucked in too close to the far end of the library table, making it impossible to launch a shot from my desk chair.

Anyone searching the place would look in the wastebasket.

I had nothing related to the Bruckner case except the files I'd hidden out in the yard. My computer was on, and it would have been simple to access my e-mail. I checked my messages. Nothing sensitive from Daina.

I couldn't be certain someone had been in the house. After all, Archie could have bumped the wastebasket, and he could have been reacting to a skunk or a raccoon that had been nosing around outside. Still, I locked all the doors and first-floor windows, then retrieved the Glock 19 I kept in a shoebox in my bedroom closet. The gun was on permanent loan from Nando Mendoza. He'd become concerned about my personal safety while we worked a particularly dicey case together a while back. I sat on the bed, loaded the clip, and snapped it into the handle of the weapon. I set the safety and put the gun on the nightstand. It was a ritual that was supposed to make me feel safer. But in my untrained hands? Not so much.

I had to chuckle. A person with such a conflicted view of guns should probably not own one.

But I took the Glock with me later that night when Archie and I took our customary walk before going to bed. The clouds moved across the waning moon like gray smoke, and the southerly wind carried the smell of rain. The only sound was the barred owl's *who-cooks-for-you, who-cooks-for-youuuu.*

I found myself wishing I could ask the owl what he'd seen that afternoon from high in his perch.

Chapter Thirty-one

The alarm jolted Archie and me awake at four-thirty a.m. A dream I couldn't remember left me with a vague sense of anxiety that only began to lift as I made a double espresso and started pulling my gear together for the day's fishing with Philip. I had nearly finished when I realized I had no fishing knife since Escalante and Dorn had taken *both* of mine. As an afterthought, I put a small pocket knife that had belonged to my dad in the tattered old fishing vest I used as a spare. My newer vest had been impounded. Then I discovered that the old vest was missing a carbon dioxide cartridge, so it was out to the garage, grumbling all the way, to get a spare, the last in the box.

As I finished packing I had to remind myself that fly-fishing with my friend was just what I needed to clear my head. But things had moved swiftly since I'd agreed to the trip, and now a part of me wished that, instead, I was on my way to Portland to try to corner the woman at the martial arts studio. That would have to wait. When I finally backed the car out of the garage, Archie stood watching with a tilted head, and when I didn't offer him the backseat, plopped down on the porch and put his chin on his paws. As I pulled out I called through the open window, "Guard the house, big boy."

Traffic was light on the I-5 until I turned onto I-84, where I fell in line with a stream of eighteen-wheelers heading into the rising sun. Ordinarily, the Columbia River Gorge acts like a natural wind tunnel, but that morning the wind was calm, the river a dark mirror in the low light. The serenity of the scene made it hard to imagine the violent, stone-carving floods that formed the place an ice age ago. I turned off at the city of Hood River and headed south. Mount Hood was dead ahead, and from this angle reminded me of the bent-thumb silhouette of the Matterhorn.

Following Philip's directions I veered right at a narrow dirt road across from a gas station and descended into the Hood River watershed through a lush pear orchard. I parked in the small gravel lot next to Philip's rig. Ours were the only cars there. I pulled on my chest waders over a pair of sweats, put on my wading boots over neoprene booties, and grabbed my fishing vest and six-weight graphite rod.

I found Philip leaning on a rusted iron railing, watching the river sluice down the sloped narrow spillway of the dam. His fly rod leaned against the railing next to him, and he was sipping coffee from a stainless steel thermos cap.

"Any fish down there?" I called out over the muffled roar of the water.

"Oh yeah." Philip looked up and shaded his eyes with one hand while pointing at the area where the overflow churned into the river with the other. Suddenly two silvery steelheads leaped from the boil and began fighting their way *up* the spillway.

"Whoa!" I said. The fish were quickly swept back into the river. Another tried and was beaten back as well. Built to divert water to a small power station down river, the dam was tiny by Northwest standards, but large enough to impede the migration of salmon and steelhead to their spawning grounds on the glacial slopes of Mount Hood.

Philip pointed across the river. "Fish ladder's over there. Takes 'em a while to find it. Some never do." He looked up and smiled. "Get your cup. I've got more coffee in my thermos."

We talked a little but mostly watched as fish after fish attempted to clear the spillway.

After finishing our coffees, we headed out. I was excited to get a fly in the water but at the same time couldn't get the images of those determined fish out of my head. I found myself wondering how much dynamite would be needed to take the dam out.

We walked downstream on a narrow path, picking our way through pine and scrub oak. After a mile or so Philip stopped. "Okay, I'll start here and fish back toward the dam. There's a trail that tees into this one another mile and a half downriver. Start fishing there. When I finish up, I'll come back down and meet you."

I gave him a skeptical look. "The water we just passed looked pretty good."

Philip made a wounded face. "I'm giving you the best water, man. Wait till you see it down there. You think I'd cheat for a lousy free lunch?"

"Yep," I said, turning to go downstream.

"Remember," he called after me, "the steelhead have come all the way from the Pacific. They're looking for a break in the current and plenty of dissolved oxygen. Shade's good, too. And keep your belt cinched tight. The water's high, and it's easy to come loose in this river."

The trail narrowed, and the trees crowded even closer to the bank, which dropped away steeply to the swift water. I knew Philip would give me the best section to fish, and he had. The rub was he would probably outfish me anyway, which would give him even more bragging rights.

At the junction of the two trails a rough patch of water tailed out into a nice, deep boulder garden, ideal holding water for steelies. I tied on a fly, eased down the bank, and worked my way out into the current until I was waist-deep. I gave that boulder garden a good strafing, putting each cast out a little further and then swinging the fly in an arc across the best water. Nothing. Migrating steelhead are mostly on the move, and apparently there were none resting in that stretch of water.

I moved upriver, repeating the process without encountering a single fish. No matter. Dappled by the trees, the morning light moved on the water like levitating silver coins. Noisy crows, nesting tanagers, and a couple of chittering kingfishers seemed to be enjoying the morning as much as me. The tension that had built over the past week began to melt away, reminding me once again why I fly fish.

I came to a wide, deep pool—so deep I couldn't see the bottom through the silt-tinted water. At the top of the pool, the river funneled down between a pair of half-submerged boulders before churning over a short waterfall. As I moved around on the bank hoping to spot a fish, crows in the trees behind me suddenly took flight. I looked behind me but didn't see anything.

Almost immediately I saw a glint of silver as a fish rolled at ten o'clock, maybe forty feet from where I stood. My pulse ramped up. The fish didn't break the surface, but it looked *big*. I took a deep breath and snapped a roll cast out at two o'clock, then gently swung the fly in the fish's direction. Because of the eddy currents in the pool, the fly took a meandering course, and it took a bit of body English to finally hit the target.

They say you never forget a steelhead strike, which is certainly the case for me. The fish, pushing a yard in length, came halfway out of the water, inhaled my fly, and dove like a porpoise. I brought my rod tip up and yanked, setting the hook. The fish reversed course and came out of the water like a chrome missile, thrashing its head to throw the hook. Landing with a smack, it dove again and ran for the center of the pool, line screaming off my reel. I'd spooled off a lot of line before the fish finally stopped running and turned to face me, digging in like a bulldog on a leash.

It was a standoff. I started to take some line back, and the fish yielded grudgingly for a few cranks on my reel. Then it dashed downstream, taking all the line I'd gained and then some. I swung around and we faced each other again, its strength together with the full force of the river threatening to pop my eight-pound leader or one of the knots I'd tied.

I cranked in some more line and the fish responded like a gymnast doing a floor routine. It paused. I took more line. I wanted to land the fish before it became dangerously exhausted. Just as suddenly it broke for the bank and then, sensing the shallow water, reversed course and leaped a final time. A few moments later I had the fish in front of me.

Far from exhausted, the steelhead thrashed about. I bent down, slipped my hand under its belly and lifted gently. The fish became completely still as its speckled, olive green head came out of the water. "Thanks, big fella. You were magnificent. Remember, the fish ladder's on your left." I slipped the hook free. The steelhead rested in my hand for a few moments, crimson gills pumping rhythmically, and then with a flick of its tail, was gone.

I got out and found a stump further upstream in the full sun. I sat down, feeling more at peace than I had in a long time. I'd landed my first summer steelhead. Claire was safe and on her way home. And I wasn't in jail for murder. Things were looking up.

Behind me a couple of crows lifted out of the trees, cawing with annoyance. "Philip, is that you?" I called. "I need coffee." No answer.

I started heading upriver. The bank became high and steep, the water deep and featureless. I heard a twig break behind me, and suddenly it dawned on me what those crows were trying to tell me. Somebody was back there in the trees.

But it was too late. An arm clamped around my chest, and a sharp blade pressed against my throat, releasing a trickle of warm blood.

"Move or make a sound and I'll cut you ear to ear." The voice was irritatingly high, as if originating from a lung full of helium, and his breath reeked of tobacco, a stench I recognized. No trace of an accent. Then just as quickly the knife was gone. I felt a tug at my waist and winced involuntarily. My wading belt fell at my feet, cleanly sliced in two. Then a squeaky laugh and the words, "Enjoy the swim, asshole," before he shoved me off the bank.

Chapter Thirty-two

Falling into a river in waders without a safety belt is the nightmare of every fly fisherman. I tried to right myself but hit the water chest first. The impact knocked most of the air from my lungs. Fifty-degree water flooded into my waders, filling the legs, which were tightly sealed at my boots. I sank like a brick. Fighting back panic, I reached across my chest and pulled the cord to inflate my vest. The carbon dioxide cartridge fired, and I felt a moment of buoyancy and a flicker of hope. But my inflated vest was no match for the weight of my now flooded legs. I bumped merrily along the river bottom as my vest rose up around my head like a noose.

The pocket knife! It was in one of my vest pockets.

I yanked down on the vest with my left hand, and searched frantically through the pockets with my right. My hand clutched the knife just as I smacked headlong into a large boulder. A supernova exploded in the space behind my eyes. The vest tore free, but I managed to hold onto the knife. I opened it and slashed at my pants legs, releasing the trapped water.

Suddenly buoyant, I started to fight my way to the surface. The water brightened, and I could almost taste the air. But before I could take a breath, the current slammed me into a boulder and pinned me there. Sensing the pull of the current to my left, I frantically swung my legs around and was flushed over the falls and into the big pool I'd just fished.

I went in deep, churning in the boil below the falls like a dead fish. I knew my attacker was on the left bank somewhere, so I decided to go right with the two or three molecules of air left in my lungs. My boots were like cement galoshes, so I pulled with my arms with everything I had until I burst to the surface, giving me a new appreciation for fresh air. I made for a tangle of logs and branches another twenty feet downstream and tried to hide myself.

But my attacker had followed me downriver. He stood directly across the pool, bouncing on the balls of his feet in a little dance of frustration. Sunlight reflected off the long blade in his hand. I could just make him out through a bleary left eye and a right eye nearly swollen shut. When it came to clothes, the guy had no flair. He had on the same outfit he'd worn on the Deschutes—a black hoodie, dark jeans, and a backpack.

I caught a fleeting impression. He was tall and slender, a face with no distinguishing features, definitely Caucasian.

A hot transfusion of rage filled my fast-numbing body. I lifted my arm partway out of the water and displayed the pathetic little pocket knife I'd somehow managed to hang on to. Through stiff, thickened lips I yelled, "Come and get me, you son of a bitch."

I think he smiled, but I'm not sure. I took my eyes off him for a moment to push a branch out of my face. When I looked back, my attacker was gone.

The bank was too steep to climb out, and setting off downriver would make me a sitting duck. So, I just hung on there for I don't know how long, wondering if my attacker could find a way across the river. Finally, I didn't care where the hell he was. I had to find a place to crawl out or die of hypothermia. I shoved off and cleared the pool okay but realized to my horror I didn't have the strength to navigate the swift water downriver.

My body seemed to shrink down to a point, leaving only my mind. Nancy came to me, her face pinched with worry. I shrugged, as if to say I couldn't help what was happening to me. Then I saw Claire. She was furious, telling me not to give up. The last thing I felt before blacking out was overwhelming guilt.

Chapter Thirty-three

I heard a distant voice, then felt two strong hands pull me out of the water and up a steep bank. I remember wondering where the knife was going to go—into my chest or across my throat? Either way I was too weak to resist. But instead of execution by knife I realized my clothes were being stripped off. My eyelids felt sheathed in lead, but I forced them open and blinked hard to clear them. I hadn't really noticed that Philip Lone Deer's green eyes had tiny flecks of yellow in them, like flecks of gold in a mountain stream. Or at least that's the way they seemed to me as I lay there looking up at my friend.

I coughed up some river water and shivered. "See him?"

"See who?" he said, pulling a deliciously warm, dry sweatshirt over my head.

"The guy…pushed me."

"*What?* Someone pushed you in?" Philip jumped up and looked around. "Where is he?"

I coughed up some more water and shook my head. "Don't know."

Philip dropped back on one knee and hurriedly pulled a pair of thermal underwear over my legs. The fog in my brain began to clear, and I noticed Philip was in his skivvies.

"Knife. He's got…knife," I said, trying to sit up. Philip eased me back down and laid his fishing vest over my upper body for more warmth.

"*Who* has a knife?"

"Deschutes killer. Cut my belt…Shoved me."

Philip stood up again, hurriedly slipped his waders and boots back on and pulled a knife from a sheath on his belt. It was a lot bigger than my knife. "Well, I've got a knife, too. Where is the bastard?"

I was still shivering, but managed to sit up. "I don't…know.… I was standing on the bank…he was shadowing me, came out of the woods…river noise made it easy."

Philip glanced over at my waders. They were lying in a shredded heap. "What the hell did you do?"

I'd stopped shivering and begun to warm a little. "Once I hit the water, I fired off a CO_2 cartridge. It kept me buoyant just long enough to find a pocket knife I had in my vest. Used the knife on my waders." I shook my head. "The cartridge and the pocket knife almost didn't make the trip. The knife belonged to my dad." I looked around, then pointed upriver. "It's somewhere in that deep pool back there." I went on to describe my submarine tour and the across-the-river, face-to-face confrontation with the killer.

Philip shook his head in disbelief. "I *just* missed the whole thing. I came looking for you and saw your pole on the bank. Figured you'd gone into the woods to pee or something. I poured a cup and waited around for you to show. When you didn't, I began to get worried and started downriver again. At the pool, I saw something swim out from under that snag of branches." He laughed. "Thought it was a pregnant beaver. Then I realized it was you, partner. I waded in and grabbed your ass as you floated by. You were finished, man."

I finally made it to my feet, and we started back upstream, moving warily, Philip with his knife still drawn. As we walked, my brain began to defrost. When we got back to the parking lot I reluctantly called the local police to report the attack. I knew it would take a lot of time, and I was worried the story would attract the Portland media. But I wanted the incident on the record, and you never know—the locals might have seen something or picked up our guy on an unrelated charge. By the time we took the officers back to the crime scene and completed the interviews it was two hours later.

We never found my wading belt. My guess was our guy took it with him to make it look like I'd neglected to wear one in the first place. I had a throbbing headache, and my right eye was pretty swollen. I also had a couple of nasty gashes on each leg from the pocket knife. Philip expertly closed them using steri-strips from his medical kit.

I declined the officers' advice to go to the hospital. Philip rolled his eyes at this but knew better than to say anything.

We decided to head back to Dundee. Philip would follow me in his rig and stay the night, even though I tried to convince him I didn't need a babysitter. On the way home I kept turning over the events of the day. How did the attacker know I would be fishing the Hood River? Did he simply follow me this morning? No way. He knew exactly what I was going to be doing. No, it must have been the break-in last night. The e-mail from Philip giving directions and the time of our rendezvous was sitting there in my inbox without password protection. The killer knew something about fly-fishing, too. How else would someone know that a pair of flooded waders would quickly and efficiently drown a person?

Why didn't he just slit my throat and be done with it? I had a good answer for that, too—I was the fall guy for Bruckner's murder. It wouldn't look good for me to turn up murdered. No, much better that I had a convenient accident. Suspected murderer drowns in fishing accident. Case closed.

Another thought occurred to me: The attacker couldn't have known ahead of time that he was going to find the e-mail describing our fishing trip, so what was he looking for? The files I'd lifted from Bruckner's study perhaps? Maybe, but I was sure no one knew about that. Maybe he was just hoping to get lucky, find out what I knew. But would *that* be worth undertaking a risky burglary? It didn't seem probable.

Another thought hit me, one that caused my stomach to tighten—instead of taking something, suppose the burglar left something? Dorn and Escalante had searched my place once, but there was nothing stopping them from looking again, particularly if guided by an anonymous tip.

When we got to my place, Philip called his wife and filled her in on the day's excitement. I went immediately to my study and started searching it. When he joined me he said, "What are you looking for?"

I smiled a little sheepishly. "I haven't the slightest idea, but whatever it is, I'd better find it."

Chapter Thirty-four

Philip left early the next morning for Madras. I sat out on the side porch enjoying a second cappuccino as a light breeze blew crisp morning air off the valley. Sonny Rollins was holding forth on the outside speakers when Archie let me know we had visitors. I padded around in my comfy moccasins to the front of the house just in time to see Detectives Escalante and Dorn get out of their car. A uniformed sheriff's deputy from Yamhill County got out of a blue-and-white that had pulled in behind them.

"Morning, gentlemen," I said in a melodious tone.

Dorn folded his arms across his chest, leaned against the car, and smirked.

Escalante approached me with a clipboard in his hand. "Mr. Claxton, we've got a new warrant here to search your storage unit in Dundee."

I took the clipboard and read the warrant through carefully. "My storage unit? You're kidding, right?"

Dorn made a grunting sound. Escalante said, "No, sir."

"You acting on a tip? Did a little bird tell you something?"

Out of the corner of my eye I saw Dorn straighten. I couldn't see Escalante's eyes through his Ray-Bans, but his eyebrows rose slightly before he caught himself. He said, "We'd like to get this done straightaway, if you wouldn't mind, Mr. Claxton. We called the facility but got a recording. We assume you have a key."

Archie moved from my side past Escalante to position himself in front of Dorn. He stood looking at the detective with his head cocked slightly to one side. Dorn shifted his stance but didn't say anything. I called Arch back to my side before saying, "Okay, I'll get the key. You're wasting your time, but it's your show, detectives. Knock yourselves out."

Dundee Self-Storage consisted of three rows of storage units on a half acre of asphalt just off the 99W on the east side. I'd stored some belongings there I didn't want at the Aerie but wasn't quite willing to part with after the move from L.A. The security system at the facility consisted of a locked gate at the entrance for which I had a key and a four-digit combination lock on the retractable door to the unit. The place was deserted when we arrived, which was a relief. I'd already had enough public exposure with the cops to last a lifetime. I let us in the gate and unlocked my unit while Dorn and Escalante donned booties and latex gloves in preparation for the search.

Boxes and furniture were packed in the small enclosure along with an old steamer trunk I'd used to store some of Claire's childhood toys and the small amount of family memorabilia I hadn't managed to destroy during my bouts of depression following Nancy's death. Dorn and Escalante entered the small space and set to work like a couple of archeologists on a dig. King Tut's tomb, maybe, judging from a palpable sense of anticipation emanating from them both.

I glanced at my watch, wondering how long this was going to take. I had a busy day lined up.

Fortunately, I hadn't squirreled away that much junk, and it couldn't have been more than thirty minutes when the only item left to search was the steamer trunk. I definitely got the impression they had saved the trunk for last. Wheezing with exertion, Dorn knelt down next to it, striking a kind of bovine pose. Escalante stood behind him, hands on his hips. Out came teddy bears, framed certificates, basketball and soccer trophies and a half dozen family photo albums. Detritus of a former life. I fought back a surge of emotion, even though I'd seen it all the night before.

When Dorn had emptied out the trunk and it was clear they'd found nothing, he struggled back on his feet and turned to Escalante. "What the fuck? There isn't a goddamn thing in this shithole."

Escalante shook his head and leveled his eyes at me. "This isn't your idea of a joke, is it, Claxton?"

I raised my hands, palms out. "I enjoy your company, gentlemen, but not that much."

The disappointment coupled with my sarcasm must've pushed Dorn over some kind of line. He faced me, met my eyes with a mocking, cocksure look and said the thing he figured would provoke me. "I heard your old lady killed herself down in L.A. Ate a bottle of pills." The corner of his mouth lifted. "Heard you were such an uptight prick you drove her to it."

The comment struck like a blow, separating my mind from my body. I heard myself laugh in disbelief that he'd actually said that and felt my face flush with anger as my fists clenched involuntarily at my side. My eyes narrowed, and I spoke slowly through tight lips. "You need to watch your mouth, Dorn."

He cocked his head and smiled, as if considering my remark. Then in a move that caught me completely off guard, he clamped my shoulders with his huge hands, yanked me forward and kneed me hard in the groin. As my head dropped he smashed my bowed neck with the base of his fist. I dropped to my knees and rode a runaway wave of screaming pain.

"That's what we do to wiseasses in Madras, hotshot."

"Bull! Stop it!" It was Escalante. He sounded twenty miles away.

I knelt there looking at Dorn's shoes. Tiny flecks of unbuffed black polish came into focus. His right sole was beginning to delaminate at the toe. I took a breath and tried to push myself up, but there was nothing there. I took a deeper breath and choked on the inhaled dust. Finally I forced myself up to face him, weaving like a boxer after an eight count. Dorn's arms were at his sides, palms facing me and fingers wagging in an invitation to try something.

I'm not particularly proud of what I did next. But in the moment it seemed my only choice. I began to turn away from him in a gesture of surrender. Then I whirled around and caught him flush on the nose with a straight right. *Pop.* The sound reverberated like I'd struck a ripe melon. Cartilage snapped and flattened beneath my fist.

The punch staggered but didn't fell him. "My nose! You broke my nose, you bastard! You broke it," he screamed as blood poured through the fingers of his left hand, which he'd clamped over the wound. With his right hand he drew his service revolver and leveled it at me. The barrel looked like the muzzle of a Howitzer, and the tips of the unchambered rounds glinted back at me in the attic light like rodent's eyes. I froze, waiting for a bullet to rip through my chest. For the second day in a row, I wasn't sure whether I was going to live or die.

But before Dorn squeezed off, Escalante jumped between us. "Enough! Both of you. Holster your weapon, Bull."

Dorn didn't move, and neither did I. "Keep out of this, Vince. Just get the fuck out of the way."

What Vincent Escalante did next probably saved my life. "I'm not moving, Bull," he said. "You'll have to shoot both of us." No one moved for what seemed an eternity. I heard my heart thumping in the silence.

Dorn finally holstered his gun, fished a handkerchief from his pocket, and pressed it to his nose. "Cuff him and get him the fuck out of here."

Escalante turned to me. He'd drawn his weapon, as well, but hadn't raised it. "Mr. Claxton, please turn around and put your hands behind your back."

"Look, detective, you witnessed what happened. You'd better think about this."

"No choice, Mr. Claxton. You're under arrest for assaulting a police officer." Then he snapped the cuffs on and read me my rights. The cuffs didn't pinch this time.

Escalante put me in their unmarked. "Listen, there're some things you need to know." I was speaking fast now. I didn't want Dorn to interrupt us. "There was an attempt on my life on the Hood River yesterday. Almost got my throat cut. I filed a police report, and I have a witness. You can check it out. I got a partial look at my attacker. He fits the description of the guy the young skaters saw near the switching yard. You know, the guy I told you killed Henry Barnes as well as Hal Bruckner. Also, somebody broke into my house night before last. That was your tipster. I'm being framed, detective."

His chin came up slightly, and he started to speak just as Dorn came up behind us holding his blood soaked handkerchief to his nose. Escalante broke eye contact with me and looked at his partner. "I'll keep that in mind," was all he said.

It was a slow day at the Yamhill County Jail, so I was processed through in twenty minutes. Anger overrode the anxiety I should have felt about the deteriorating mess I was in. I called a bail bondsman I knew in Portland and told him I was going to need a good chunk of change for bail. I'd know the exact amount after my arraignment in the morning. "Think in the range of fifty to one fifty," I said and shuddered at the thought of losing ten percent of that. Next I called Murray Felding, the best defense attorney I knew, and told his assistant I needed to see him straightaway. It was clearly time for me to hire someone to help me work my way out of this situation.

Murray had a court case and came in around eight that night. A thin, energetic man with a penchant for three-piece suits, he had small, intense eyes that seemed in constant motion. I gave him the broad outline of my situation, then described the incident that got me arrested. He took detailed notes and said he'd meet me at the arraignment, scheduled for ten-thirty the next morning. He took photographs of the reddish-purple bruise forming below my beltline and the contusion on the back of my neck.

After he left, I lay on my bunk listening to the echoing chatter of the evening's guests at the jail—curses, laughs, and the whimpering of someone in acute withdrawal. The last time I'd spent a night in jail, I'd been arrested on suspicion of murder, but I beat that wrap in a hurry. The fact that this was a lesser charge didn't make me feel any better.

Things quieted down when the lights went out, and I found myself thinking back on the frantic search Philip and I had conducted at the storage unit the night before, a search that started when we discovered that two items were missing—the key to the storage facility and an attached tab bearing the combination for the lock on the unit.

The discovery was all Philip's doing. He was poking around in the desk in my study when he held up a ring of miscellaneous keys, and almost as an afterthought asked, "Anything missing?"

I glanced at the keys and shook my head. "We're looking for something *planted*."

He shrugged and tossed the keys back in the drawer.

We were searching upstairs when I suddenly thought about my storage unit. I went back downstairs and checked the key ring. My stomach kind of dropped when I realized the gate key and tab with the combination were gone. I stood there for a few moments thinking about the last time I'd used them. No doubt in my mind—they should've been on the ring.

When I called Philip down and told him he asked, "How would this guy know what the key is for?"

"There's a tab attached to it with Dundee Self-Storage along with the number of the unit written on it."

"Do you have a spare?"

"Yep. In my glove compartment."

We finished searching the house without finding anything suspicious and waited for the cover of darkness to check out the storage unit. In less than fifteen minutes we had located the plant at the bottom of the steamer trunk—my fleece jacket that had gone missing at the river, the right sleeve stained with dried blood—Hal Bruckner's, no doubt—and in the jacket pocket, a handsome gold ID bracelet with thick chain links and Hal Bruckner's initials engraved on it in an elegant script. I moved under the light and read out loud the inscription on the back: "To Hal from Alexis with much love. Maui, 2000." The simplicity of the inscription struck me as heartfelt, and I was surprised to feel a pang of pity for the new widow.

"This is the bracelet Alexis was talking about out on the Deschutes, remember?"

"How could I forget?" Philip responded. "Man, this creeps me out."

I felt a wave of revulsion as the brutality of that morning on the Deschutes came back. "I think we found what we're looking for. Now the question is, what in the hell do we do with it?"

We went back to the Aerie and had a beer while my jacket burned in the fireplace. We discussed what to do with the bracelet. When I told Philip we needed to get rid of it, he said, "The man is dead. The bracelet belongs to his widow. This is a matter of respect. I'll keep it. When this is over, you can give it back to her if she's not in jail."

I looked at the inscription again. He was right. The bracelet would mean a lot to Alexis. "Okay, but make sure it's well hidden."

I walked Philip to his truck. He got in and rolled down the window. "So, dodged another bullet, huh?"

"Looks like it. If they'd found the coat and bracelet, they would have arrested me on the spot. And being arrested for murder's bad news. There's no possibility of bail, so you ride out the whole run-up to trial in jail—twelve, eighteen months."

Philip shook his head slowly and exhaled. "But I don't really get this. I mean, first off how could anyone possibly know you had something stashed in that trunk?"

I thought for a moment. "Well, the so-called anonymous tipster probably told Dorn and Escalante that they had seen me putting something in my storage unit. After all, I'm a person of interest in the Bruckner murder. Probably said it looked a little suspicious and that they were just doing their civic duty."

"Okay, but who would be stupid enough to keep incriminating evidence around, even if it's hidden away?"

"Yeah, I would argue in court that this stunt was too dumb to be believed. But the prosecution would turn right around and say I'd kept them as souvenirs or some damn thing. Murderers do that all the time, even ones that should know better. It would have been a deep hole to dig out of, believe me"

"I see your point," Philip said as he started the big diesel engine in his truck. "Well, in any case you owe me, partner. That makes two times in two days I saved your ass."

I laughed. "I'll owe you even more when you forget this night ever happened."

Chapter Thirty-five

Murray Felding dropped me at the Aerie after my arraignment. Considering that I'd just given him a three thousand-dollar retainer (he'd asked for five), it was the least he could do. I groaned as I got out of his Cadillac, and he said, "Have your stomach looked at."

"Yeah. I had blood in my urine this morning."

"Great. Make sure you get that in your medical record." Then he roared off.

There were no surprises at the arraignment. I was charged with assaulting an officer. We planned to counter with a charge of police brutality. Bull Dorn attended so the judge could see his face, which sported two black eyes and a large bandage across his swollen, distorted nose. We showed the photograph of my bruised groin, and then Murray had me approach the bench so the judge could see the swollen lump on my neck. But in light of the damage I'd inflicted on Dorn, I didn't expect the judge to go easy.

I was right—he set bail at one-hundred thousand dollars, which forced me to put my property up as collateral. The bail lender's fee plus Murray's retainer blew a huge hole in my meager savings. I looked straight ahead as I was escorted out of the courtroom, but I could feel Dorn smirking.

I had to admit he'd won round two.

I wasn't hungry when I got home, but Archie was. I'd left him to fend for himself this time. I fed him while the Sonny Rollins from the other night played out and *Solo Monk* came up. I went out on the porch and sat for a long time just listening to

Thelonious' eccentric musings and watching the finches swirl around the feeder. Archie sensed my dark mood and lay next to me with his body against my foot. A big feral cat I called One Ear, for obvious reasons, crept to the opposite end of the porch and dropped her head to drink from Archie's water dish. Archie eyed him but didn't move from my side. I took this as a show of support.

Even thought I was mad as hell at myself for making such a sophomoric mistake, I was also righteously indignant about being baited. I was charged with a felony. I might beat it, but only if Escalante stepped up and told the truth or convinced his partner to drop the charges. Fat chance of that.

I sat there with my mind churning, feeling stymied, pinned down, and uncertain about what to do next.

By the time Monk finished, the wrecking ball bouncing around in my head had stopped. I decided to put Dorn and the assault rap aside. It was a complication I didn't need, and Felding was on it, anyway. The real issue was that I was in somebody's crosshairs, and the mischief he or she had in mind made my doing time for a felony look like a pleasure cruise. That decided, my next step became crystal clear.

At 9:15 that night I sat in my car across and down the street from the martial arts studio, patiently waiting to see who emerged when it closed at ten. A light rain made it hard to see, and I had to run my wipers every couple of minutes to clear the windshield.

Just after ten, four people trickled out. The woman I was looking for was not among them. At a quarter past, the man with the spiky yellow hair came out, locked the door, and got in a low-slung sports car, cherry red with a double white stripe down the hood. What the hell, I thought, he may be a harder nut to crack, but I had a hunch he knew the killer, too.

I followed him up Milwaukie into the Brooklyn neighborhood, where he turned right onto a side street. We hadn't gotten more than a block before he abruptly pulled over. I had no choice but to cruise on past him, at which point he pulled out and fell in behind me, right on my bumper. It was clear I'd been busted, so I pulled over and he followed suit, parking a fair distance behind me. I was thankful I'd brought the Glock along but panicked at the thought of actually carrying it. I tucked the revolver in my belt and reluctantly got out of the car.

Spiky Hair was already out of his car. "Why are you following me, dude? You a cop?"

"No, I'm not a cop," I replied as I walked toward him. "I just want to talk to you. I need some information."

"Oh, it's you," he said as I became illuminated by a streetlight. "Why the fuck should I tell you anything?"

"Uh, because I'm willing to pay you for the information?"

He considered that for a moment. By this time, we were facing each other. Spiky Hair's small, narrow-set eyes and squat nose seemed at odds with his jutting, block-like chin, thick neck, and watermelon shoulders. Haloed in the light reflecting off the mist in his hair, he turned a corner of his mouth up. "Let's see the money."

I opened my wallet and teased out two crisp one hundred dollar bills brought just for this purpose. Without saying a word he reached for the bills. I tensed but let him take them. "Okay," I said with false optimism. "All I want is the name of the guy at your gym who smokes the smelly cigarettes. And anything else you know about him."

He put the bills in his hip pocket and shook his head. "Fuck off," he said with a laugh and turned to go.

"Hey! You can't just walk away," I said in a voice filled with indignation but lacking conviction. The last thing I needed was another fight.

He whirled around and stepped up in front of me. "*What?* You want a receipt?"

He tried to shove me, and I pushed his hand away instinctively. Infuriated, he threw a short, powerful jab that I just managed to slip, his thick fist grazing the side of my head and ripping at my ear. His leg came up, and I twisted just in time to take a powerful kick in the hip instead of my bruised groin. I grunted as a shock wave of white-hot pain surged through me. He shifted his weight and unleashed another kick. I twisted again and braced for the blow, but it never came. Instead, his leg flailed past my head as his other foot slipped out from under him on the wet pavement. He landed flat on his back in front of me with a very surprised look on his face. The hazard of kickboxing out of doors in Portland. As he scrambled to get up, I moved behind him, pulled the Glock out of my belt, and shoved it behind his ear.

He froze. I slowly turned him around, and when he opened his mouth to speak, I jammed the barrel in. His body became rigid as steel. I definitely had his attention.

"Now, listen to me," I said in a hoarse voice between breaths, "I'm sick and tired of people pounding on me. You can either give me the information I just paid for, or I'll blast you a new windpipe. *Do you understand?*" The safety on the Glock was still engaged, a point he had failed to notice. I slowly pulled the barrel out of his mouth and positioned it between his eyes, which were now the size of dinner plates.

"Talk to me," I said.

"Chuck. His name's Chuck. That's all I know, man."

"Not good enough." I slid the barrel down his nose, stopping at the tip. "What's his full name?"

"That's the only name he uses. Pays cash. Started coming in four or five weeks ago."

"Where's he live?"

"Some place off 26 on the way to Hood. On a river."

"The Sandy? What river?"

"I don't know. I just heard it was a cabin on a river. You know, rustic."

"Who told you that?"

"One of my client's been there."

"Give me a name."

"Aw, come on ma—"

I pushed on the gun, flattening his nose. "*Tell me.*"

"CJ, CJ Manion. She was the woman working out when you came in."

"Does Chuck know about me?"

"I don't know. Maybe CJ said something. Chuck stopped coming in after that."

"Where does CJ live?"

"Southeast 16th . I don't know the address."

The pain in my hip was easing. Spiky Hair's breathing was coming in ragged gasps. There were tears in his eyes. I said, "If Chuck lives way out by Mt. Hood, why would he come all the way into Portland to work out at your gym?"

"The girl, CJ. She's worked out there for a long time. They have some kind of history."

I waited for a long time without speaking. "Anything else you know about Chuck?"

"No, man. Nothing. Honest."

"Then get out of here." As he started to leave, I added, "And keep your mouth shut about this. Understand?"

He already had his back to me, but he nodded. I stood there in the rain as he got in his car, started it up, and drove off. I got back in my car and started to shake from the shock of the encounter. I took a couple of deep breaths to calm myself. I'd been lucky. If I hadn't dodged that first punch or if he hadn't slipped on that second kick, I'd probably still be sprawled in the street with a broken jaw and an empty wallet.

But even so, I felt guilty about what I'd just done. That look of stark terror in the man's eyes lingered like a shameful after-image. That wasn't me, I told myself. I don't do things like that. At the same time, I can't say a part of me didn't enjoy his transformation from someone bent on felony assault to a model of cooperation. And it's fair to say that I now understood at the gut level the enormous power a gun can impart to someone. It wasn't a revelation that brought me much comfort.

I did take comfort in the fact that I now had the name of someone who might lead me to the killer. But as I headed back to Dundee I had an uneasy feeling that these events were changing me, like I was on some kind of slippery slope.

Chapter Thirty-six

I got back to the Aerie just after midnight, dragged myself into the house, fed Archie, and hobbled upstairs. The spot on my hip that had caught Spiky Hair's kick had taken on some color, but nothing like my stomach, which looked like a swirling abstract painting in purples and yellows. It would have been amusing, I suppose, if I hadn't been in so much pain. I took two aspirin and eased into bed like a nonagenarian.

I got up early feeling tired, edgy, and sore. A cool wind gusted off the valley, promising rain. Sipping a cappuccino at the breakfast table, I opened my cell and scrolled down to Nando Mendoza. "I need you to search ViCAP for me," I told him. ViCAP's a national law enforcement database open only to law enforcement agencies. Nando could access it. He never told me how, and I didn't want to know. "I'm looking for a contract killer. He uses a knife. Nearly decapitated that guy on the Deschutes. He's using the name Chuck. That's all I've got. No last name. I'm guessing late thirties to mid forties. Caucasian, six three or so. Slender build."

"Such minimal information will run the cost up."

"Oh, and he smokes foul smelling cigarettes."

"I would rather have his last name."

"It's all I've got. I need this, Nando."

"Okay, my friend. I will do what I can."

On a whim, I also asked him to see what he could dig up on Daina Zakaris. I had no reason to suspect her of anything, but her reluctance to talk about her background had left me a little curious. "She's Lithuanian, late thirties or early forties, lives in Seattle," I told him. "Just run a background check on her."

I was making another coffee when the phone rang. "Cal? Philip. What the hell happened, man?" I hesitated a moment, not quite getting the question. "Have you seen *The Oregonian*? You made the front page again."

My heart sank. "Shit. I was hoping to stay under the radar. Did they at least use a good picture?"

"Under the radar—are you kidding? Let me read you the headline." I heard the rustling of newspaper. "'Deschutes Slaying Suspect Assaults Investigating Officer.'"

I literally winced, then let out a deep sigh. "Well, it kind of got out of hand. Dorn got pissed when they didn't find anything in the storage unit, so he kneed me in the balls. Then I broke his nose." I left out the part about what Dorn had said about Nancy and the fact that Escalante had saved me from getting my head blown off.

Philip snorted a laugh. "You okay? I mean, how're they hangin'?"

"They're bruised, but not broken."

"Well, the good news is your stock went up around here. I checked it out. You're not the first guy Dorn's roughed up. Half of Jefferson County wants to give you a medal."

"Tell them to send money instead." I went on to tell him that Murray and I were fighting back with countercharges, that the whole thing was costing me an arm and a leg, and that I'd get suspended from the bar if I was convicted.

Philip wasn't upbeat about my chances with the white man's justice system, but he did tell me that if I lost my license for assaulting Bull Dorn, I could always guide for him. Assuming, of course, I wasn't convicted of murdering Hal Bruckner.

Changing the subject, I said, "Everything good for picking Claire up tomorrow?"

"You bet, buddy. I've got you covered. I'll spend tomorrow night visiting my cousins on my mother's side. See how the white folks are living down there."

I chuckled. "I'm sure they're just as curious about you. Maybe you could demonstrate some Piute war chants or something."

After Philip signed off I checked the online white pages and found a C. Manion on SE 16th. I jotted down the address, but I was in no shape to drive back to Portland. I had nothing pressing at the office, so I decided to visit the urgent care center in Newberg to have my groin examined and the visit duly recorded. I'd drive to Portland in the morning to see if I could catch CJ Manion at home.

On the way back from Newberg I stopped by Pritchard's Animal Care Center to check in with Hiram. I'd seen that he called, and I figured it was about the latest article in *The Oregonian*. The waiting room was crammed with people and nervous dogs and cats. I got a couple of strange looks when the receptionist called my name and I went in without an animal. Hiram was stitching up a cat that had lost a fight. As he stitched and snipped, I explained what had happened. "Well," he said, "it looks like Dorn was banking on that planted evidence to allow him to make an arrest. Hence the frustration. Perhaps the case against you is not going so well for them."

"Maybe so. My knife was accessible to everyone in the camp. So the big thing they have is my affair with Bruckner's wife as a possible motive. Of course, now, after the fight with Dorn, I've shown that I have a violent nature. Whether I was baited or not, that'll go against me. Of course, if the assault charge sticks, I'll get disbarred, too."

Hiram shook his head. "I know you had cause, Cal, and I don't want to pile on, but, honestly, was it worth putting your law practice in jeopardy?"

I nodded and cast my eyes down. "I know, Hiram. I, uh, he brought my wife into it, and after he hit me, everything just sort of went red." It was all I could think to say.

He waited for me to look back up, met my eyes, and nodded. "We all draw lines beyond which no one should cross." He dropped the subject. "This killer you know only as Chuck, do you have reason to believe he's still in the area?"

I shrugged. "My guess is he's long gone, but I can't say for sure. I do know he stopped coming into the martial arts studio."

Hiram stroked his chin. "I see."

He didn't want to say it. He was worried about Claire coming to the Aerie in the middle of all this craziness.

So was I.

Chapter Thirty-seven

That evening I was having a glass of pinot noir out on the side porch. I'd selected a pricey bottle of Beaux Frères from a case I kept for special occasions and ambitious meals. Owing to the battering I'd taken over the last few days, I figured I'd earned a little enjoyment. The grapes for the wine grew not far from my place, and I marveled at how a simple fruit like a grape could produce such rich, complex flavors. I sipped it slowly and watched the bats swoop and dive as the last rays of the sun filtered through the Doug firs, thankful to be off my feet and to have all the medical probing and prodding done with.

I had just finished leaving Philip a message on his cell when Archie started barking. I walked around to the front just in time to see Alexis Bruckner's silver Jaguar pull though the open gate. She stayed in the car as Archie continued to bark. As I approached, she rolled down her window and shot me a look. "Can you call him off?"

"Hush, Arch. Mind your manners. What are you doing here, Alexis? This isn't a good idea."

She locked both hands on the steering wheel. "Oh, it's okay if you come to my place, but not the other way around?"

"I wanted to warn you about the break-in, and about the fact that I'd told Escalante and Dorn about the affair."

Her eyes flashed. "Yeah, thanks a lot for that."

I shrugged. "They would have found out on their own. They check phone records, you know."

She glanced at Archie, then got out of the Jag and faced me. She wore skinny jeans, a lavender tank top, and calf-high leather boots. Her eyes were puffy and slightly bloodshot with bluish circles under them. "That's not why I came, Cal. My house was broken into last night. The prowler you told me about. He must've come back. I'm a little freaked, and I, uh, don't know who to turn to."

"Did you call the police?"

"*Of course*. Look, Cal. I know you didn't kill my husband. And I'm sorry about the impression I left with those detectives from Madras about you. After all, I was blindsided by their knowledge of the affair. And it was mostly my attorney's spin, not mine, anyway."

I nodded. "Does your attorney know you're here?"

"*No*. Nobody does. Christ, Cal, you live in the middle of nowhere."

She was here. Might as well see what's on her mind, I decided. Besides, she seemed genuinely upset. I ushered her to the side porch, flipped on the lights, and invited her to sit down. She eyed my quarter-filled wineglass, but I didn't offer her a drink. Archie lay down next to my chair, propped his chin on his paws, and watched her.

"So, what exactly happened last night?"

"Well, I was out for the evening. They jimmied a window off the deck. Came in and apparently went straight for Hal's study. I'd been busy in there packing up some books and files that Mitch had asked me for. Hal did a lot of his work in that office. Anyway, the room looked like a bomb had gone off. Paper scattered everywhere."

"Any idea what they might have been looking for?"

"No. Not really. Mitch looked around afterward. He thought maybe some personnel files and files concerning the Diamond Wire work were missing, but he wasn't sure."

The files I filched, I said to myself. I made a mental note to have another, more careful look at them.

Alexis leaned back in her chair, breathed a long sigh, and looked me in the eyes. "You know more about this situation than you're telling me, don't you?"

I didn't answer. "How are you and Hannon getting along?

She blew a dismissive breath. "Oh, another one of my stupid mistakes, I suppose." Then she smiled and added, "I don't put *you* in that category, dear. Mitch is a man on the rise. You know, the usual—ambition and greed. I shouldn't have turned the company over to him so quickly. That was a mistake."

"NanoTech's yours, then?"

"That's what Hal's will states, yes." She paused and dropped her gaze to the splintery floor boards of my porch. "I don't trust Mitch. Hell, I don't trust anyone at NanoTech. Hal's murder, now this break-in. She leaned forward, tears in her eyes. "I'm scared to death, Cal."

"What's not to trust about Duane Pitman and Andrew Streeter?"

"Nothing specific, I suppose. Andrew's a creep. Plays the Southern gentleman. What a joke. And he's no gift to women, despite what he thinks. He seemed to idolize Hal, but Hal didn't like him from the get-go. He was going to fire him, I think. But Mitch wants to keep him. Mitch likes yes men."

"So Streeter's staying at NanoTech?"

"That's the plan."

"What about Pitman?"

Alexis laughed. "Duane's such an ingrate. Hal was so good to him. Now Mitch is worried that he's going to leave the company and take his inventions and secrets with him."

"He could do that?"

"Oh, I don't know. Apparently Hal and Duane did everything on a handshake. Now Mitch is worried that the right security papers didn't get signed or something," she answered, shrugging her shoulders.

"I see. Sounds like Hannon would like to get rid of Pitman."

"Oh, in a heartbeat, but only if he can locate those papers."

"What about Daina Zakaris? How does she fit in?"

"Daina's fine by me, but Mitch wants her out as soon as possible."

I raised my eyebrows.

Alexis laughed again. "Not surprising. Mitch's threatened by intelligent women, myself excluded, of course. But Daina has a six-month contract she negotiated with Hal. Mitch is looking at buying her out."

I wondered why Mitch would be so anxious to get Daina and her people out of NanoTech. Alexis looked down at her hands, which were fidgeting in her lap. I studied her for a couple of beats. If this was an act, it was a damn good one. "There's not a lot I can tell you at this point, Alexis, except to be very careful until this thing gets sorted out. I don't think anyone in our party actually killed your husband, but I think someone on the inside helped set it up. I don't think it was a random killing."

Alexis shivered perceptibly. "Oh, God, don't say that. What if they come after *me*?"

"I don't think they will, but keep things locked and don't open the door to strangers." That felt like lame advice, but it's all I could offer.

She managed a weak smile and looked down at Arch. "Maybe I should get a guard dog."

I chuckled. "Wouldn't be a bad idea. Uh, one more thing. Did Mitch know about you and me?"

She hesitated for a moment. "Well, I might have mentioned something."

"Did he, or for that matter, anyone else at NanoTech have any way of knowing I was going to be on the trip?"

"I don't really know. I suppose Hal knew you were coming. I mean you're the one who sold him on the idea that night at the Lyle Hotel. But I don't know if he told anyone else."

I stood up, stretched, and glanced at my watch. "I've got to run to a meeting tonight," I lied. I was happy for the information, but the longer she stayed, the more nervous I got.

I walked her back to her car. She turned to face me, glancing down at Archie, and smiled. "That dog of yours never did like me."

"Yeah, well, it's a two-way street, Alexis."

She stepped in close to me. Her eyes came up to meet mine, and the tips of her breasts nearly touched my chest. "I'm, uh, sorry things didn't work out for us, Cal." Her voice was soft, almost a whisper.

I smiled and stepped back. "It was for the best, Alexis."

Chapter Thirty-eight

At seven the next morning I sat in my car down the street from CJ Manion's place, trying to decide how to play it. Should I wait for her to come out or just go up and knock? Had Spiky Hair warned her about me? Probably, although I held out some hope he had bought my tough-guy routine the other night and kept his mouth shut.

At eight-thirty with no sign of her, I decided to just go up and ring the bell. She lived in a small, unkempt bungalow set back from the street behind a low chain-link fence laced with weeds and vines. Three newspapers were on the porch, and there were no lights on inside. I rang a couple of times and wasn't surprised when no one answered. I doubted she'd left before seven, and wondered how long she'd been gone and why.

I went back to my car and glanced at my watch. Philip should be at the airport by now, I figured. He'd received the confirmations for the ticket and the rental car, but I wanted to make sure everything was okay. I punched in his speed dial digit. "It's Cal. You all set?"

"Yep. Just checked in. The flight's on time. It's all good, Cal."

On my way back to Dundee, I felt anxious and depressed. Philip was the best stand-in I could ask for, but I wanted to be there to meet Claire in person, damn it. Frustration tinged with panic swept over me when I considered my situation. I was caught between someone bent on framing me for a murder and a sadistic cop who would like nothing better than to make that happen. It certainly wasn't the kind of atmosphere I wanted to bring Claire into, either. And one thing was crystal clear. I couldn't afford to wait around for Jefferson County's finest to crack this case. That job was mine.

My mind drifted to the last time I was in L.A. I'd gone to Forest Lawn Memorial Park to pay my respects at my wife's grave. It was a hot day, and I remembered feeling agitated as I sat down next to her marker. I laid a dozen yellow roses, her favorite, on the grass. My thoughts were jumbled, but after a few minutes a light breeze materialized, and although I was too far inland, I thought I could smell the ocean. My mind began to clear. It was as if she had joined me.

"Claire's doing great at Berkeley," I remember saying in a low voice. "She's almost through with her course work and has started her thesis research. She's going to make a great environmental scientist. She's a young woman now, and I'm trying to let go, you know, like you used to tell me. Don't hover. I wish you could be here to see this. God, I miss you, Nancy." I started to choke up but caught myself. I hadn't gone there to wallow in self pity.

The traffic ahead of me on I-5 slowed abruptly, jerking me back to the present. I switched on the radio, punched in the 89.1 jazz station, and turned the volume up. When I swung off Eagle Nest onto our long drive, I could see Archie waiting at the gate. He took off across the field, and when I pulled through the gate, circled around behind the car and herded me into the garage. When I got out of the car, he stood there whimpering and wagging his stump of a tail, a grungy tennis ball in his jaws.

We played fetch the slobber ball until my arm began to ache. I was rescued when my cell buzzed with a call from Nando. "Calvin, I have the ViCAP information for you."

"Wow, that was fast."

"Yes, well my source was quite accommodating. It seems your man Chuck could, indeed, be a contract killer. There is a gentleman the Zetas cartel uses for single hits north of the border, usually somebody they are very upset with. This assassin likes to get in close and use a knife."

My stomach fluttered. "Sounds like my boy."

"Your *boy* is a sadistic psychopath and very good at what he does. At least ten assassinations have been attributed to this man. The Zetas call him El Cuchillo, which means The Blade. The general description you gave me fits, along with the viciousness of the attack."

"But this doesn't look like a cartel hit."

"It could have been a freelance contract. He is known for it, a believer in free enterprise. There is considerable demand out there for competent hit men, you know. And he's not Latino. He's Anglo."

"Do you have any photos of him?"

"Only one, of poor quality. The man is like a ghost."

"Scan it and e-mail it to me right away, okay?"

"Very well. I trust you are keeping your Glock handy. You should take it with you when you go out at night. This man is very dangerous, Calvin."

"I'll consider it." Then I thought of Daina. "Did you turn up anything of interest on the woman, Daina Zakaris?"

"Actually, I did. She's Lithuanian, like you said, good credit, no criminal record, owns a consultancy business up in Seattle—"

"Good."

"But something weird came up when I looked to see if she'd ever shown up in the press."

"Weird?"

"Yes, I ran across a short newspaper article that said a Daina Zakaris had died in a gas explosion down in Los Angeles fourteen years ago. I guess it was just a coincidence, but the name is rather unusual."

"Huh, I think you're right, Nando. Has to be a coincidence."

Sure. It had to be a coincidence. Really.

Chapter Thirty-nine

I went into the study and booted up my laptop. The photo of El Cuchillo came in first. The grainy, poorly focused snapshot showed a man getting into a taxi, his head partially turned toward the camera, grim-faced, watchful. I had seen the guy who pushed me into the Hood River only briefly and through bleary eyes—the slender body, the non-descript features. But I was sure. It was him.

A scanned copy of the newspaper article on Daina Zakaris popped up a few moments later from Nando. It was a short article with no photograph. I read through it quickly. The woman had lived in Inglewood, in an apartment complex called Las Brisas. The blast destroyed her apartment. Gas water heater implicated. Killed her instantly. Her next-door neighbor, a woman named Svetlana Tetrovia was wanted for questioning in the explosion. Tetrovia was missing, and an investigation was underway.

I sat back in my chair and rubbed my temples. My stomach felt hollow, my chest tight. I googled Las Brisas. It was still there. I jotted down the directions from LAX to the apartment building and glanced at my watch. Philip would land in another forty minutes. I pecked around impatiently on my computer, then went out and played some more ball with Archie. Forty-five minutes later I had Philip on his cell. "Hey, Cal. I just got off the plane. What's up, Buddy?"

"I've got another favor to ask." I gave him the gist of the article about Daina that Nando had e-mailed me. "You're maybe twenty minutes from the Las Brisas. I'm wondering if you could, uh, drive over there and see what you can find out. I just want to confirm that the Daina Zakaris we know isn't the one who reportedly died in the blast."

He laughed. "You're kidding, right? This is your department. I'm just a lowly fishing guide."

"Come on, man. No false modesty. I've seen you handle those wealthy clients of yours. This is a chip shot. All you have to do is go over there and sweet-talk the manager. The website said her name's Florence Castro. Tell her, or whoever's in the office, that you're an old friend of Daina Zakaris' from Oregon. Uh, tell her you know about the tragic accident and that you were serving your country in Iraq and didn't make the funeral. Ask her if anyone is still around there that knew Daina, that you'd like to talk to them, maybe see where the apartment was. You know, kind of pay your respects, hear about her last days, that sort of thing."

"I don't know, Cal."

"It'll work, Philip. Trust me. People love to talk about stuff like this."

"A friend, huh?"

"Right, but keep it vague. Don't offer too much. And remember, she's Lithuanian. And get a picture of her if you can."

The line went so quiet I thought the call had dropped. Finally, Philip said, "Okay, Cal. I'll give it my best shot. Am I breaking any laws here?"

"Nope." I gave him the directions, and he agreed to call back when he'd finished.

I suddenly realized I was starving. I went into the kitchen, separated a sesame bagel and put both halves in the toaster. I got out the cream cheese, red onion, a tomato, a ripe avocado, capers, and smoked salmon. When the bagel came up, I built one helluva sandwich, which I washed down with a Mirror Pond while standing over the sink and looking out on the valley. A silvery haze muted the colors and a lone hunter, maybe a bald eagle, spiraled lazily in an updraft. That damn bird, I thought to myself. Not a care in the world.

It was nearly two hours later when Philip called. "Are you sitting down, Cal?"

My stomach tightened. "Yeah. What'd you find out?"

"At first the woman at the desk was wary, but I played the Iraq vet thing to the hilt. Turned out she has a daughter who's over there now. She directed me to a woman named Gladys who's lived there forever, just a few doors down from where the explosion happened. Everyone in the place thought it was either a plane crash or a terrorist attack. Anyway, Gladys was all too happy to talk about it. She was good friends with Daina, she—"

"*Jesus*, Philip. Give me the bottom line." My normally laconic friend had suddenly become annoyingly verbose.

"I'm coming to it," he shot back. "Daina Zakaris was in her mid-twenties, worked downtown. A naturalized citizen. I asked for a photograph, and Gladys hauled out an album. She showed me shots of a birthday party she'd held for Daina. Daina was a tall, attractive blond. Very Nordic looking." I felt a rush of relief and started to speak, but Philip cut me off. "There was another woman in almost all the shots. She was shorter, with dark hair. Cute as a button. Gladys told me her name was Svetlana Tetrovia. A Russian, on a visa. Everyone called her Lana. Cal, that woman is the one we know as Daina Zakaris."

We both fell silent for several beats. "You're sure?"

"Gladys gave me one of the photographs of the two of them together. There's no doubt in my mind. She told me Lana and Daina were the best of friends. She said Lana disappeared after the explosion. Apparently the police and some of the people in the building thought she might have had something to do with it. But Gladys never bought it. She said Lana was a sweet kid."

"Spotting that photograph was great work, Philip."

"Yeah, well, she just kind of jumped out at me. She's got the kind of face you don't forget, and she's hardly aged at all. What do you suppose it means?"

I exhaled a long breath. I felt like my canoe had just gone over a waterfall. "Man, I wish I knew. At the very least, Daina's an identity thief. Listen, Philip, scan that photograph and e-mail it to me, if you can. I need to see it, too."

"No problem."

"Are you all set for tomorrow morning? Claire's flight gets in at 9:06."

"Don't worry about a thing, Cal. I'll be there."

I had no sooner gotten off the phone with Philip when Claire called from Dubai, her voice as clear and bright as a silver bell. Her flight would be boarding in an hour, she told me. She couldn't wait to get to the Aerie and was looking forward to seeing Philip in L.A. If she was disappointed that I wasn't meeting her, she hid it pretty well, saying only, with a tease in her voice, "This long story you promised me better be a good one, Dad."

Arch and I drove over to the Fred Meyer in Newberg and laid in extra provisions for her stay. I tried to remember all her favorite treats, too—Chai tea, dark chocolate-hazelnut bars, Greek yogurt, and Tillamook Mudslide ice cream. I think I got most of them.

Later that night, I lay on the couch in the study trying to sort everything out. On the bright side, I now had a solid lead on the man who had killed Hal Bruckner, Hank Barnes, and nearly me. If CJ Manion cooperates, I might have a shot at his location, maybe even his name. If I could get Oliver Dan and his skateboarding buddies to identify El Cuchillo as the man they saw drop off the stolen Ford F-150, then I'd be on my way to proving the train theory. That might even be enough to persuade Escalante and Dorn to pick him up. That is, of course, if he was still in the Northwest.

The situation with Daina Zakaris, also known as Svetlana Tetrovia, was another matter completely. The photograph of the two women had come through an hour earlier. Philip was right. There was no question the Daina I knew was Tetrovia. The news hit me with a shotgun blast of emotions—anger at being duped by someone I trusted, shock at losing an ally in my fight to clear my name, and fear of what this could mean for me. And there was something else—a sense of loss. I found myself thinking about those nights on my deck and the lunch we'd shared and realized she'd managed to capture a bit of my heart. You know better than that, I told myself, and now look what's happened.

No, I couldn't afford to trust Daina, or I should say Svetlana, anymore. All bets were off.

I went to my office in Dundee the next morning, met with one client, then left for the Portland airport. It was smooth sailing until I got to the I-205, which was stop and go. But I'd left in plenty of time, and for once didn't find the traffic so onerous. After all, I was on my way to pick up my daughter, and despite the troubling news about Daina, found myself in a fine mood. I parked in the near-term lot and made my way through the terminal to the entry way for arriving passengers.

About ten minutes before her scheduled arrival, two TV camera crews showed up along with reporters, who were easy to spot because they were the two best-dressed of the lot. Maybe the local media had picked up Claire's story, I mused. Having a basic distrust of the media, particularly TV, I found myself hoping that wasn't the case, then realized that wish was more about me than my daughter. Why shouldn't she be recognized? She was a hero as far as I was concerned.

When passengers from the L.A. flight began filing out, I worked my way to the front of the crowd that had gathered. "There she is!" I blurted out when I saw her. Claire was in a wheelchair being pushed by Philip, who had a broad smile on his face. Sheathed in a plaster cast, her right leg jutted forward. She had definitely lost weight and looked tired, but her face lit up when she saw me, her auburn hair bouncing on her shoulders. She wore a navy blue sweatshirt with BERKELEY scripted in gold across the front and a pair of sweatpants that had been split up the right leg to accommodate her cast.

With Philip's help she stood up from the chair and called out, "Dad!" As we embraced, klieg lights came on behind us. The media was, in fact, there to cover her homecoming, and they obviously weren't going to give us much private time. I quickly moved aside and watched in awe as, poised and articulate, she handled them effortlessly.

At one point a reporter not much older than Claire asked, "What did you worry most about while you were in captivity?"

Claire looked over at me, smiled, and said, "My dad. I worried that my dad would worry too much about me."

Several people in the crowd said "Ooh" in sympathetic tones, and then the reporters turned to me. I put up a hand and tried to wave them off, the emotions so strong at seeing her that I wasn't sure I could get an intelligible word out. But they persisted, and I managed to say something about how proud of her I was. In midst of my fumblings, I caught a glimpse of Philip standing off to the side. He was chuckling, but with me, not at me.

We escorted Philip to his truck and I thanked him for the umpteenth time for being there for me and Claire. I invited him to dinner, but he begged off. "I've got to get back to Madras," he explained. "Got a client who wants a single day on the Deschutes tomorrow."

Claire said, "Isn't the salmon fly hatch on right now? Isn't this your busy time of year on the Deschutes, Philip?"

Philip looked at me and didn't speak. I said, "Uh, that's part of the long story I owe you, Claire."

Chapter Forty

I awoke the next morning to sunlight streaming through my bedroom window and the insistent cawing of the crows—that excited tone they use when the morning is clear and fine. I immediately noticed that Archie wasn't in his customary corner. Then it hit me. Claire was here, safe under my roof. She was exhausted when we arrived and, after an emotional reunion with Archie, had gone straight to bed. Archie would be in with her now. He knew instinctively that she needed special attention. Not that he needed an excuse to shadow her. She was definitely his favorite person, eclipsing even my vet, Hiram Pritchard, for the top honor.

I went down the hall and looked in. My daughter was sound asleep, and my dog, having heard my approach, lay at the side of her bed with his head erect, looking up at me. I stood there watching Claire sleep for a several minutes. There was no doubt she had her mother's face. The delicate trace of her nose, the high, sculpted cheeks, and the mouth that seemed to smile, even in sleep, were all maternal gifts. But the line of her jaw was more sharply drawn than Nancy's, reflecting a resolve that some called stubbornness. This—together with her five-ten height and broad, freckled shoulders—had more to do with me. She was lovely to behold, and I felt an immense sense of gratitude that she was finally back, safe and sound.

I left her sleeping and made my way down the back stairs to the kitchen, where I made myself a double cap before calling Hiram.

"Is she home?" my friend said in answer to my greeting.

"She sure is. She's tired, sleeping now, but she looks great." I went on to describe the status of her injured leg and to tell him about the surprise press interviews and how well Claire had handled herself. We agreed to get together as soon as Claire regained her strength.

Next, I went into the study and forwarded the picture of El Cuchillo to Philip with the following note:

Philip,

This is the guy who sent me swimming. I know you're on the river today, but please run this photo by Oliver Dan and his buddies as soon as you can. I'm hoping they can put him at the railroad yard.

Cal

By mid-morning Claire was up, and after breakfast we were sitting on the side porch taking in the view. The sun fought through thickets of low clouds scattered across the valley, and out near the horizon, the colors of the coastal range changed restlessly from greens and blues to deep shades of violet and back again. Closer in, fields and vineyards throbbed with early summer colors in the shifting light. Claire's broken leg rested on a chair, and her crutches leaned against the porch railing. Archie was laying against her other leg. I knew he wouldn't let her out of his sight.

I nodded toward her crutches. "You seem to be getting around okay."

"Yeah. Getting around on crutches is no problem. I spent six weeks on crutches when I blew my knee out playing basketball. Remember?"

"Oh, I remember all right. I never heard so much whining in my life."

"Very funny," she answered, and we both laughed. Her laugh, sweet and carefree, cut straight to my soul, and the pillars that supported me seemed to firm up.

"You want more tea? It's your favorite."

"I know, Dad, thanks. Sure, I'll have another cup."

I came back out with a tea for her and another coffee for me.

We were bringing each other up to date, but very cautiously it seemed. I didn't know where to begin about my mess, and I wasn't sure why Claire seemed reluctant to talk much about her experiences. In any case, I didn't push it.

She was much more interested in what I was up to, and telling her it was "the same old, same old" didn't cut it. At one point she fixed me with her eyes and said, "Okay, Dad. What's going on?"

I dropped her gaze and stroked my mustache with my thumb and index finger, searching for the words. "Well, I've got a situation I'm dealing with. Actually, two. But they're related."

She raised her eyebrows and leaned her head forward slightly. Her smile faded.

I sketched in an admittedly sanitized account of Hal Bruckner's murder on the Deschutes and the effort to frame me for it. When I told her about the affair with Alexis, the smile came back. "You had an affair? *Really?*"

I shook my head and tried not to smile. "It was stupid. I got involved with her against my better judgment, and I wish I could erase the whole episode. Feels like bad karma to me."

"No. It wasn't bad karma, Dad. And she came on to you, right? Don't beat yourself up. Besides, since when does having an affair constitute a motive for murder?"

"I need you to talk to a couple of gentlemen in Madras who have a contrary view," I said with a laugh.

"Their case is a joke, Dad. Trust me." She raised her chin and gave me a look taken whole-cloth from her mother. "I don't have a Dad who's a lawyer for nothing."

When I finished telling her about the train-hopping killer I knew only as El Cuchillo, she said, "So, when are you going to track down this woman who might know where to find this dude?"

I felt a twinge of anxiety at having found CJ Manion's place vacant. I hoped she hadn't left town. "Just as soon as we get you settled in. She lives in Portland."

"Well, you need to get on that, Dad. Don't worry about me. I can take care of myself."

Then I came to my run-in with Bull Dorn. She listened as I described how he'd baited me from the beginning, our encounter in the storage unit, and my subsequent arrest.

Claire's face clouded over and tears brimmed in her eyes. "Thank God his partner was there. I think he would have shot you and claimed self-defense."

I nodded like a guilty school boy. For the first time I saw clearly how my reckless actions could have impacted her as well as me. She'd be an orphan now, for God's sake.

"You just can't lash out, Dad. You roughed up that witness in the Parker Center, and what happened? They made you give up the job you loved. This guy, Dorn, *wanted* you to try something."

I studied the planks on the porch like a shamed little kid. "Yeah, I know. He definitely knew what button to push." I looked up at her. "He said he heard I caused your mother's death."

Her eyes closed, squeezing out a single tear that slid down her cheek and stopped just above her jawline. She dried her eyes with a paper napkin before replying. "I'm not surprised he said that. He's a sociopath, Dad. You're a good man. You're just trying to cope with a violent world." Then she gazed out at the valley for several moments. "I guess we all are."

I knelt beside her chair and hugged her until the tears in my own eyes stopped flowing. "I'm glad you're home, Claire."

"Me, too, Dad. Me, too."

We had dinner out on the side porch. The sun died slowly behind the trees and the twilight sky deepened to a violet glow. I barbecued some fresh halibut and served it up with a mango salsa and sweet potato slices I fried in hot oil. The dinner was a big hit, and we both ate with gusto. Afterward, we sat in the Northwest gloaming, talking softly and half listening to Dylan's "Blood on the Tracks," one of Claire's favorites. Claire began talking about her experiences in Darfur, and I listened, silently pleased she'd decided to open up about what had happened there. I knew the basic story, of course, and I also knew there was more. I could sense it. So I listened and at the same time steeled myself.

She spoke with affection about her teammates, the interesting people she'd met, and the strange things she'd seen. She spoke with pride about the wells her team had dug and what that basic act meant to villages lucky enough to be selected for the Well Spring program. I learned that in addition to clean water and better sanitation for all, the women of those villages were much less likely to be raped by marauding militiamen, because they didn't have as far to go for water. I stiffened involuntarily at the mention of rape. The word seemed to stand there between us like an unwelcome guest.

As she began to relate the story of her captivity, tension seeped into her voice. "After we wrecked our jeep trying to escape, the Janjaweed took us out at gunpoint and put us in the back of a pickup. The ride back to the village where we'd been working was really rough, Dad." Tears filled her eyes.

"Hey," I said, "we don't have to talk about this if you don't want to."

She smiled, fought to regain control of her emotions, and continued. "It's okay. I need to tell you this, Dad."

I struggled to keep my expression neutral; it seemed important to do that. I nodded for her to continue.

"Instinctively, I knew I shouldn't let them know I was hurt. But by the time we got back I couldn't stand it anymore. When I tried to climb out of the pickup I collapsed." She paused, gazed at the space between us and grimaced slightly as that scene played out again in her mind.

"Did they give you any medical help?"

Claire laughed sardonically. "We had a few ibuprofen, but they didn't cut the pain much. Jerry, our team leader, complained bitterly to the guy in charge of the group left to guard us. His name was Mustafa. The guy was right out of the Arabian Nights. Tall, with a full beard. His eyes. I remember his eyes. They flashed at you. And he carried a scimitar. No kidding. Anyway, Mustafa listened to Jerry, then just shrugged his shoulders and walked away."

"Bastard," I said under my breath.

"Wait, Dad. Let me finish. About an hour later two scruffy looking guys came in and said they'd been sent by Mustafa to take me to a doctor. Jerry was suspicious, but since he'd complained so much, he let them carry me out on a slab of plywood. He started to go with me, but the guards at the door stopped him. There was a struggle, and I heard him shouting, but I didn't give a damn. I was in so much pain I would have gone with the devil himself if he promised to get me a doctor."

As I listened my hands got cold, and my heart shrunk inside my chest.

Claire continued, her voice wavering again. "They carried me down an alley, and after a block or so they started laughing hysterically. Like kids who'd gotten away with something. I knew I was in deep trouble when they brought me into a deserted house."

"Oh, no," I said, half to myself. I wasn't sure I wanted her to continue, but I didn't say anything more.

"Anyway," she continued, "Jerry told me later what happened after I was taken. Mustafa came back with some narcotics for the pain. Jerry told him about the two men. Without a moment's hesitation, Mustafa turned and took off running as fast as he could down the street."

I must have gasped, because Claire stopped speaking for a moment. Then she continued, "He got there while the two creeps were still arguing about who was going to go first. There was a violent shouting match in Arabic. I was afraid they would kill Mustafa. But the two backed down when he drew his sword. Mustafa made them carry me back to the holding room while he walked behind us."

I exhaled and muttered, "Thank God."

Claire straightened up in her seat. "I never saw either one of those creeps again." Then she looked me full in the face and added, "They didn't touch a hair on my head, Dad."

After Claire was in bed, I went to my study and poured a glass of Rémy with a shaky hand. I felt profound relief and a sense of closure. Claire was back, and she was back *whole.*

It was over now. A stranger had intervened on behalf of my daughter. I was willing to bet this man had a daughter of his own. I raised my glass and said aloud, "To Mustafa, wherever you are."

Chapter Forty-one

I was still nursing my Rémy and trying to think my way forward when my cell rang.

"Cal?"

"Yes?"

"It's Daina. I just called to see how your daughter's doing. Is she home now?"

"Uh, yeah, she is. Everything's fine. She's in bed now. I'm, uh, just relaxing."

"Oh. Well, I'm glad to hear everything's okay." She paused, and I searched in vain for something casual to say. Finally she said, "Are you all right, Cal? Is something wrong?"

"Uh, no. Everything's fine." I tried to keep my voice light but didn't quite manage it. I wasn't ready for the call. I hadn't come to terms yet with how to handle the situation with Daina.

There was another pause, and then she said, "You know, don't you?" Her voice was low, fearful.

"Know what?"

She hung up. I stood there with the phone in my hand and shook my head. I'd forgotten that this woman didn't need a lot of information to figure out what was going on. I thought about driving over to Wilsonville and confronting her, but there was no way I was leaving Claire alone.

I poured another Rémy, went upstairs and checked on Claire before settling back with a James Crumley. Whatever I needed to do, it would have to wait until morning. It wasn't long after that that Archie growled and barked a couple of times from his spot in the corner. I got up and went to the window just in time to see the lime green VW pull up in the dimly lit driveway. I took the Glock off my nightstand, and after pulling my shirt out, concealed it in my back waistband. I wasn't taking any chances.

By the time I got downstairs, Daina was knocking softly on the front door. I opened it, and Archie moved around me to greet her, his tail wagging furiously. She knelt down to hug him, then stood but made no move to come in. Her hair was swept under a paisley kerchief, and her baggy jeans made her look disarmingly child-like. Her eyes were huge, luminous discs, registering fear. I stepped back and she came into the hall without saying anything. "Hello, Svetlana."

Her eyes were down, her shoulders slumped. "How did you find out?" Her voice was husky, yet I caught a hint of defiance in it.

"I had a friend run the name Daina Zakaris. Did it on a whim. I didn't suspect a thing".

She showed a bitter smile. "Then why did you run my name?"

I shrugged. "Instincts, I guess. Anyway, Philip Lone Deer was down in L.A. to pick up Claire for me. He drove over to Inglewood and talked to someone who knew you as Svetlana Tetrovia, here on a visa from Russia."

Her face brightened like a flickering light. "Was it Gladys? Did he talk to Gladys?"

I nodded. "Yeah. She gave him a picture of the real Daina Zakaris, and there you were, standing next to her."

Her eyes filled, but she didn't speak.

"Look, I need to know what the hell's going on."

She sighed like she'd just caught the weight of the world on her shoulders. "Can we at least sit down?"

The near-perfect American accent had cracked, and I could hear a little more of the eastern European inflection. I nodded in the direction of the living room, followed her in, and sat down across from her. "What happened in Inglewood?"

She sat on the edge of a small sofa and wiped a tear from her cheek with the back of her hand. I handed her my handkerchief, and she dabbed her eyes. "Daina was very sweet. We'd become good friends. She was Lithuanian. All alone here, but a naturalized citizen. I'm Russian. We understood each other. One morning there was this terrible explosion in her apartment—hot water heater or something. I never heard exactly—"

"I know about the explosion, about Daina's death, and the fact that you vanished afterward."

She shrugged. "Okay. Well, the blast blew me out of my chair. At first I thought it was a plane crash. I ran to what was left of her apartment and found her in the kitchen. I knew she was dead the moment I saw her. A small fire had started in the living room, and as I was putting it out, I saw a desk drawer on the floor. The contents had spilled out—her passport, birth certificate, and other personal papers. I scooped up the passport and birth certificate and left the other papers to smolder there. It all happened so fast. I told myself I was just trying to save them, that I would return them. But deep down I knew I wouldn't. My visa was about to expire, and I dreaded the thought of going back to Russia. Don't you understand, Cal? This was a gift. *Pure freedom.*"

I didn't answer.

"The rest was fairly easy. I moved to Seattle and hired some Russians skilled in the art of helping people like me stay in the U.S. I became Daina Zakaris, U.S. citizen, Lithuanian by birth. She was dead. What was the harm?"

"So you stole the identity of the dead Lithuanian woman and went on to reinvent yourself? These Russians who helped you—are any of them working for you now?"

She puffed a breath from her lips in a distinctively European manner and looked at me through tear-soaked eyes. "No. None. I built my company on my own. I made a clean break with those people. I didn't want anything more to do with them."

I raked my fingers through my hair. I wanted to believe she wasn't mixed up in Hal Bruckner's murder, but every skeptical bone in my body screamed for me not to. "Look, I really don't give a damn what you did fourteen years ago, and why you did it. We all have our secrets. All I want is to clear my name and get on with my marginal existence."

She blinked rapidly to clear the moisture from her eyes and scanned my face. "I want to help you do that, Cal."

"Okay," I continued, "we both know that *someone* at Nano-Tech helped plan the murder of Hal Bruckner. Tell me why the hell I shouldn't suspect you?"

The tears had stopped, and her huge eyes were now burning with a passion I hadn't seen before. "Let me explain. You Americans, you have so much, and you take so much for granted. But in Russia, it is different. We learn early in life to fight for what we want and what we need. We learn that *nothing* is given."

I raised my eyebrows and nodded slightly.

"When I came here it took me very little time to realize that I *had* to find a way to stay. Going back to Russia was simply out of the question. It would be like dying. I decided I would behave as though I was staying in L.A. Like a citizen. I enrolled in school and worked full time. Daina Zakaris was my mentor. She encouraged me. I knew the woman well, Cal. She would have wanted me to have her identity, *I know it.*"

I still didn't speak.

"No, I'm not proud of taking those papers, but I'm not ashamed of what I did with them, either." Then she met my eyes. "And I think you know, in your heart of hearts, Cal Claxton, that I had nothing to do with the murder of Hal Bruckner."

I broke eye contact and raked my hair again. She was partially right. Part of me did believe she wasn't involved, but the skeptical side of my nature wouldn't shut up. I was stuck somewhere in the middle.

All I could do was shake my head.

"Someone broke into my house and tried to kill me, Cal. Think about it. And the information I've given you, think about that. I've gone out on a limb for you. And why would I want to harm Bruckner? Christ, I need this account."

I had to think fast and ruthlessly. Suppose she's telling the truth about Bruckner? If I turn her in I lose an invaluable source inside NanoTech, to say nothing of getting her deported, which didn't sit well with me. If she's involved in the plot to kill Bruckner there still might be some upside to playing along, provided I could make her believe she'd fooled me. The decision seemed clear, but it made me queasy. What were the chances of fooling this woman?

I exhaled a decisive sounding breath. "Okay. Like I said, I'm not interested in your past. And you're right, I don't think you had anything to do with Bruckner's murder, but you can bet I'm going to check out your last fourteen years."

Defiance flashed in her eyes. "Go ahead. You won't find anything."

"Good." I allowed myself a tentative smile. "Uh, so what am I supposed to call you now?"

"Daina. It's Daina Zakaris. That's my name."

"Daina it is, then."

A long silence ensued before she said, "What about the police? Do they know about me?"

"No, don't worry about that. The source I used will keep the information confidential."

She nodded and tried to smile but didn't quite succeed. After all, now I knew her deepest secret. She brought her eyes up and met mine. "Thank you, Cal. You won't regret this. What else can I do to help you?"

I hesitated for a moment, not liking myself for what I was about to propose. But I was up against it. Hard. "Well, there is one thing."

Chapter Forty-two

Forty-five minutes later Hiram Pritchard pulled up in his Saab. He had agreed to house-sit while I ran a "late night errand." If Claire woke up I wanted someone she knew there, someone I trusted. I met him on the front porch and thanked him again for coming. He said, "This must be damned important, Cal. I know you're not anxious to leave Claire at night."

I nodded. "Look, Hiram, trust me on this."

He raised an eyebrow. "No risk of disbarment?"

I had to chuckle. "I hope not."

He let it drop there and followed Archie into the house. He was a good friend, and, frankly, nothing I did surprised him much anymore.

I blinked my lights when I saw Daina's VW on the side of the road down the hill from my place. She pulled out and I followed her to NanoTech's headquarters in Wilsonville. She was horrified at my plan, but she reluctantly agreed. A quick look in the execs' offices, I told her. That's all I was after. Whoever was on the inside in the Bruckner murder didn't know that I knew about the use of the trains. Maybe they were careless. Maybe I'd find a link. It was low risk and worth a shot, I told her. And it beat sitting around waiting to be framed.

Daina parked in a far corner of the employee lot, away from the lights. I parked a couple of blocks down on the street in an unlighted spot. When I joined her in the lot, she gave me a resigned look. "It looks clear, no cars, no office lights. The cleaning crew has come and gone. When we go in, I'll go to my office. You'll take the fire stairs to the fourth floor. The doors are marked. Remember—thirty minutes, and *nothing* gets taken away."

"Right. I'm not after the company secrets here."

She frowned. "This is a high-tech company, so people pop in at weird hours. I'll keep an eye on the lot. If someone comes, I'll call you. Take the back stairs and wait for me."

"Got it."

She exhaled a long breath and surveyed the lot and the building once more. "Okay, let's get this over with. Don't disturb a thing."

When we got to the gate, Daina said over her shoulder, "You're lucky the security cams I ordered haven't arrived yet. She swiped her master key against the lighted security pad. A loud metallic click reverberated in the still night, like a pistol shot. I winced, feeling like everyone in Wilsonville had heard it, and hesitated for a moment before following her in.

You're not breaking any laws here, I reminded myself. Just accompanying a friend while she picks up something at her office.

Daina repeated the process to gain entrance to the building. She pointed to the fire door at the back of the lobby leading to the staircase. "Thirty minutes, Cal." She glanced at her watch. "I'll meet you back here at 12:35."

I took the stairs fast and was breathing hard by the time I reached the fourth floor, which contained the executive offices. I started down the hall and stopped at the sixth office on my left. An engraved brass plate read, Dr. Duane F. Pitman, Ph.D., Director of Technology. I didn't even need Daina's master. The door was unlocked.

Pitman's office was pitch dark. I paused to put on a pair of latex gloves and take out a pen light. I felt my way to the window, closed the blinds, and switched on the light. The place was a mess. There were stacks of scientific journals and books and papers on virtually every flat surface. Equations, sketches, and diagrams covered a white board spanning one wall. It reminded me of the office of one of my favorite law professors at Boalt. I knew that, like my professor, Pitman could quickly find anything he'd stashed away, and would know instantly if I left anything out of place.

I tried his computer, but it was password blocked. A drawer in one of his file cabinets had been left open, with a couple of files pulled halfway out as if they were being actively consulted. I checked those first and found schematics of laboratory equipment. The rest of the cabinet was similarly uninteresting. A second cabinet contained reprints of scientific papers and a dozen or so of Pitman's old laboratory notebooks. Nothing caught my eye.

I was sweating, and my stomach had turned sour. I started to have second thoughts about my snap decision to wring this favor out of Daina. I scanned through several files jammed with letters he'd written and received and didn't see anything remotely interesting. As I closed the drawer I noticed a gap between the last file and the back of the drawer. I reached over the files into the gap and pulled out a large, half-inch thick envelope. It was sealed, taped shut, and unmarked. My pulse ticked up a beat. Pack rats, I thought to myself. They can't help themselves.

A quick search turned up a stack of matching envelopes on a shelf below his computer. I slit the sealed envelope open and began to rapidly scan the contents, which consisted of correspondence between Pitman and Jean Claude Clivas, the U.S. sales director for the French firm Daina had told me about, Technologie Micro-Electronique.

The letters detailed a rather lengthy negotiation between Pitman and TM-E, which culminated in Clivas proposing "a salary of $350,000 per annum, a $750,000 signing bonus, 50,000 stock options, a group of ten degreed professionals, and a fully equipped lab, if you should decide to accept our offer of employment."

I whistled, shook my head, and said out loud, "Who said lawyers make all the money?" This confirmed what Bruckner was worried about—Pitman intended to bolt, taking his knowledge of the Diamond Wire technology with him.

But there was a caveat. Toward the bottom of the letter, Clivas, most likely at the insistence of their lawyers, had inserted the following: "It is our understanding that you are free to accept this offer and that you are not bound to your current employer by prior legal agreement. This offer is contingent upon this."

I tried to sort this out in my mind. It sounded like Pitman had told TM-E that he was free to leave NanoTech, so he must have known the security document was missing. Quite a gamble on his part. If Bruckner's copy of the agreement was found, Pitman and TM-E would become legal sitting ducks in any court of law.

I used my phone to photograph the offer letter from TM-E, then slid the whole packet into a new envelope, sealed and taped it, and put it back where I'd found it.

I searched the rest of the room with increased enthusiasm. Give me something, *anything,* that ties Pitman to Cuchillo or shows he had a sudden interest in train schedules.

I found nothing else.

I had to use the master key to gain entrance to Andrew Streeter's office. It was 12:16. In contrast to Pitman's office, it was neat to the point of sterility.

I took a quick look at his executive bragging wall first. A formal portrait of Streeter's father, State Senator Paxton K. Streeter, scowled out at me, two sets of tiny South Carolina and U.S. flags adorning the bottom of the frame. A much younger and slimmer Andrew stood proudly in a photograph between Strom Thurmond and Lindsey Graham , and in another, with George W. Bush's arm draped around him. There was also a graduation diploma and a shot of Andrew in a football uniform to attest to his glory days at The Citadel.

Streeter's filing cabinets were a bust. His desk drawers were equally disappointing—a couple of thick working files, some Harvard Business Review reprints, and an Accelerated Management Development manual. The manual looked untouched.

The desktop was clean except for a massive brass pen holder with Streeter's name engraved on the base and a flip-page calendar with daily words of inspiration for the aspiring business leader. That day's message was "A leader isn't born; he's forged on the anvil of challenge. " I rifled through the calendar but found nothing of interest.

As I moved around the desk, my foot bumped something under it. I fished out a black nylon gym bag that spewed a cloud of sweat and mildew odors when I unzipped it. Streeter's unimpressive workout routine, a combination lock, and a tattered business card were zipped in a side pocket. The card belonged to a masseuse named Zina at the Mystic Hands Whole Body Massage Center. The center was up on Mississippi in northeast Portland, a tough neighborhood that was rapidly gentrifying and, I guessed, a lengthy drive for Streeter.

Zina's hands must be truly mystic, I thought to myself. On the back of the card the name, Rey, and a local phone number were written in a flowery script. I jotted down the information in a notebook I'd brought and put the gym bag back under the desk.

A plaque on the counter behind his desk read *FAC UT GAUDEAM*. I had no idea what the Latin meant. Next to his computer sat something completely out of character for a high-tech executive's office—an old-fashioned Rolodex. Some habits die hard. I spun through it and saw nothing that caught my eye until I got to the Zs. There on a blank card, written by hand, were the following words—*Nemo Me Impune Lacessit.* More Latin. I didn't have a clue what the phrase meant, but I jotted it down out of curiosity. After all, it wasn't filed alphabetically.

It was 12:29 when I hurried down to the hand-carved, double doors marking the corner office. No brass plate on the door, just four screw holes marking where the plate had been. The office was twice as big as Streeter's with a desk made from a small forest's worth of old growth hardwoods. The bookcase on the south wall was only half stocked, books sat in boxes on the floor, and there were stacks of file folders on the counter behind the desk. Mitch Hannon, the new CEO of NanoTech, was apparently moving into the late Hal Bruckner's office.

I was working my way carefully through the file folders when a light flickered on the blinds I'd drawn upon entering. It was gone in an instant. A passing car, I decided.

I went back to the search, kicking myself for not demanding more time from Daina. After all, I held the leverage. But I was trying to strike some kind of crazy balance. This was, after all, an enormous risk for her business. On the bottom of the shortest stack of files I found a thin manila folder with Deschutes Trip written in what I assumed was Hannon's handwriting. I opened it hurriedly. A map of the Deschutes River was on top, a circle drawn around the Whiskey Dick campground and the Kaskela switching station. A chill worked its way down my spine.

As I started to rifle through the file, my phone vibrated. *"Cal, it's me. Get the hell out of there. Someone's coming in the building."* I turned to put the file back and brushed one of the stacks of folders with my hip. It avalanched into the next stack, and they both cascaded off the counter, taking an expensive windup clock with them.

"Shit!" I hissed at the sound of breaking glass. I shone my light on the floor. The face of the clock was shattered into a dozen pieces. I was frozen for a moment, not believing what had just happened. The clock was hopeless, but I tried to put the files back the way I'd found them. I quickly realized this was hopeless, too.

I was halfway to the office door when I heard the ping of the elevator being summoned. I dashed out the door and headed down the hallway, which now seemed much longer. Just as I closed the door to the stairwell, the elevator pinged again. Someone was entering the fourth-floor hallway.

Chapter Forty-three

I careened down the stairwell, berating myself with every step. Daina met me at the bottom. We collected ourselves and walked calmly out of the building to the parking lot without saying a word, hoping all the while no one was watching us from the fourth floor. Ten minutes later I pulled in behind Daina's VW in her driveway, turned off the ignition and lights, and sat there letting my heart rate recover. I went over my escape again. Nothing left behind. No way to trace me.

Daina got out of her car and waved me into the house. Dylan eyed me with suspicion and barked his displeasure as we entered. She scooped him up, hugged him, and put him back down. Her eyes grew to saucers as she raised her hand to her mouth and let out a burst of nervous laughter. "*Oh, shit, that was so close.* I forgot all about that little parking lot in the back of the building. Whoever it was must've parked back there."

I nodded and tried to smile. "I saw the headlights flash but figured it was a passing car."

She eyed me more carefully. "You got out clean, right?"

"Not exactly."

The smile died, and her face lost some color. "What does that mean?"

"I was in Hannon's office when you called. I, uh, knocked some files over in my haste to get out of there."

"You put them back, right?"

"Sort of. But his clock got broken, too."

Her eyes narrowed. "You mean, they'll know someone was in the office?"

"Afraid so. But they won't know who. I didn't leave anything behind."

Her eyes flashed anger mixed with fear. "Oh, that's great. Just great. A chip shot. Isn't that what you called it? In and out. No problems." She laughed bitterly.

"Shit happens, Daina. Does anyone know Bruckner gave you a master?"

"No. I don't think so. He told me not to tell anyone."

"Then you're probably okay."

She didn't say anything, but anger, like the latent energy in a thunderhead, still shone in her eyes. Dylan rubbed at her leg, begging to be picked back up, but she ignored him. Finally she said, "Well, did you find anything?"

"No. I hate to admit it, but it was a complete bust." I'd decided, at least for the present, not to tell her about the Pitman document I'd photographed or the map I'd seen in Hannon's office. I needed time to think it through.

"You mean you're not any closer?"

"You could say that." I shook my head and sighed. "God, I'm tired. I'm tired of this whole mess." It was a true statement.

Daina shook her head, sighed, and motioned toward a chair. "Sit down for a minute." When I complied she began to gently massage my neck.

I closed my eyes and exhaled slowly. "I'll give you exactly an hour to stop that," I said in a near whisper.

"I'm still pissed off at you, but try to relax, damn it. Your neck muscles are like a box of rocks."

After a couple of minutes I stood up, and the next thing I knew she was in my arms. I could feel the contours of her body firm against me. She looked up, showing a hint of a smile. Her eyes were calm, like shadowed pools, and I could smell a hint of lilac in her hair, soap on her skin. I released her and stepped back. "I've got to go. I'm anxious to get back to Claire."

"I know," she answered. "Go."

Chapter Forty-four

I drove back to the Aerie and found Hiram in the kitchen with a mug of coffee and a Richard Dawkins book he'd taken off the shelf in my study. He looked up and smiled. "You're back with no bleeding wounds. Was the foray a success?"

I shrugged. "I'm not sure. It didn't exactly go the way I drew it up."

We chatted for a while. My friend didn't ask for details, and I didn't volunteer any. Before he left, he agreed to meet Claire and me for lunch later that day.

After Claire got up and had breakfast, she, Archie, and I took a walk down to the mailbox. Claire used her crutches, making it down and back without incident. I didn't look at the newspaper until we were back in the kitchen. There we were on page two of the Metro section, father and daughter human interest story. The article and photo had been picked up from the wire services with some modifications to play up the local angle. Mercifully, the paper left out the fact that I was a person of interest in a grisly murder and had recently been arrested for assaulting a police detective.

Later that morning Claire was out on the deck, catching some sun. "You want to venture into the metropolis of Dundee?" I asked. "I've got some work to do at the office, then we could grab lunch at the Brasserie. Bettie's dying to see you, and Hiram said he could join us." Bettie was a dear friend. She owned the Brasserie Dundee and was crazy about my daughter.

"Sounds like a plan. It would be fun to see Doc, and Bettie, too."

At a little past one, Claire swung herself into Bettie's restaurant as I held the door. The Brasserie was always inviting. Sunlight streamed in from high windows, mingling with a barrage of good smells—sage, garlic, chops and fish on the grill—and the low buzz of conversation amidst fresh flowers and white tablecloths. I saw several folks I knew. I'd handled a zoning dispute with the county for Mervin and Aurora Thompson. They looked up from their menus, smiled weakly and dropped their eyes. Teddy Wilcox was chatting up an anorexic-looking redhead. I'd handled his second divorce. He pretended not to see me. Only Gus Foster, another ex-client of mine, looked up and smiled with genuine friendliness. Maybe he didn't gossip or read the newspaper.

Claire and I made our way back to the booths in the bar area. Hiram was already there, talking to Bettie. When they saw us Hiram stood up, and Bettie met Claire with a warm hug. Then, holding her at arm's length she said, "You're lookin' good, hon. How's that leg of yours?"

"It's feeling better every day. Look, I can even wiggle my toes." We all watched as she made good on her boast.

Bravo, Claire," said a beaming Hiram, who moved in for the next hug. "We're so relieved to see you, child, but we didn't doubt for a moment that you would return to us unscathed."

"That's the truth," I chimed in, although I realized Hiram was being generous in his use of the word "we." After all, it was his optimistic tone that kept my doubts from overwhelming me during Claire's ordeal. And, come to think of it, Daina had a lot to do with that, too.

"Come. We're anxious to hear about digging wells in the Darfur and all the rest of it," Hiram continued.

"Sit yourselves down," Bettie said. "I need to check on lunch. I'm cooking us something special."

We settled in around my daughter and listened as she retold her story, with gentle probing from Hiram. Claire was a very private person, and I wasn't surprised when she left out the part about being nearly raped.

We talked and laughed and devoured Bettie's lunch—pan-seared sea bass served with apple-cranberry chutney, thin-cut French fries, and an arugula salad with goat cheese, pears, and walnuts. We washed it down with a bottle of Argyle reserve chardonnay. I sat there looking at my friends and my daughter, and for the first time in a long time my life seemed…well…as close to normal as it gets.

I had my phone on vibrate, and I nearly spilled my wine when it went off. I'll never get used to that feeling—like having an angry bee in your pocket. I excused myself and took the call by the bar.

"Cal? It's Philip. Can you talk, buddy?"

I could tell by his tone that this was business. "Yeah, I can talk. What's up?"

"I managed to corner Oliver Dan and his boys this morning. Man, I worry about those kids on the Rez."

"What happened?"

"First off, I didn't like their attitude. All of sudden, they don't want to talk to me. I had to remind them I knew about them boosting the F-150."

"And?"

"Oliver called me a 'fucking apple', you know, red on the outside, white on the inside. Can you believe that? I mean, I love my mother, but I'm red *all* the way through, man."

I tried to suppress a laugh, but part of it escaped through my nose. At the same time, I was alarmed. "Tell me you didn't scare them off."

"I came close to mopping the floor with them, but I kept my cool. I told 'em I needed them to make an ID, that if they didn't cooperate, I was going to their parents. I know every one of them."

"So, you showed them the picture of El Cuchillo?"

"Yeah. I showed them."

I was losing my patience. *"And?"*

"Not a sure thing, Cal."

"Shit. So, what exactly did they tell you, Philip?"

"First off, Oliver was the only one who really got a look at him. He said the build was about right, and the face *could* have been a match. But the guy was a ways off and wearing a hood.

"Did he say anything else?"

"No. That was pretty much it."

"Okay. So we can't prove Cuchillo was at the Barlow Northern train yard, at least not yet," I said, fighting back the disappointment. Without Dan's corroboration, I could hardly go back to Escalante. "So be it. If he's still in the area, we need to figure out how to flush him out."

"You got a plan?"

"I know someone who knows where Cuchillo's holing up."

"You're kidding."

"Nope." I went on to tell him about CJ Manion, the woman at the martial arts studio, and my intention to look her up in Portland later that afternoon.

"Sweet. Take good notes, because I'm dying to meet that son of a bitch Cuchillo. And Cal, watch your step. This is getting dicey."

◇◇◇

It was after four when I headed out for Portland. I'd dropped Claire off at my neighbor, Gertrude Johnson's, place. I promised to be back at Gertie's for dinner, a treat I never missed.

I parked a block and a half down from CJ's place. The bungalow had charm once but was losing the fight against time and the wet Oregon climate. Hanging by a single hinge, the front gate opened to a brick walkway encrusted with moss and bristling with weeds. The front steps felt spongy and sagged under my weight, and after ringing the doorbell several times, I gave the door a couple of sharp raps. No response. She's got to be home, I told myself. The lights are on, and the newspapers I'd seen the other day are gone.

Maybe she's in the back somewhere. I followed the driveway around the house to a one-car garage that was listing to the right about 15 degrees. I peeked in a side window. It was empty except for a Kawasaki motorcycle and some gardening tools. I approached the back door of the house, which was slightly ajar. I knocked again, harder this time. Nothing.

Through a window in the back door, I could see another door that led into a darkened basement. She's either down there, in the shower, or asleep, I concluded. I glanced at my watch, and grumbling all the way, headed back to the car, determined to wait her out.

Twenty minutes later, I stood at the back door again, after getting no response out front. I rapped hard and waited. Still no response. With frustration mounting, I eased the unlatched door open slightly and yelled into the house, "Hello in there. CJ? It's Cal Claxton. I'd like to talk to you." That's when I heard the faint, rhythmic drone and occasional clink of a load of clothes being dried, the sound drifting up from the basement.

Laundry day.

Through the window in the back door, I could see the top of the stairs disappearing into the darkened basement. I called out again to no effect, then stood there, a bundle of indecisiveness as visions of the NanoTech disaster danced in my head. But sometimes there's no way out except through. I sighed, let myself in, and called down the stairs. "CJ? Are you down there?" Nothing came back except the sound of the dryer, louder now. But as my eyes adjusted, I saw a shadowy form lying on the steps, maybe halfway down. I flipped on the wall switch, and there she was, sprawled head first down the steps, one leg tucked under her, an arm flung to the side. The blood from CJ Manion's ravaged neck was dark but still had a reddish cast. A fresh kill.

I heard a strange noise, then realized it was my own voice. "*No. Oh, no.*"

No question CJ Manion was dead. My only question was how fast could I get out of there. Being implicated in a second throat-slashing would not help my standing with Escalante and Dorn. I literally backed out, desperately wiping down the surfaces I remembered touching. Did I get all my prints? Who the hell knows?

I let myself out the door. As I came around the house a woman walking a border collie stopped and shot me a curious look. I avoided eye contact and walked past her, trying to assume an air of casualness, but I could feel the heat of her gaze on the side of my face.

You can't just leave her body lying there, my better angel argued as I drove away. The hell I can't, my self-preservation instinct countered. Pretend you weren't there. Let someone else handle it. You're in enough trouble. But no, I couldn't do that. I pulled off the I-5, bought a burner phone at a discount electronics house near the freeway, and called in the crime through the triple-folded sleeve of my windbreaker. I told them I was a neighbor who stopped by, and no, I didn't want to give my name.

I should have felt better, but I didn't. I couldn't get the image of that young woman out of my head. The viciousness of the attack, the savagery of it, was numbing. And something else bothered me even more. I felt like the slippery slope I was on just got steeper, that my life was spinning out of control.

How many more sketchy choices was I going to have to make, anyway?

Chapter Forty-five

I arrived at Gertrude Johnson's at about six-thirty. Claire met me at the door, and when I walked into the kitchen, Gertie looked up and frowned. "Good grief, Calvin. You're as pale as a ghost. Sit down and let me get you a beer." I tossed the first beer down and asked for another. I had to summon up every scrap of willpower to hide the shock of what I'd seen in CJ Manion's basement. I kept seeing her nearly decapitated body, and the realization sank in that El Cuchillo hadn't gone anywhere. There was the guilt, too. I couldn't get away from the thought that CJ had died because of me, because of my snooping around at the martial arts studio, and I'd just left her body lying there. It was like a fresh bruise on the unhealed wound that was my conscience, or what was left of it.

Then there was the crime scene. Like a wave of nausea, the thought that I might have left behind a fingerprint, or something else incriminating, kept returning. The woman I'd encountered on the street was even more worrisome. She could probably pick me out of a lineup in a heartbeat. And what about Spiky Hair? When he hears about CJ, will he give me up?

My neighbor and friend, Gertrude Johnson, was a semi-retired forensic accountant who did the books for my law practice more out of pity than need for money. A fifth-generation Oregonian, she loved a good joke, straight Scotch, and a rough and tumble argument. She could cook like a wizard, too. So having dinner with her would ordinarily be high on my list of enjoyable things to do, but on that particular night I must have been dreadful company and insisted on leaving before she had served the pie and coffee. We said awkward good-byes and made our way home on foot across the set of fields connecting the two properties.

"Are you okay, Dad?"

"Yeah. Sure. I just drank a bit too much is all."

"I can *see* that," Claire said in a tone that reminded me of her mother. "I meant you seemed totally preoccupied tonight. Is something wrong?"

"Nothing," I reassured her. "Just need some sleep."

I slept fitfully that night, the beer triggering a pounding headache that three aspirin couldn't subdue. I got up early and went down to get the paper. There was no mention of the murder yet. Claire and Archie accompanied me to my office in Dundee, where I caught up on some paperwork while she read and Archie snoozed. I felt better that afternoon, managing to rid the garden of some weeds and throw together a more than passable dinner.

The headline in the Sunday paper read:

Woman Found Brutally Slain in Brooklyn Neighborhood

Next to photographs of CJ and her bungalow was a composite sketch of a white male who looked an awful lot like me. The text beneath the drawing asked, "Have you seen this man?"

Anxiety spread out from the pit of my stomach like water on a dry sponge. I made a cup of coffee and drank half of it before I went back to the paper. I looked at the drawing again and felt slightly better. After all, I told myself, the sketch looked like a lot of white males out there with dark, graying hair and a full mustache. I had no prominent scars, birthmarks, or tattoos, thank God. And the sketch showed an elongated face. I had a much rounder face, like all the males in the Claxton family.

I read the article carefully. There was no specific information about the time of the murder, just the time when the body was discovered. I figured CJ must have been hit *after* she'd loaded the clothes dryer and was on her way back up from the basement. El Cuchillo probably lay in wait at the top of the stairs. Since the dryer was still going when I arrived, the murder occurred probably no more than sixty minutes earlier, at the most. That seemed consistent with the blood I'd seen, which hadn't darkened and congealed.

So, the lady with the dog could put me smack at the scene within the window of time that CJ was murdered.

I leaned back and raked the fingers of both hands slowly through my hair. I had unwittingly set myself up to be blamed for another murder, and far worse, I knew El Cuchillo was still out there, taking care of business. One thing was crystal clear—time was running out. Even if Escalante and Dorn weren't faithful readers of *The Oregonian*, I knew the composite sketch would be on its way to the Jefferson County sheriff's office. I wondered how long it would take them, or for that matter someone else who knew me, to make the connection with that sketch.

My first impulse was to put the paper away before Claire got up. Then I realized how absurd that would be. Instead I left it out on the kitchen table with my simulated mug shot in clear view. It would be a good test.

She breezed in a half-hour later, sat down, and pulled the paper to her. I watched her across the kitchen as I cooked some oatmeal. She read the front page headlines and wrinkled her nose in what I took to be a negative reaction to the grim image they conjured up. Then she went on to skim the rest of the front section. I breathed a little easier. When I served breakfast she closed the paper, glanced at the front page again, and then looked up at me.

"Now I know what you were doing yesterday afternoon," she said, looking me square in the eye.

I stood there like a post, trying to smile while fighting back an urge to swallow.

Finally she laughed brightly. "Look at this dude, Dad. I mean, if it weren't for the skinnier face he'd be a dead ringer for you."

I leaned over the paper and pretended to look closely at the drawing for the first time. "Are you kidding me? I'm *much* better looking than he is."

We both had a good laugh as I sat down and we tucked into our oatmeal. Claire failed to notice that mine went uneaten.

Chapter Forty-six

After the sun burned off a thin layer of clouds that afternoon, Claire went out on the porch, using one crutch while lugging a hefty environmental tome in her other hand. She may have a broken leg, I remember thinking, but she's still strong and agile. I retreated to my study on the pretense of planning my work week. Not that it needed all that much planning. Hell, two more clients had cancelled their appointments. A definite trend.

I felt so jangled that it took half an hour of deep breathing while listening to a CD of crashing surf before I felt reasonably centered.

Focus on what you know, I told myself. Sadly, that wasn't much. Aside from his identity, all I had on El Cuchillo was that he was holed up somewhere out by Mount Hood, "near a river." In western Oregon, that doesn't tell you much. What about the inside person? The only tangible evidence I had was that Duane Pitman planned to leave NanoTech. I could argue he was angry enough to have Hal Bruckner killed, but without a link to El Cuchillo, this didn't get me very far. As for Alexis, Hannon, and Streeter, I had nothing on them except that all three benefitted handsomely from his demise. Daina was a wild card in this deck.

I pulled out the little notebook with my jottings from the NanoTech foray and read over them again. All I'd found in Streeter's office was the name of a masseuse named Zina, who worked at a place called Mystic Hands Whole Body Massage Center, and a phone number for someone named Rey on the back. I wondered what kinds of services were offered at the massage center and what role Rey played. The somewhat unusual name, Rey, caught my eye. A woman's name? Or short for Reynaldo?

I had to laugh when I thought about tipping the files over in Hannon's office, but I was still disgusted with myself for not having grabbed the folder that had *Deschutes Trip* written on it. That boat's sailed, I told myself.

The Latin phrase I'd seen on Streeter's desk—*fac ut gaudeam* popped into my head, which reminded me of the other, longer phrase I'd seen in his Rolodex. I couldn't remember all of it, so I looked it up in my notebook—*nemo me impune lacessit.* I could have googled both phrases, but since Hiram Pritchard was always spouting Latin and extolling the virtues of a classical education, I decided to call and ask him to translate.

Hiram chuckled when I repeated the first phrase to him. "*Fac ut gaudeam?* That one's easy. It means 'Make my day,' an homage to Dirty Harry, no doubt." I read him the longer phrase I'd found in Streeter's Rolodex. "Hmm. Let me consult a text and call you back."

Five minutes later he had it. "*Nemo me impune lacessit* means 'No one attacks me with impunity.' Has a rather vindictive ring to it, wouldn't you say?"

"For sure," I replied. We talked for a while, trying to wrest some hidden meaning from the second phrase or to find some connection between the two, but nothing came of it. I hung up feeling a little foolish about having bothered Hiram in the first place.

I sat with my feet up on my desk, crumpling up pieces of paper and glumly tossing them at my wastebasket. No way to paper over it. The NanoTech gambit hadn't yielded a damn thing. What did I expect? It was a hail-Mary to begin with. When I'd finally plunked three baskets in a row, however, I picked up my cell phone and made two calls.

First, I called the Mystic Hands Massage Parlor and asked for an appointment with Zina. She had an open slot for three the next afternoon. I booked it, using the name Robert.

Next I called Daina and told her I needed another favor.

What the hell, I figured, it never hurts to ask. "Oh God, what is it now?" she said.

"Uh, it's about a manila folder I saw in Mitch Hannon's office. It's marked *Deschutes Trip* in what's probably his handwriting. I saw some interesting things in it but didn't come away with it. I'm wondering if you could, uh, borrow it for me? I'll give it right back."

There was a long pause. I could hear her breathing. "You're serious?"

"Yeah. Things are breaking the wrong way, Daina. I feel like I'm running out of time here. Surely you or Rusty Musik can come up with something." It was an unfair request, for sure, but I needed to know what was in that file. And if she brought it to me, that might restore my trust in her. If she didn't...well, I just couldn't see any downside.

I waited through another long pause. "I'll see what I can do," she finally answered, then hung up.

That evening I grilled some thick portobello mushrooms slathered with olive oil, steamed a handful of asparagus, and made a huge salad, which I served with a baguette. The weather was pleasant, so Claire and I ate and talked out on the porch. I tried to enjoy myself, but a feeling of anxiety draped over me like an itchy blanket. I half-expected another phalanx of cop cars to show up at the gate due to the composite sketch. But it wasn't just that. It felt like some fuse had been lit. Nothing mattered now, I decided, except movement, action.

Gertie called that evening and invited Claire over to watch a couple of episodes of *Prime Suspect* on Netflix. Archie and I walked her over, and I didn't have to tell him to stay with her. As I walked back across our north field, I saw headlights coming up our drive and tensed up. When the approaching car passed through our open gate, I could just make it out in the fading light. It was Alexis' silver Jag.

I picked up my pace, and by the time I reached the house, she was up on the porch leaning on the bell. "You left your car unescorted. This must be urgent."

Alexis whirled around. "*Jesus*, Cal, you scared the crap out of me."

I raised my hands, palms out. "Sorry. What's on your mind, Alexis?"

"Can we talk for a few minutes?"

I climbed the porch steps, opened the door, and showed her into the front room. Her hair was pulled back in a careless tangle of blond curls, and she wore no makeup except for a thin swipe of pinkish lipstick. She sat down, crossed her legs, and gave me a wry smile. "Surely, I get a drink this time."

I popped to my feet. "I think I have some Glenlivet. I don't stock a lot of the hard stuff."

She gave me a look. "I know, dear. That would be fine. Pour it over ice. A double."

When I returned with her Scotch, she eyed my other hand, which was empty. "Not joining me?"

"I'm good."

Her eyes clouded, as if my refusal was a personal rebuke. We waited through an awkward pause. I said, "So, how's Mitch Hannon doing?"

She drank some Scotch, put the glass down and let out a deep sigh. A faint series of food stains in the shape of the Capricorn constellation adorned the right side of her silk blouse. When she leaned into the light, I saw little clusters of wrinkles around her eyes and mouth. "I own the company. He runs it. We don't talk much."

"I see," I said, wondering what had caused the falling out. "Did you tell him about our last talk?" I tried not to sound accusatory.

She drank more Scotch, crunched some ice, and shook her head. I waited for her to continue.

"I told him you weren't some Podunk fishing guide, that you were an ex-DA from Los Angeles, a damn good one. I said you wouldn't sit around and let someone blame you for Hal's murder. I told him you thought someone in our fishing party was involved in Hal's death, too."

I nodded.

"Mitch doesn't think those two detectives from Jefferson County know what they're doing. He's worried that if the crime goes unsolved, it might screw up the deal."

"You mean an IPO?"

"Yes, haven't you heard? NanoTech's going public. We're going to be filthy rich."

"Who's we?"

She put an open palm to her breast. "The grieving widow, Mitchell Hannon, and Andrew Streeter."

"What about Duane Pitman?"

She laughed again. "Oh, Duanie—pooh. He wants a full equity share, but Mitch and Andrew are saying no. You know, the pie's only so big."

"How's he taking it?"

"Oh, he's furious. Threatening dire consequences if we don't deal him in."

"Like what?"

"He's going to leave, or sue us, or *something*. I don't know. Mitch says the man's a legend in his own mind. But, frankly, he scares the hell out of me. You know, the mild-mannered geek who goes postal." She laughed, then drew her face into a serious look. "Listen, Cal. I think Mitch wants to talk to you. Don't be surprised if he calls. Talk to him, please."

"I'll talk to him anytime. No hard feelings." I met her eyes. They were watery and seemed to have lost some of that deep ocean color. "Sounds like you trust Hannon all of a sudden."

She shrugged. "Woman's intuition, I guess." Then narrowing her eyes, she added, "I'm not sleeping with him. It's strictly business now."

I held a neutral expression. "Let me ask you something about that night on the river."

She gave me a pained look as if it wasn't a place she wanted to revisit.

"Did anyone in the party know ahead of time you were going to banish Hal from your tent?"

"With the exception of Daina, I'm afraid they all did, dear. It's a small company. Hal's snoring was legendary at NanoTech. I think they all knew he'd be sleeping outside on this trip."

"Of course. The sleep apnea."

She dropped her eyes and spoke in a low, halting voice. "Yeah, Hal made light of his condition, and I complained about it all the time. Imagine—*me* complaining because *he* was sick. The truth is, he suffered a great deal. She shook her head slowly, then raised her eyes, which brimmed with tears. "God, I'd like to have that last night back, Cal. I was such a bitch."

I finally spoke into the silence. "What can you tell me about Andrew Streeter?"

She wrinkled her brow and took a long pull on her Scotch. "Not very much, I'm afraid. Mitch tells me he's great at what he does, but he's, ah, a little hypocritical for my taste."

"Hypocritical?"

"He hails from an upstanding Southern family, but I understand he can be quite a naughty boy at times."

"How's that?"

"Oh, you know, he likes to party, drugs, alcohol, women who charge for their services, that sort of thing." She chuckled. "And he undresses me with his eyes every chance he gets. But I'm told he never misses church on Sunday."

I raised my eyebrows. "Drugs?"

She nodded. "Puts a lot of money up his nose."

"How do you know this?"

She laughed. "Hal's secretary told me. She's the epicenter of NanoTech gossip."

I continued to dig for information on Streeter but didn't learn anything more. Finally, Alexis glanced at her watch and said she had to leave. We stopped at the front door, and she turned to face me. She flashed a brave smile, but fear clouded her eyes. "You haven't told me a thing, Cal. I hope you're getting somewhere. I'm, uh, not sleeping so well." She folded her arms across her breasts as a tear broke loose and slid slowly down her cheek. "Every time I close my eyes, I see Hal in that sleeping bag." A shiver rippled her body.

I put my hands on her shoulders and met her eyes. "I'm working this thing as hard as I can. Look, Alexis, keep your eyes and ears open. I need all the help I can get."

She nodded. "I miss him, Cal. Damn it. I never thought I would, but I do."

"Yeah, I can see that."

Chapter Forty-seven

Zina was a tall redhead with green eyes and breasts that seemed too large for her thin frame, reminding me of a Barbie doll. In addition to her surgically enhanced breasts, her hair was dyed, and her eyes most likely tinted with contacts, rounding out the package. My session was underway at the Mystic Hands Whole Body Massage Center, a ramshackle, two-story commercial building that had been superficially retooled for a massage therapy operation of somewhat questionable legitimacy.

I was sprawled on my stomach with my head wedged into a padded hole in the table watching Zina's bare feet as she worked my neck and shoulders. Her toenails were painted black, and both her little toes were oddly curled up over their neighbors. Considering the duplicity of my intent, I felt vulnerable as hell lying there in the nude with nothing but a sheet covering the lower half of my body.

Candlelight flickered, incense smoldered, and something haunting by Loreena McKennitt played softly on the sound system. "So, Robert, how did you hear about me?" Zina asked, as she gently kneaded the left side of my neck. She'd found a spot, a hard nodule, in which I had apparently stored a good portion of my angst. She was not as good as Daina at kneading my neck, but she was good enough. I had to remind myself why I was there.

"It's Rob. Call me Rob," I replied through the hole. "I heard about this place from a friend of mine. He said I should check it out. And he recommended you, too."

"Well, that's nice. You'll have to thank your friend for me. We try to keep our customers satisfied." She didn't ask for the name. I didn't think she would. After all, discretion is everything in this line of work.

There was a long pause while she worked her way down my back. I began to relax and made a mental note to schedule more massages, if not here then somewhere. We made a little small talk, and it wasn't until she was working on my calves that I said, "My friend also mentioned Rey, said you could put me in touch."

The pressure from her fingers increased slightly. "Rey? You mean Reynaldo?"

"Uh, yeah, Reynaldo." I didn't know where the hell this was going, but at least I had a name, and what do you know? Hispanic. I thought about El Cuchillo and his connection with the Zetas cartel. It was a stretch, but better than nothing.

She paused, and I wished I could see the expression on her face. "Why didn't your friend just give you Reynaldo's number himself?" Her voice was cautious now.

I chuckled. "Oh, you know, he's Mr. Disorganized. Since I was coming here today, he said to just ask you." More chuckles.

Her fingers relaxed perceptibly and she replied, "Okay, Rob. I'll take care of it when we finish."

"A phone number will be fine," I added quickly. I wasn't anxious to confront Reynaldo in person.

After I declined the additional services Zina was offering, she left the room in a bit of a snit. I started to get dressed. The massage had revived me, and I was relieved that Zina had apparently bought my story. I was thinking maybe Nando could help me get a line on Reynaldo.

I was lacing up my shoes when the door opened. I looked up. A man stood there, backlit by the harsh hall light. His face was shadowed, but there was no mistaking his girth. He blocked out most of the light from the hallway.

He closed the door behind him. "I'm Reynaldo. I hear you looking for me," he said with a thick accent. His eyes peered out through the cracks formed between his bulbous cheeks and the bony ridge of his brow. His left earlobe sagged under the weight of a large hoop, and his smile was more gold than enamel. But it was his stomach that got my attention. It pressed on his knit shirt, oozing over his belt like a massive water balloon.

I reminded myself to stay in character and struggled to keep my eyes off his gut. "I'm Rob," I said, extending my hand.

Reynaldo just stood there and looked at me, his meaty arms at his sides. I withdrew my hand. "What do you want?"

Crap, I said to myself, I wasn't planning on this. "Uh, I hear you're a stand-up guy, Reynaldo. I'm interested in some blow. For my own consumption." I held my breath, and hoped *blow* was still a reasonably current street term for cocaine.

"Who told you I sell something?"

Moment of truth. This was obviously how he vetted new customers. If I didn't mention Streeter's name, I'd have no credibility whatsoever. I decided to risk it. "Guy named Andy Streeter."

There was a long pause while Reynaldo's beady eyes examined me through those horizontal slots. It was like being watched by archers inside a medieval fortress. Drops of sweat coalesced in my armpits, broke loose, and slithered down my rib cage. Finally he said, "Where've I seen you?"

I opened my hands and shrugged, trying to appear casual. The composite sketch, I thought. I'm screwed.

He pointed a bejeweled finger that looked like a Polish sausage at me and asked, "You the guy who slugged that cop from Madras?"

"Uh, yeah. That would be me," I answered, feeling like I just dodged a very large caliber bullet.

He smiled, showing even more gold, extended his hand and, when I reciprocated, nearly pumped my arm off. "You really nailed that *carbón, amigo*." Then he added, "You a friend of Andy's? He's a good customer. When you need the blow?"

"Tell you what. Give me a number and I'll call you. I'm in town all the time."

Reynaldo's face brightened. "I've got some pharmacy grade, *amigo*. It will take your head off."

I walked out of there on slightly rubbery legs. When I got to my car, I let out a long breath and just sat there for a while. Then I phoned Nando Mendoza and asked for a rundown on a drug dealer named Reynaldo who operates out of the Mystic Hands Whole Body Massage Center.

After dinner that evening, Claire and I sat locked in a fierce game of Scrabble. I was getting my butt kicked, as usual. I think it was somewhere around the age of sixteen that Claire started to whip me at the word game. Her mother always could, so I'd been schooled in the art of losing graciously.

Archie barked first—a single sharp note—and then I heard the purr of a small engine. I went out on the front porch in time to see Daina getting out of her VW. Archie made a beeline for her, and she dropped to one knee to embrace him. I watched them, thinking about what I'd always said about my dog—that he was an excellent judge of character.

Daina marched up and handed me a manila folder held shut with rubber bands. "Don't ask where I got it," she said with a look that held anger tinged with resignation. "I didn't look at it. Look it over, make copies, whatever. Then give it back. I'll wait." It was clear I'd forced her to do something she detested. It occurred to me she might never forgive me. Suddenly that mattered.

I took the file and tried to meet her eyes, but she looked away. "Thanks, Daina," was all I managed to say.

Breaking a moment of awkward silence, Claire came up behind us on her crutches. I moved aside and introduced the two women. Daina said, "I've heard so much about you, Claire. And I just want to say how much I admire what you were doing over there in Darfur. That kind of hands-on work makes a huge difference and takes real courage, too. You're a hero in my book."

Claire shrugged in modesty, and they immediately launched into a deep conversation about the role of volunteer work in the Third World, the threat of global warming, and the general state of the world's ecological balance. I was impressed at how knowledgeable Daina was, and it became evident rather quickly that my daughter, like my dog, thought highly of this woman.

I excused myself and took the file into my study and shut the door. Of course, I didn't expect to find a smoking gun. After all, I told myself, Hannon was a bright guy and wouldn't leave incriminating evidence lying around. The map of the Deschutes River was lying on top, just like the night I'd seen it in Hannon's office. The Whiskey Dick campground was circled and someone, presumably Hannon, had written, Camp First Night. I looked carefully at the path of the railroad tracks running parallel to the river. The Kaskela junction was shown clearly on the map next to the circle Hannon had drawn. I was disappointed to see there were no markings or notes to indicate whether Hannon knew that Kaskela was where the trains would pass each other that first night on the river.

I sifted through the rest of the file page by page. A detailed checklist of items to be brought on the trip attested to Hannon's attention to detail, and a sheaf of printouts from the Internet describing the Deschutes River, desert redband trout, and how to fish for them during the salmon fly hatch showed he was a fly fisherman who did his homework. A phone number was jotted in the upper right hand corner of the checklist. I called the number and got the recording of the Riffle Fly Shop in Madras.

So I didn't have squat. As I was closing the file I looked at the map again and noticed something I'd missed. Hannon had circled the campsite for the *first* night but downriver from Whiskey Dick, he hadn't marked anything else. The float trip was to take three days with *two* nights on the river.

Why the hell hadn't a stickler for detail like Hannon noted the second campsite? Could it be that he knew there wouldn't be a second night? Or, was the second site still being debated?

I found Daina and Claire still engrossed in conversation in the living room. When I walked in, Daina got up immediately and announced she had to run along. I gave the file back and walked her to her car. When she got in her car she looked up at me. "You look really stressed, Cal. Are you okay?"

I gave her a blank look. It was either that or unburden myself about the whole catastrophe coming down on me, and I still couldn't bring myself to do that. "Thanks for letting me see the file, Daina. I appreciate it."

She nodded curtly, started up the VW, and looked back up at me. "Cal, you can trust me. Let me help you."

I thanked her again and told her to drive carefully.

After Daina left, Claire and I went over to Gertie's to catch the Lakers and Nuggets in the first round of the playoffs. Gertie was a big basketball fan and had a fifty-five-inch high def TV and a larder full of homemade snacks. Five minutes into the second half my cell went off. I took the call out in the kitchen. "Is this Cal Claxton?" The back of my neck tingled momentarily.

I knew the voice—it was Mitch Hannon. "Are you free tonight? We need to talk."

Chapter Forty-eight

Mitch Hannon and I agreed to meet at a little bar called The What's Up, located on the southeast side of Newberg on the St. Paul Highway. The bar looked like a converted Grange Hall, which it probably was, since farm country started just a few miles south, after the highway crossed the Willamette River. Hannon had suggested the place, which was roughly equidistant from Dundee and Wilsonville. It sat on a large, treeless lot with no buildings on either side and a parking area in the back. It struck me as an odd choice for a meeting. I'd left the Glock at home, figuring we were meeting in a public place. I began to regret the decision.

The rutted, thinly graveled lot behind the place was unlit except for a single bulb dangling above the back door, where a sign said *For Employees Only*. I parked behind a dumpster reeking of rancid grease and other less savory aromas and made my way through a thicket of parked cars and motorcycles toward the front entrance.

It was a Saturday night, and the place was still filling up. The playoff game was winding down on a TV above the bar, and something not too twangy by Carrie Underwood played on the sound system. An older crowd, mostly couples, populated the tables clustered around a small stage, waiting, I assumed, for a band to arrive. The guys at the bar were younger and into the game. All in all, a friendly crowd.

Hannon had a kind of Clark Kent look about him, with the dark, wavy hair, horn rims, and strong chin, but his eyes were small and deep set, giving him a bookish aspect. Every inch the executive in casual attire, he wore a teal-colored golf shirt, tan chinos, and Armani loafers with tassels. He tried to strike a relaxed pose, but his right hand was curled too tightly around a glass filled with ice, which, judging from the fullness of the cubes, had been quickly drained.

He looked up and nodded at a chair across the table from him. "Have a seat, Claxton. Thanks for coming."

I sat down, propped my elbows on the table, and grooved my fingers between the knuckles of my other hand. The ball was in his court.

He smiled and shook his head. "I, uh, had quite a laugh when I read about you smacking that cop from Madras. That guy Dorn's a real piece of work."

I didn't smile. "He hit me first, but I'm looking at a felony charge for hitting him back."

Hannon killed the smile. "Yeah, well I assume you can beat that."

"Maybe. What's on your mind, Hannon?"

Before responding he flagged down the waitress and ordered another Scotch, which seemed to be the NanoTech drink of choice. I ordered a Mirror Pond pale ale. He turned back to me. "I don't think those idiots from Madras can solve my uncle's murder. That bothers me."

"It bothers me, too. Why am I suddenly off your suspect list?"

He rattled the ice cubes in his glass and watched them for a few beats. "I have some good contacts in L.A. I checked you out. You were a DA down there, for Christ's sake. Spotless record. I don't think you'd kill someone with your own knife, then throw it in the river where it could be easily found." He hesitated for a moment, and I sensed what was coming next. "And I was sorry to hear about your wife."

I nodded. "So, why are we here?"

Our drinks came. Hannon took a long pull before answering. "I'll be blunt. We have big plans for the company, and having the murder of the owner go unsolved is unacceptable. And the longer this drags out, the less likely we are to find who did it, right?"

I nodded. "That's generally the case."

"So, I'm thinking, why not hire a top-notch detective agency to investigate the murder? The detective could work with you, get this thing wrapped up. I'm sure you know a good outfit."

I nodded again. "Interesting idea, but let me ask you about a couple of things before we go any further. First, Bruckner told you ahead of time the name of the campsite for the first night on the Deschutes, right?"

"Yeah, Whiskey Dick. He got a kick out of the name." Hannon smiled wistfully and shook his head.

"What about the second night? Did you know the name of the campsite ahead of time?"

He wrinkled his brow in a confused look. "Uh, no. The only campsite I remember hearing about was Whiskey Dick. What's that have to do with anything, anyway?"

It was a reasonable answer, and I felt a little better about the guy. I waived a hand dismissively. "Never mind. Just a loose end I was trying to tie up."

My next question was a lot tougher. "Why shouldn't I suspect you of killing Bruckner?"

He placed both elbows on the table, leaned forward, and looked me square in the eye. "I'm no more a killer than you are, Claxton. Jesus, Hal was my mom's brother. Okay, I had a dalliance with Alexis. That was a mistake, and it's over." He stopped at this point and deadpanned, "Come to think of it, you made a similar mistake."

That remark broke the tension, and we both smiled, despite ourselves. I waited for him to continue.

"Look, Claxton, let's not dance around. I think I know who killed my uncle, but I can't prove it, and those idiots in Madras are not listening to me. As you know, they've got a hard-on for you."

I nodded. "I've noticed. Go on."

"Duane Pitman wants to jump ship and take his technology with him. He can name his price at one of our competitors. But he signed a security agreement with Hal stating that the technology he develops belongs to NanoTech, not him." Hannon shook his head and clinched his jaw in frustration. "But the Goddamn document has been misfiled or something."

"Doesn't seem like a motive for murder."

"Hal would've sworn in a court of law they entered into an agreement. He's dead now. Very convenient. And Duane's been on a rampage looking for the document. Hell, he broke into my office the other night. And I'm willing to bet he was behind the break-in at Alexis' place and the rental where Daina Zakaris is staying.

Whoops! Pitman was being blamed for my bungled break-in at NanoTech. Finally, an unintended consequence with an upside. "You're sure Pitman was behind these burglaries?"

"Who else would've broken into the three most likely places to find the security agreement?" Hannon raised his hand and ticked them off on his fingers—Hal's study at home, his office at NanoTech, and Zakaris' place."

I asked a few more questions, but it became evident Hannon's suspicions of Pitman were grounded more in emotion than hard evidence. I had to agree the other two burglaries might have been Pitman's, but I didn't say that to Hannon. And I was having trouble getting Pitman from burglar to murderer. The security document was the key thing for him, not the removal of Bruckner. Unless I was missing something.

I decided to change the subject. "What about Andrew Streeter? What would *he* gain from your uncle's death?"

Hannon removed his glasses and rubbed his eyes before answering. "Andy? Hell, Hal didn't like him, but, you know, I'm a strong supporter of his."

"You mean Hal was going to fire him?" I asked, pretending a bit of surprise. I'd read the memos and knew the answer to that question, but wanted to hear Hannon's response.

"Yeah, he was making noises to that effect before the trip, but I would have talked him down."

"Did Streeter have that kind of assurance, that he wouldn't be fired and lose out on the public offering? I understand it's going to be a very big payday for all the officers."

Hannon cleaned his glasses and put them back on. "Andy knew I was behind him."

"Yeah, but Hal had the final word, right? And Hal was the boss."

"Come on. What are you saying? Andy killed Hal?"

"No, he didn't kill your uncle. But he could've hired someone to do it."

"So could Pitman. You're reaching, man."

"Did Streeter know I was going to be on the trip?"

Hannon glanced down at his glass and swirled his ice cubes. "Uh, Andy and I are drinking buddies. I might've mentioned something about one of Alexis' ex-flames being a guide."

"Did you know Streeter has a serious cocaine habit and gets his drugs from some pretty tough elements in Northeast Portland?" I decided to risk disclosing that but wasn't about to tell him about El Cuchillo and the rest of what I knew. I felt better about Hannon, but had no basis in fact to rule him out.

Hannon set his drink down, swallowed, and licked his lips. "Uh, no, I didn't know that. I suppose you can back that up?"

I nodded. "I talked to his dealer in person."

"What else have you got?"

"What've *you* got?" I shot back. "Think about the trip. Did Streeter act unusual in any way?"

Hannon sat there for a moment, swirling his ice cubes and staring down at the table. Then he shrugged. "I don't know. He was keenly interested in the trip, wanted to know all the details." He looked up. "But that's just Andy. He's a detail guy like me."

That's all I got from Hannon on Streeter. He agreed to keep his eyes open at NanoTech, and I agreed to come up with a private detective agency that might be able to help us. We even exchanged business cards.

Hannon left the bar first. I stayed behind to finish my beer and think through what I'd just learned, which, I had to admit, wasn't a lot. I did find it interesting that Hannon had assumed a personality distinctly different from what I'd encountered on the river and at Alexis' place. Hell, I almost liked the guy now. The scent of money can do that to a person.

When I left the bar I stood out front stretching and gulping in the fresh air. The night was as black as shoe polish. As I headed around the building to the back parking lot, the smorgasbord of smells hit me again. Just as I got up to the dumpster, I became aware of two things. First, the light above the back entry was now out and, second, a new smell was riding on the odors from the dumpster, something pungent and familiar.

I sniffed the air again, and a chill sprinted down my back. It was a tobacco smell, and it came from the same brand of cigarettes El Cuchillo smoked. I was sure of it.

Chapter Forty-nine

That rank, unmistakable tobacco smell hit me like a sharp slap in the face. I stopped abruptly. I couldn't see a damn thing except the shadowy outlines of cars, trucks, and bikes, but I had no doubt Cuchillo was out there somewhere waiting for me. The objective this time was to kill me outright. No more faked accidents. I'd moved up in the pecking order. I backed out of the lot and didn't stop until I was around the corner of the building. I heard a car start up. A couple of moments later, a dark, late-model SUV with its lights off sped out of the lot and screeched out onto the highway, heading toward the bridge.

I broke for my car in a dead run, as visions of bled-out corpses and my near-drowning flashed in my head, and anger bloomed in my chest. I would catch the bastard, no matter what it took. But when I reached my Beemer, I had a dog-chases-car moment—what happens if I catch him? I started the car up anyway, figuring I might get close enough to him on the highway to get a plate number. But it was no use. By the time I pulled out, got the Beemer up to speed, and crossed the river, the SUV was out of sight.

I picked up Claire and Archie at Gertie's. When we arrived home, Arch started to dash into the yard for his nightly game of tag with the skunks and raccoons, but I told him to stay close. Once we were in the house, I went upstairs for the Glock before taking him for a quick walk. The barred owl was across the field in a Doug fir watching our place. It was reassuring to hear his familiar greeting. Stay vigilant, big fella, I told him.

Claire was waiting when we came back in the house. "Okay, Dad. I know that look. What's going on?" Her tone made it clear she wanted answers. No bullshit.

I exhaled and shook my head. "Look, this guy who killed the CEO on the river, it looks like he's still around trying to clean up the mess he's in. I guess he figures he's at some risk of being exposed."

Claire's eyes narrowed, and she drew her mouth into a tight, defiant line. "Is he a threat to you?"

"Yeah, he's definitely a threat. He killed a woman who knew him just to keep her quiet, and he, uh, tried to ambush me tonight when I was going to my car."

She sucked a breath involuntarily, but her expression remained unchanged. "When are you going to the police?"

"I already laid out the whole story to Escalante, but that was right after I'd hit Dorn, so it probably didn't take. I mean, they want me for the first murder, so it's going to take a lot to derail that train. And I don't have enough on the killer to go to the local cops for protection, either."

"So, what are we going to do?"

I met her eyes. "First thing tomorrow morning I'm calling Hiram to arrange for you to stay with him until this thing gets resolved."

Claire's eyes widened in disbelief. "*What?* No way. I'm staying with you, Dad."

"Trust me on this. This guy's not just a threat to *me*."

She gave me an indulgent smile. "Don't worry, Dad. He can't be any worse than the Janjaweed. I can take care of myself."

I didn't return the smile. I knew I'd have to take the gloves off to convince her, so I did. "I know you can, Claire, but this guy's an utter psychopath. That young woman he killed, he ripped her throat from ear to ear and left her to bleed to death on her basement staircase."

The smile faded. "The murder in the paper?"

"Yeah. That was his work. I don't want you to go either, but the killer knows I know too much about him."

"But, Dad—"

"*Please*, Claire. It'll just be for a little while. I'm close to busting this thing open."

She reluctantly agreed, and we said our goodnights. After rechecking all the locks, I went up to my room, knowing sleep would be hard to come by. The night was the deepest black, and I cracked a window open just to smell the jasmine that had begun to bloom on the front porch pillars. The frogs sang down at the pond, but without enthusiasm, and the barred owl was silent. With no light at my back, I stood at the window as waves of frustration, anger, and fear washed over me like storm surf.

Finally, I changed, got into bed, and tried to read, but I was too wired. Had Cuchillo followed me to the bar, or had Hannon set me up? I kept asking myself. I had no way of knowing. My mind was drawn back to that night on the Deschutes. I thought about the phone calls on the tracks, the speaking-truth-to-power session after dinner, the positioning of the tents, and the light that Blake had seen going back up to the tracks after the session. I combed through each detail over and over again.

I was missing something—a small piece in a nearly complete puzzle. Whatever it was, it was just beyond my grasp.

Chapter Fifty

Like a burial at sea, I finally slid off into merciful sleep, sinking to a place where light and sound no longer penetrated. It was peaceful there, until the dreams started. Visions of genocide in Darfur played across my mind like an endless documentary. Claire would appear periodically, holding a shovel and saying, "I came here to dig wells, not bury people."

Then I was fishing in the Deschutes. The nearly decapitated bodies of Bruckner and Manion floated by. I vomited into the clear water. Next, I was leading the NanoTech execs up a steep ravine adjacent to the river. They were grim-faced and silent, riding pack animals. I stopped and pointed to a sign at the top of the ravine, like the famous icon in the Hollywood Hills, except the sign read, *Fac Ut Gaudeam*. I looked back and realized Pitman and Hannon were riding sleek, muscular horses, but Streeter was on an old, broken-down mule that could barely support him.

I awoke at a little after four. It was like coming out of a coma. I snapped on the light and sat slouched on the edge of my bed, scratching my head with both hands. The dreams had been stark and vivid, like black and white movies. And I couldn't get that last one out of my head. It had to mean *something*. But what?

Why the hell was Streeter riding a mule, while the other two were on horses? And the Latin? What was that all about?

I sat there, sifting back through the last dream and getting nowhere, haunted by the feeling I was missing something. I needed somebody to talk to, and it wasn't going to be Claire. I'd already told her more than I wanted to.

I thought of someone but still wasn't sure I wanted to risk it. As if he'd read my mind, Archie came over, put his chin on my knee, and looked up at me with his big, coppery eyes. I stroked his head and scratched him gently behind his ears. "You trust her, don't you, big fella." He whimpered a couple of times and wagged his tale. I sat there turning that over in my mind, absently running my fingers through the fur of his broad back.

He looked up at me again. "Okay," I said, "you win." I picked up my cell phone and called Daina.

"Hullo," she answered on the eighth ring, her voice thick with sleep.

"Daina, it's Cal. I'm sorry I woke you."

"That's okay." Something about her tone made me feel as if my call was not unexpected. "Are you all right?"

"Yeah, I'm fine. Listen, does your offer to help me still stand?"

She chuckled. "Yes, but I'm not filching any more files for you."

"No, no, nothing like that. Uh, I've had a helluva night, and I need help sorting it out."

"I'm glad you feel like you can talk to me, Cal. What's happened?"

"I had a chat with Mitch Hannon at a little bar in Newberg last night."

"How did *that* happen?"

"Alexis told him to call me. She says they're all business now, no more hanky-panky. Anyway, I question whether Hannon would ever hurt his uncle." I paused here to see if Daina would comment.

She went silent for a few moments, and I could hear her breathing. "Well, I can tell you that Hannon seemed genuinely grief-stricken over his uncle's death. To tell the truth, Alexis was distraught, too. It's hard to fake something like that."

And put it by *you*, I said to myself. I went on to tell her about the discussion at the bar, Hannon's suspicion that Duane Pitman was behind the murder, and his offer to hire a detective to work with me.

"I'm not surprised Hannon wants this wrapped up," Daina responded when I'd finished. "The NanoTech public offering is hanging in the balance."

"What about Pitman? Are you in Hannon's camp?"

She sighed deeply. "All I can tell you is that when I'm around him, my skin crawls. He broke into my house, Cal, I'm sure of it."

"Yeah, well, Hannon thinks Pitman broke into his office, too."

She laughed. "I'll bet you didn't tell him what really happened."

I had to chuckle. "Yeah, I let Pitman take the fall for that. Collateral damage. But there's more to the story." I went on to tell her what I'd learned about El Cuchillo and the trap I'd almost stepped into when I left the bar.

"Oh, Cal, that was close. Thank God that man's a nicotine addict."

"The wind was blowing in the right direction, too. Hannon had done a fair job of convincing me he wasn't the inside man. But all bets are off now, despite what you and Alexis think."

"What are you going to do?"

"I'd like to hunt him down tomorrow and confront him, but that probably wouldn't advance my cause. I need to link him to Cuchillo, and I need to do it fast."

"I'll have Rusty Musik go back over his e-mail to see if the name El Cuchillo comes up."

"Not likely, but it's worth a shot. Thanks." I heard her yawn, so I added quickly, "Uh, there's something else. Don't think I'm bat shit crazy, okay? I had this weird dream, and I think it means something. I thought you might be might be able to help me interpret it."

"All right, tell me about it."

When I got to the part about the Latin sign, she interrupted me. "*Fac Ut Gaudeam?* Where have I seen that?"

"On Streeter's desk. It means 'Make My Day' in Latin."

She laughed. "Oh, my God, you're right, that's where I've seen it. Why do you think you put *that* in your dream?"

"Beats me. Maybe it was my subconscious making sure I noticed him. He's fond of Latin. I found another phrase in his Rolodex. Uh, let's see, it was *Nemo Me Impune Laccessit.* It means 'No one attacks me with impunity.'"

"The second phrase sounds militaristic, like something from his Citadel days. I think you're right, though. The Latin probably shows Streeter was on your subconscious mind. Okay, go on."

When I finished describing the dream, she said, "Okay, you were leading Hannon, Pitman, and Streeter up a trail. You were walking. They were riding."

"Right. Like I said, Hannon and Pitman were on these chestnut-colored horses, sleek, beautiful beasts. Streeter was on a swayback mule that looked like it was on its last legs. After I pointed up to the sign, I woke up."

"Nobody spoke?"

"No. It was like a silent movie."

"That mule set Streeter apart in your mind. Did you notice anything *different* about him on that trip? It couldn't simply be his Southern accent or his flabby build, could it?"

"No. It has to be something else."

"How he acted? His equipment? Did he have inferior fishing gear? You know, a cheap fly rod or something? What set him apart?"

I think it was the word "cheap." I sat there for a moment, frozen. *"Could it be that simple?"*

"What, Cal? What is it?"

"Streeter's *phone.* What kind does he use?"

"Uh, a smartphone, of course. Why?"

"That first day on the Deschutes, he was using a cheap phone, not a smartphone. I saw it when we were up on the tracks." He didn't notice me, but he was definitely hiding the phone from the others. At the time, it just didn't register."

"Okay, but—"

"That phone must have been the communications link. It was most likely a prepaid. That's how the killer knew exactly where Bruckner was sleeping. That's how he knew to take my coat and use my knife and then toss it on the gravel bar. Streeter gave him last-minute directions using that phone."

"Oh, a burner. Right. Can't be traced."

"*Exactly*. It's the only way someone would have communicated with Cuchillo. No way Streeter's going to use his own phone. Blake saw someone go up to the tracks when everyone was turning in. It was Streeter on his way to call in the final instructions."

"Maybe he lost his phone before the trip and picked up the burner as a stopgap?"

I chewed that over a few moments. "No. I don't think so. First off, if he'd lost it, he would have bitched and moaned about it, right? I mean he's as attached to his phone as the next person. And, besides, it probably takes just as much time to buy a disposable phone as it does a new smartphone. And if he'd lost his phone, why didn't he want anyone to see the phone he was using?"

We both fell silent. Daina said, "Well, Streeter certainly has a motive. If Hal would have fired him, he would have missed out on a multimillion-dollar payoff when the IPO takes place."

"For sure."

"Do you have anything else on him?"

"I learned from Alexis that he's a user, cocaine. I managed to track down his dealer, a man named Reynaldo. I'm checking to see if Reynaldo has cartel connections. El Cuchillo's a favorite of the Zetas cartel according to my sources."

"You *talked* to this Reynaldo guy?

"Yeah, well, I've had to take a few risks here."

"Maybe Reynaldo told Streeter about you, and Streeter sent Cuchillo to follow you."

"The thought crossed my mind."

"So your guy Musik can't bust into Streeter's e-mail? I'd love to know who he's been talking to."

"Nope. Rusty's good, but not that good. We'll have to find another way."

"Well, I've got some checking on Reynaldo to do. Maybe I'll get lucky." A ghostly visage of El Cuchillo waiting for me in the shadows of that parking lot popped into my head. "I'm running out of time, Daina."

"Cal, surely you have enough to go to the police?"

I thought of the witness who'd described me for the composite sketch. She'd identify me in a heartbeat, and I'd be up for CJ's murder, too. "Not yet."

After going over everything one more time, we decided to call it a night. I didn't know how to thank Daina, but I tried. She said, "I was worried things were broken between us, Cal."

"Someone put a good word in for you."

"Who?"

"Archie. He's an excellent judge of character."

She laughed, and I heard that girlish ring. "Well, you can tell him thanks for me."

The phone fell silent for a few moments, and I could hear the sound of her breathing again, soft and rhythmical. It occurred to me I could listen to that sound all night, and if I get out of this mess, I promised myself that's exactly what I was going to do.

Chapter Fifty-one

At eight sharp the next morning I called Hiram to arrange for Claire to stay with him. I'd considered having her stay at Gertie's, but that was too close to home. I wanted her completely out of the picture until Cuchillo was off the board. Hiram was delighted to help out, no questions asked, of course, and offered to come pick Claire up.

I made an espresso and sipped at it while standing in front of the kitchen window. The Cascades were obscured by a bank of low clouds, but closer in, the valley popped with color and a narrow thread of the Willamette glittered in the sun. My conviction that Streeter was the inside man had been tempered somewhat by a few hours of sleep. After all, I really hadn't eliminated Hannon, or even the possibility of the two of them working together. No question, I needed something more on Streeter to close the deal in my mind.

As it turned out, I didn't have long to wait.

I'd gone back upstairs to change when my cell chirped. It was Nando. "I do not know what your interest in that bag of scum Reynaldo is," he said after we exchanged greetings, "but my sources in Drugs and Vice tell me he is a major drug supplier in Portland."

"Any known cartel affiliations?"

"Yes. Most certainly Los Zetas, the worst of the worst. They have oozed up into the Northwest from the border. The veneer of civilization is showing some cracks, my friend."

I was stunned. As far as I was concerned, the picture was now complete. Streeter had to be the inside guy. I had no clue how to take Cuchillo down, but Streeter would be an easier target. What I needed now was a way to smoke him out.

I'd just finished dressing when I glanced out the second-floor window and froze. Two blue-and-whites and an unmarked were coming up the drive. I grabbed my cell phone and the Glock and dashed downstairs to the study, where Claire was working on her laptop. I cupped her face in both hands and locked onto her eyes. "The police are in the driveway. Tell them I left earlier this morning to play golf with a friend, and you don't know who or where. Hiram's coming to pick you up. Stay in the house till he comes. I'll explain later."

I wanted to assuage the fear and confusion that clouded my daughter's eyes, but there was no time. I burst out of the sliding door and ran full tilt to the hole in the fence leading to the quarry. Archie was right on my heels. I whirled around and pointed toward the house. "Stay, Archie. Stay with Claire."

Stands of stunted cedars that had been missed by the strip-mining provided the only cover in the quarry. I picked my way down and across, dashing from one stand to the next, hoping I wouldn't be observed from above by the cops. I finally reached the lower edge of the quarry and took refuge in a dense cluster of trees next to the dirt entry road. I allowed myself a breath of relief, which was followed immediately by second thoughts about what I'd just done. But that show of force coming up the drive meant I was going to be arrested for certain. I was so close to busting this thing that I couldn't let that happen.

But what the hell was I going to do now?

I didn't debate it this time. I called Daina and asked if she'd be willing to come pick me up. Not wanting to explain the situation over the phone, I told her only that it was a dire emergency. She agreed to help me without hesitation. I felt bad about dragging her into this even more, but at this juncture, at least, I could claim I didn't know I was a wanted man.

I gave her directions to my hiding place, and she said she'd be there in thirty minutes. I was tempted to call Claire but decided against it. The cops might still be at the Aerie.

When Daina's VW pulled up I hopped in, slouched down, and said, "It's Streeter. I'm sure of it." I explained what Nando had told me and then came clean about finding CJ's body and the witness who'd seen me at the scene.

She said, "Cal, this has gone far enough. You've got to go to the police. You have enough to clear yourself."

"I want to do that, believe me, but I don't have enough hard evidence yet. Trust me on this, Daina."

We were still discussing the issue when my phone rang. It was Claire. "Dad, what's going on? The police just left. They said you're wanted for questioning in the murder of that woman in southeast Portland. They said you're supposed to surrender yourself to the nearest police station. Was that drawing in the paper really you, Dad?"

"Don't worry, it's all a mista—." I heard what sounded like a car go by. *"Where are you?"*

"I'm walking out to the road with Archie to meet Hiram. I was upset and needed to get out of the house."

"No, Claire. I don't want you out on the street. Turn around and go back. *Now."* My voice was harsh, but I didn't care. I was frightened and angry she'd blown off my instructions.

"Okay. Okay. We'll head back. When are you coming home?"

"Right away."

We were nearly back to the Aerie when my cell rang again. "Calvin? It's Hiram. I'm at your place. Where's Claire?"

"She's out on the road walking with Archie. You probably just missed her." I forced down a sense of panic and told myself nothing was wrong. After all, she was with Archie.

"Okay, then. I'll turn around and pick them up."

I punched off and looked at Daina. "What is it?" she asked.

"Claire's not at the house." I scrolled down to her name. Her cell went immediately to voice mail. I tried again and got the same result. My chest tightened, making it suddenly difficult to breathe. I flipped my phone shut and said, "Hurry, Daina. I don't like this."

We arrived at the Aerie a couple of minutes later. Hiram's Saab was in the driveway. I immediately saw he was the only one in the car. I jumped out, hoping Claire had gone inside to get her things. "Where is she?" I asked.

"I don't know, Cal. I didn't see her out on the road, so I came back. I checked inside. She's not there."

"Look, check over at Gertie's. Maybe she popped in there. We'll go up toward the cemetery. Call if you find her."

We tore down the driveway ahead of Hiram, hung a right on Eagle Nest and another right at the highway.

Halfway to the cemetery I screamed out, "Stop! That looks like Archie. "

Daina slammed on the brakes, and I jumped out of the car. Archie was lying in the ditch on the side of the road. I ran over to him and dropped to my knees at his side. His eyes were closed, the base of his right ear swollen and badly cut, leaving his head covered in blood. I put my hand on his ribcage and thought I felt him breathing weakly, but I wasn't sure. I gently picked him up. Daina opened the back door, and I got in while holding his neck and head steady. In his good ear I said, "Stay with me, Arch. Keep breathing, big boy."

To Daina, I said, "Keep going toward the cemetery. Maybe they got separated, and Arch was hit by a car." But I knew that Arch would have never willingly become separated from Claire. When we were well past the cemetery with no sign of her I said, "Go back to Gertrude's." Claire wasn't there either. Hiram examined Archie, taking his pulse on the inside of his rear leg, and announced that if my dog didn't get immediate medical attention, he wouldn't make it. We transferred him to Hiram's car and I watched through tear-stained eyes as they drove off for the Animal Care Center.

Moments later my phone rang again. I recognized the high-pitched, grainy voice immediately. I'd heard it out on the Hood River. "I've got your daughter, asshole," El Cuchillo said. "If you want to see her alive again, you need to do *exactly* what I tell you. If you even think about contacting the police or the FBI the deal's off, and I'll slit her throat slowly, while you're listening. Got that?"

"I got it. Can I—"

"Good," he interrupted. "I'll be in touch."

The line went dead.

Chapter Fifty-two

I stood there staring at the cell phone in my hand while I tried to deny the reality of what I'd just heard. This couldn't be happening. It had to be a nightmare.

From far away I heard Daina say, her voice quivering, "Cal. Who was that? Tell me."

My brain had shut down, and I couldn't speak. I dropped the phone and grabbed my head with both hands. My chest folded in on itself, and my heart started thrashing around in the shrunken space like a trapped animal.

From far away, again, "Cal, speak to me."

I dropped my hands and turned to face her. "That was El Cuchillo. He's got Claire." The words came, but it was as if someone else had spoken them.

"No! God, no."

"I'm supposed to stand by. No cops."

My cell phone rang again. We both recoiled involuntarily. It was Hiram. He told me Archie's skull had been fractured with something heavy, probably a tire iron, and that he was doing everything possible to save him. I grimaced at the news. "Do what you can." Then, forcing my emotions down, I added, "Listen carefully, Hiram. I don't want you to call the police or breathe a word of this to *anyone*. Got that? Not a *word* until I get back to you."

I was over the shock. My mind began to hum with a crystalline clarity and a single purpose—*get my daughter back or die trying.*

I turned to Daina. "Where does Streeter live? He doesn't know we're on to him. Maybe we can take him by surprise."

Daina had the directions to Streeter's house up on her phone in an instant. We were there in forty-five minutes, an upscale neighborhood in West Linn. My gut told me they wouldn't chance holding Claire there, but I felt certain Streeter would know where she was.

We parked on Willamette Drive, and to be less conspicuous I walked up the hill toward Streeter's development alone. The neighborhood was quiet, but I worried about Neighborhood Watch types. I was relieved to see that the windows were curtained off on the side of Streeter's house I was approaching. I quietly opened a narrow gate and let myself into his backyard, which was completely enclosed with a high hedge. I clicked off the safety on my Glock and crept to the back door. It was locked, but I found an open window on the other side of the house.

I climbed into the attached garage without making a sound. My heart sank. His yellow Hummer wasn't there, only a late-model Corvette with the top down. Nevertheless, I swept the house with my gun drawn.

Streeter was gone.

My knees felt rubbery as I fought off a sickening rush of anxiety. The only people who could tell me where to find Cuchillo were CJ Manion and Andrew Streeter. One was dead, and the other, God knows where.

I called Daina and told her to come up the hill and ring the front bell. If there was a hint of where they'd taken Claire, I intended to find it. I let her in. Daina took the first floor, and I took the second.

A few minutes later I called down to her, "Daina. Come up here. I need help."

She bounded up the stairs and found me in Streeter's study, standing over his computer. "It was hibernating. When I nudged the mouse, his e-mail account popped up. "Maybe Cuchillo got sloppy and sent him something unencrypted," I said as I double-clicked the icon. His inbox listed several unencrypted messages, but they contained no useful information. The last e-mail had come in at 8:35 that morning. The message consisted of a title and several lines of text composed of scrambled letters. The title read: XXFTYQAG23#. "Encrypted," I said grimly.

Daina put her hand on my shoulder and squeezed.

"What do I do next to open this?" I demanded.

"You can't."

"*Tell me.* What's the next step?"

"Click on that icon." She pointed to the upper right corner of the toolbar at what looked like a tiny treasure chest with a big lock on it. I clicked it and the following message came up: *Welcome to Strong Box E-Mail Encryption Service. To decrypt your message, please enter your personal pass code in the box below.*

I sat there for a moment, motionless. The room was still, and all I could hear was the blood thumping in my ears. "The Goddamn Latin phrase," I heard myself say.

Daina was squeezing my shoulder, hard. "What?"

I sat down at the keyboard without answering and began to type with a shaky hand—*Fac Ut Gaudeam.*

Halfway through Daina said, "What are you doing, Cal?"

"Betting the farm," I answered through clinched teeth. When I finished typing, I hesitated for a second before hitting the enter key. The screen jumped and the following message came up: "Access denied. Please re-enter your personal pass code."

"*Shit!*" I hissed.

This time I entered the longer Latin phrase, the one I'd copied from Streeter's rolodex. When I entered it, the same message came up.

Denied again.

Daina's grip tightened on my shoulder. It'll give you only one more try, Cal."

I grabbed a pen from a cup next to the computer and wrote the phrase out carefully on a pad of paper—*Nemo Me Impune Laccessit.* I studied it for a moment. "Damn, never could spell. *Lacessit* has one c."

I typed the corrected phrase in, took a deep breath, and entered it. The pause seemed interminable. A long, rectangular box finally appeared, and green dots started filling it from left to right.

"My God, Cal!" It's working."

I was too numb to speak.

When the dots filled the box, the screen flickered and a blank page came up that instructed me to copy and paste the message to be encrypted, which I did. I hesitated again. Daina was squeezing both my shoulders as I entered the final command. The screen jumped and flickered again, and the message reappeared. This time it was decrypted. The title read: *Heads Up.* The text: *Plan A unsuccessful. I'll be busy with Plan B this morning. Join me at cabin by noon, latest and bring your rifle. Hunting should be excellent.*

It hung together. Plan A was the effort to kill me last night and Plan B, Claire's kidnapping.

I read the postscript on the message twice before I allowed myself to believe it. "There's the address of the cabin and a set of directions. I guess Streeter didn't know how to get there. It's up at Rhododendron on Mount Hood, on a crook in the Zigzag River."

"That *has* to be where they're holding Claire," Daina gasped.

"Right," I said, finally allowing myself the tiniest sliver of hope, "This gives us a shot."

I hit the print icon and flinched when Streeter's printer clattered to life, imagining everyone in the neighborhood would be alerted to our presence. When it stopped I grabbed the print-out and turned to leave. Daina said, "Wait," sat down at the computer and pulled up Google Maps. She entered the address Cuchillo had so obligingly provided and up came a detailed satellite image of a remote cabin. "We'll need this, too."

She zoomed in, and we studied the images. The cabin was in a clearing at a sharp bend in the river. A narrow road ran from the clearing for about three miles through dense woods and connected to a Forest Service road, which continued out to I-26. The cabin, an A-frame, sat on a raised wooden deck, facing the river. We could just make out a kayak lying on the deck and what looked like an outhouse at the edge of the clearing. The terrain behind the clearing sloped up steeply through a thick layer of conifers to a boulder-strewn ridge that ran more or less parallel to the incoming road and the river. A much smaller structure that looked abandoned was closer in, maybe a mile from the cabin.

We printed one satellite image at the highest magnification and then cranked it back so we could see the overall layout as well.

As we moved down the hall toward the staircase I pointed to a wall-mounted gun case in an adjacent room I'd already searched. The door to the case was ajar, the four slots in the rifle rack were empty. A box containing thirty-ought-six rifle shells sat on the bottom shelf with its top open. Half the shells were gone. Daina glanced at the Glock I was carrying, then back at me.

"Yeah," I said, "I'm definitely outgunned."

At the back door, Daina nodded toward a large, stainless steel bowl filled with water next to a matching, empty bowl. "That feeds a big dog. Thank God it wasn't home," she said in a low tone as we slipped out.

We had just gotten back to Daina's car when my cell rang. "Dad, it's me," Claire said in a voice filled with defiance. "I'm okay, but Archie—"

Before Claire could finish, Cuchillo took the phone. "Listen, Claxton," he began in his squeaky voice, "if you want her back, here's the deal. We're calling a truce, you and me. I give you your daughter, you forget who I am, and what you know about me and my client. No harm, no foul. Got it?"

"Sure. I got it." I noticed I wasn't "asshole" anymore. Cuchillo was making nice with me now. He was pitching the deal.

"Okay," he continued, "to keep your amnesia permanent I want you to write a note of confession for that murder on the Deschutes and the one in Portland. You confess to it, like you're getting it off your chest, and that you did it for Bruckner's bitch of a wife," he said with a laugh, obviously pleased with what he considered a clever idea. I imagined my hands around his neck, the squeak getting higher as I slowly choked off that disgusting sound.

He went on to dictate the note, but I didn't bother to write anything down. When he finished he said, "You write that out, sign it, and give it to me. Then I give you back your daughter. I keep the note for insurance. Got it?"

"Right. I have no beef with you. I just want my daughter back safe. Where's the exchange?"

"Stay tuned. And remember, Claxton, if I even *think* you've called the cops or the FBI, your daughter gets my blade across her neck."

"Don't worry, I—." He cut me off.

Daina looked at me, her eyes clouded with dread. I told her what Cuchillo had said. "He doesn't mean that, does he?"

I shook my head. "No. It's just a stupid ruse. He's trying to make sure I come in alone. He intends to kill Claire and me both. We've got to go in and get Claire out *before* the exchange. It's our only chance." Then it hit me what I was asking her to be a part of. "It's going to be dangerous, Daina. Just give me the car, and I'll go alone."

She shot me an angry look, shook her head, and started up the VW. "How do we get to Mount Hood from here?"

"Straight ahead. But don't go so fast you get stopped by the cops. I'm on their radar."

Chapter Fifty-three

"Take the Estacada turnoff," I told her, "and watch your speed." We were cruising north along I-205. I called Philip, desperately hoping he'd pick up. The call went immediately to his voice mail. I left the following message—"This is Cal. Claire's been kidnapped by El Cuchillo. Come as fast as you possibly can to Rhododendron and turn off at Forest Service Road 18. I'll meet you there, right off the highway. Come armed, and don't call the cops. Time's running out."

Next, I called Philip's wife, Lanie. She told me he was somewhere on the Warm Springs Reservation, where the cell phone coverage wasn't all that great. She gave me four other numbers on the rez to try and promised to have him call immediately if she heard from him.

I kept calling Philip every couple of minutes but had no luck. Out of the four numbers she'd given me, I was only able to reach Philip's dad. I told him to spread the word that Philip needed to call me about a life and death emergency.

Just past Sandy on Interstate 26, a sheriff's car came up behind us and followed along for a couple of miles. "Are your tags up to date?" I asked Daina, who had both hands on the wheel, keeping the VW steady at 55 miles an hour.

"Oh, God, I hope so," she answered without taking her eyes off the road. She was apparently correct. After another mile that seemed like ten, the sheriff's car turned off, and I started breathing again.

We were about ten miles south of Rhododendron when my cell phone rang. "Pull over *now*," I said. "If this is Cuchillo, I don't want him to know we're on the move." We skidded to a stop on the fourth ring. I thought my heart would beat itself out of my ribcage as I answered.

"Okay, Claxton, here's—"

"I want to hear my daughter's voice," I broke in. "There's no deal unless I know she's—"

"Shut up, asshole! I'm giving the orders here!" My nickname was back.

There was a long pause. My heart and breath stopped simultaneously. "Dad, it's me, Claire. I'm okay, Dad. Just do what he says." Her voice was weaker, but still firm.

Then Cuchillo snarled back into the phone, "You interrupt me again, and you can kiss your baby girl good-bye."

He went on to explain the next step in the exchange. I was to drive to Rhododendron, park my car off the highway, and walk along the west bank of the Zigzag River to an abandoned shack. I was to arrive alone at three p.m. sharp and await further instructions. He rattled off detailed directions, which matched the route Daina and I had already mapped out. The abandoned shack was the smaller structure we'd seen on the satellite image. It all made sense.

We turned off on Forest Service Road 18 and parked at a trailhead where we could watch the highway for Philip. It was 11:26 a.m. I tried Philip again, then all the numbers Lanie had given me. Nothing. I shuddered through a wave of bitter anger and frustration, struggling to stay focused.

Daina said, "What if Philip doesn't come?"

"Then I'm going in alone. The exchange isn't until three p.m., so the earlier the better to catch them by surprise."

"You won't call the police?"

"No. There's no time," I said with finality. "By the time I untangle myself, Claire will be dead."

At 11:40 I couldn't stand it any longer. "Let's go."

FS 18 wound through a dense swath of late second-growth Douglas firs, sword ferns, and salal. Four and half miles in I had her stop. "Okay, I'm getting out. Cuchillo's road tees in about a half-mile from here. You go back to the highway and wait for Philip. If he makes it, tell him to come in along the ridge to Cuchillo's cabin. Show him the map. That's the route with the best cover." I checked my cell phone. I had three signal bars. "It'll take me about forty minutes to reach the cabin. If Philip shows, call me. My phone's on vibrate. I'll wait as long as I can. If he doesn't show, I'll call you when I'm ready to go in. Call 9-1-1, and have them bring the cavalry."

As I opened the car door to get out, Daina pulled me to her and kissed me lightly on the mouth. Her eyes were open wide, full of hope and strength. "Come back with her, Cal," was all she said. Her eyes said the rest.

After twenty minutes of tough climbing I was on top of the ridge and advancing along a narrow deer trail toward the cabin. I picked my way through the boulders and trees cautiously, watching for loose rocks that might go crashing down the hillside. My vision was sharp, my hearing acute, and my mind focused—*get Claire out alive or die trying.*

It was 12:26 when I caught a first glimpse of the A-frame through the trees. An intense mixture of relief, fear, and anger washed over me. I stopped and crouched down at an outcropping of lichen ridden boulders that gave me a fairly unobstructed view across and down the hillside.

I scanned the scene. A canary yellow Hummer and a dark-colored SUV were parked beside the cabin. I recognized both cars. I couldn't see into the cabin, because the windows, at least the ones facing me, were well covered. Nothing moved in or around the cabin.

The hillside dropped steeply away in front of me, a no-man's land of rotted logs and loose rocks. I moved cautiously toward the cabin at a diagonal, my heart in my mouth. A slip here would send a rock down the hillside like a runaway freight.

I was almost directly above the cabin when the back door opened. I ducked behind the root ball of a fallen tree that lay in shattered pieces below me. A tall, thin man in a black t-shirt and jeans and a pistol in his belt came out, lit up a cigarette, and stretched. El Cuchillo. He leaned on the railing and smoked leisurely. My nostrils flared in disgust as the first traces of secondhand smoke reached me, yet I could do nothing but hunker down and watch through a crack between roots radiating out from the trunk of the fallen tree. Finally he went inside.

Still nothing from Daina or Philip.

I moved down another twenty feet and took cover behind a canted section of the fallen tree. The back door of the cabin opened again, and Andrew Streeter came out. He was dressed in full camouflage, including a billed hat and face paint. He looked pudgy, out of shape, and ridiculous. He was obviously going to be the one to hide in the brush and pick me off at the exchange point. I fumed in silence, like a boiler being stoked.

Streeter unbuttoned his pants and urinated off the back porch in an arcing yellow stream. Too lazy to walk to the outhouse. Then he went back into the cabin.

After two more advances, I ducked behind a large tree stump on flat ground within a hundred feet of the cabin. It was 12:34. Still no buzz from Daina or Philip. Even if Philip arrived at the highway now, it would take him at least thirty-five minutes to traverse the ridge. No way I could wait that long. Not when I knew my daughter was inside that cabin with those two cretins.

I had no choice but to go in after her.

I checked the Glock and clicked the safety off. I dug my cell out of my pocket and flipped the lid open. *"Shit!"* No signal bars at all. I tried calling Daina anyway. Nothing. I shook my head. So much for backup.

The last hundred feet to the cabin stretched across open ground. I watched the curtains on the back windows for signs of movement but saw none. I made a dash for it, halting at the steps leading up to the back door. Crouching below the level of the deck, I took a couple of deep breaths and listened. I heard a low, unintelligible murmur of conversation, then a sharp honk of laughter. I pulled the Glock out of my belt. I had no interest in guns, and I didn't even know what kind of marksman I was, so I asked whoever was running the universe to steady my hand and make my aim true.

I was halfway up the steps when, to my left, I heard the distinct sound of chain dragging on deck planks and the rapid thud of heavy paws. I froze as a huge animal barreled around the corner and launched itself at my throat, eyes wide and fangs barred.

Streeter's dog!

I instinctively raised my arm to protect myself, and the collision knocked the Glock out of my hand and sent me sprawling backward. I braced for a mauling, but the brute was at the end of its chain, straining and clawing to get at me. I jumped up and spun around to find my gun, which had landed somewhere behind me.

"Touch that gun and you're a dead man." The screechy voice again. El Cuchillo was standing on the deck pointing a large caliber pistol at me.

I looked up at him and raised my hands. "I, uh, came a little early."

Chapter Fifty-four

El Cuchillo certainly didn't sound like a cartel hit man, and he didn't look like one either. He had sandy hair cut short, utterly nondescript facial features, and a lean body that was otherwise unremarkable and unmarked by tattoos. The Zetas' favorite north-of-the-border hitter might pass for an auto mechanic, a retail salesman, or the person who delivers your packages. But if you looked more closely, you would notice one distinguishing feature—his eyes. They were gray like smoke—the eyes of a wolf—and absolutely devoid of any trace of humanity.

My entire body tensed as if to deflect the high-caliber round I figured was about to tear through me. Claire, I said to myself, forgive me.

Instead of shooting me, Cuchillo turned to Andrew Streeter, who had just come up behind him. "I think we have all the players now." He turned back to me. "You came alone, like a good boy, right?"

"Do you see anyone else?"

Streeter had a rifle trained on me, the thirty-aught-six from his gun rack, no doubt. He glanced over at his dog, an overweight Rottweiler that was still snarling and straining at its choke chain. There was a nice symmetry in his choice of breeds. Streeter and his dog had similar builds and equally ugly faces. "You're a good ol' boy, Tull," he said to the dog. "You saved the day." To me he twanged, "Mister Claxton, I'm a little surprised to see ya'll.

You're a bit more resourceful than I gave you credit for." His eyes narrowed down. "How'd you find us, anyway?"

I was desperate to keep him talking. "I was the one who broke into NanoTech. I didn't just search Hannon's office that night, I searched yours, too. You'd be surprised what I found, like Reynaldo's phone number and the password to your encrypted account, you know, *nemo me impune lacessit.*"

Streeter arched his unibrow above his grease-painted face. "So that was you. *Damn,* Claxton, you *are* the clever one, and figuring out my pass code, too—"

"Enough with the fucking chitchat," Cuchillo cut in. "Go get the girl."

Claire came out on her crutches. When she saw me, she said, *"Dad."* Her eyes flickered with joy and just as quickly fell back to a mixture of fear and defiance. She had no allusions about the situation.

I desperately wanted to give her reason to hope, but all I could think to do was nod subtly to imply it was somehow going to be okay, that I had something up my sleeve. I said, "Stay strong, Claire."

She nodded. "I will, Dad."

I turned to face our captors. "You've got me now. Let her go. She knows absolutely nothing. Let her go, and I'll give you the letter you requested, money, anyth—"

"I'm not going without you, Dad," Claire said, her face set in a look I knew all too well, her voice ringing with determination.

I shot her the most withering, shut-your-mouth look I could muster. "Don't listen to her."

Cuchillo looked at Claire first, then me. He tilted his head slightly, as if he were considering what I'd just said. His face was placid, but his gray wolf eyes were flat and unyielding. "Look, Claxton, I'm sorry it has to go down this way, but this is business. I have my reputation, you know, and you've already embarrassed me enough."

"That's for sure," Streeter said, half to himself. "I should get a fucking refund." Cuchillo shot him a look that Streeter should have paid attention to. The naïve bastard, I thought to myself.

Cuchillo said, "Let's all go for a walk."

With both of them behind us, Claire and I were directed past the outhouse toward a small clearing at the base of the ridge, where a shovel leaned against a tree. Claire gasped when she saw it, and what blood was left in my head drained away.

"Ever dig a ditch, Claxton?" Cuchillo asked. "This'll be good for you. Good cardio." Streeter laughed at this. The hatred I felt for these two men twisted in my gut like a mean snake. Cuchillo nodded at me. "Go on. Get to it."

I turned back and locked onto Streeter's eyes. "You fool. He's going to kill you, too. You know too much."

Streeter's forehead furrowed above his unibrow as he struggled to compute what I'd just said. He turned his head to look at Cuchillo, his rifle still pointing at me. With cat-like quickness, Cuchillo clipped him hard on the chin with the butt of his pistol. I heard teeth break.

Streeter dropped like a sack of rocks. His rifle fell out of reach, so I grabbed the shovel and whirled around to throw it. But instead of throwing it I lowered my arms and dropped it at my feet.

Cuchillo smiled his approval as he stood calmly pointing his pistol at Claire's head.

"That wasn't very nice of you to spoil my surprise," he said in an even voice. "Now get to work. And make it a triple."

I began digging the first grave. The earth was damp and loamy. A rich, fecund smell bloomed up and touched something primal within me. I was overwhelmed with the desire to save Claire, to live. Thoughts of the time I'd wasted after Nan's death flashed through my head. I'd spent years as a shriveled, shrunken shadow of who I'd been before. Precious, beautiful time wasted. I looked over at Claire, and our eyes met. I remembered reading to her, teaching her to ride a bike, the first time she whipped me at Scrabble. My eyes must have registered sorrow and defeat, because she cast hers down, knowing that whatever plan I had

had just failed. I struggled to keep my knees from buckling and tears from flooding my face.

"Pick it up, Claxton. Keep digging or I'll shoot her right in front of you," Cuchillo said in his businesslike tone. "I've got a plane to catch."

I finished two shallow graves and then feigned exhaustion before starting the third. Streeter was sitting up now, groaning, rubbing his bloody jaw and probing for missing teeth. *Philip*, I cried out silently, *where are you?*

I would start the third grave, I decided, then try to take Cuchillo in a suicide charge. It was the only action left to me. I would scream at Claire to run, although on crutches it would take a miracle for her to get away. Maybe Streeter would come to life, affording Claire a chance to escape.

I paused at two feet of depth into the third grave, my hands tightening on the shovel, every cell in my body focusing on a single, last task—*get to the bastard alive*. Cuchillo eyed me casually, tucked his pistol into his belt and brought Streeter's rifle up into firing position. The barrel swung from Streeter to me and back to Streeter again. I placed a foot on the shovel, but lightly, as Cuchillo's eyes strayed from me to Streeter. I brought the shovel up, extending it like a lance, and charged forward. *"Run, Claire!"*

The bullet hit Cuchillo before I heard the crack of the rifle. It was a loud *smack*, like an angry fist striking a side of beef. He grunted and pitched forward. I dropped the shovel and jumped back involuntarily, trying to comprehend what had just happened.

Cuchillo fell face-first into the first grave. The pistol and rifle disappeared beneath him.

I looked back at Streeter and Claire behind me. Claire froze for a moment, then as Streeter got up, she dropped one crutch and grabbing the other with both hands, swung it hard at him. The blow caught him flush on the ear. He shrieked in pain as he spun around and started running, a hand clasped to his wounded ear.

At the same instant, a Paiute war hoop pierced the air as rocks and debris came crashing down the steep hillside. I looked up and saw Philip high up on the ridge, a scoped rifle in his hand. He was working his way down, but it was steep, the going slow.

Streeter was halfway to the cabin, moving in a half waddle, half run in his upmarket camo outfit. I looked at my daughter, uncertain what to do. She set her jaw in a stubborn line, her eyes burning with anger. "Go, Dad. I'm okay. Don't let him get away!"

I knelt next to the grave and probed under Cuchillo's limp body, digging out the rifle first, then the pistol. I handed Claire the pistol, then glanced up at Philip, who was halfway down the ridge. "If Cuchillo tries to get up, shoot him. Can you do that?"

"*Yes*, Dad. Don't worry. Go after that fat little shit."

By the time I started after him, Streeter had disappeared around the cabin. A car engine roared to life, and through the trees and I saw a yellow blur flash by out on the road. "Damn it." I'd forgotten about the Hummer.

I took a diagonal path up a small incline to the road, sprinting all the way. Dust was still hanging in the air, but the Hummer had already disappeared around a bend in the road. I started running after him and hadn't quite reached the bend when I heard a grinding crunch followed by the steady blaring of a car horn in the distance. I began to sprint again. When I rounded the bend I saw both Philip's big truck and Streeter's canary yellow Hummer. The truck was broadside in the road and the Hummer in the deep ditch at the side of the road, tilted at a forty-five degree angle.

I was breathing hard, but I picked the pace up, unsure of what the hell had happened. Is that somebody standing in the road between the truck and the Hummer? I ran faster, my lungs nearly bursting, the rifle I was carrying starting to feel like a lead brick.

Is…that…Streeter…or…Daina?…it's…*Daina!*

As I got closer, I saw she was in a wide stance, pointing a long-barreled revolver at the Hummer with both arms extended like a seasoned cop. I drew up next to her and leaned on Streeter's rifle to catch my breath. She turned her head to look at me, her face filled with concern and streaked with tears. "Oh, Cal. Thank God. I heard a shot and thought the worst. Is Claire safe?"

"She's perfect," I gasped. "Everybody is, except Cuchillo."

By this time Streeter had managed to shut the ignition off, which killed the horn, and was crawling out of the Hummer. He looked like he'd just gone fifteen rounds with Mike Tyson. His nose was bent at a new angle, he had a cherry red abrasion on his forehead, both eyes were nearly swollen shut, and appropriately enough, his right ear was a tangle of bloody flesh.

Without lowering the revolver, Daina said, "Philip gave me this cannon and showed me how to use it." She allowed herself a smile. "I was going to blow his head off if he tried to run."

I surveyed the scene. The grill and front fender of Philip's truck were smashed in. The Hummer had taken a much more damaging hit on its left fender and driver's side door. "Looks like you played bumper cars with him." I laughed. "Philip's going to be pissed. He loves this truck."

She smiled again and shook her head, a look of utter disbelief on her face. "Philip told me to drive down here where the road narrows and block it, so I did. When I heard the shot, I dialed 9-1-1. I had a single signal bar and the call went through."

"The cops are on the way?"

"Yes. I saw the Hummer coming and knew it was Andrew's. I didn't know what to think or what to do, but I felt like I was in an armored tank. I started the truck up and when I saw who was driving the Hummer, I just flew into a rage, you know? Streeter tried to go around me, so I floored it and rammed him. The air bag caught him full in the face, I think."

Streeter groaned as he cleared the wreckage. "Y'all should've buckled up," I told him. "Those air bags can be hell on a person."

I herded Streeter into the back of Philip's truck and got in with him. Daina drove us back to the cabin. El Cuchillo was still alive. Claire and Philip had pulled him out of the grave and they were using strips of bedsheets to staunch the bleeding in his lower back. Philip looked up at me. "I didn't go for a head shot. Too risky at that distance. I figured you wanted him alive, anyway."

Daina and Claire shared a long, joyous hug, and after Daina explained again how she'd captured Streeter, Philip pointed a finger at him and said, "You're gonna get the bill for my truck, too."

We heard sirens in the distance.

I hugged my daughter again. "It's over, sweetheart," I told her, "It's finally over."

She looked up at me and smiled, but her beautiful eyes were clouded with concern. "Dad, Archie—"

"I know, Claire. We found him."

"Is, is he okay?"

"I don't know, but he's with the best vet on the planet."

Chapter Fifty-five

There's no better time to fish in Oregon than autumn, which follows summer like a good glass of brandy follows a fine meal. It's a time when the deciduous trees, which float like small islands in a sea of evergreens, burst into flames of yellow, gold, and crimson, and the trout, fat with a summer's growth, are restless with the knowledge that winter's coming on.

It was early October, and I stood belly-deep in the Deschutes, the current pushing at me like a playful friend. The sun warmed the back of my neck, and a light breeze swept what few cares I had downstream. Swarms of caddisflies swirled above the water like thin wisps of smoke as I managed to coax the occasional redside up from the soft bottom grass waving in the clear current. Archie followed my progress from the bank with intense interest. It had been touch-and-go for a week, but he'd made a full recovery, thanks to Hiram Pritchard. A jagged scar at the base of his right ear was the only visual evidence of his ordeal. Each time I brought a fish to the surface he would bark wildly, spin in circles and threaten to come to my aid. I smiled and thought to myself, some folks have hunting dogs, but I have a fishing dog.

Philip was downstream, where an archipelago of grassy hummocks harbored some of the biggest fish in the river. No doubt he was taking fish after fish, the desert redband trout coming up for his flies like snakes for a snake charmer. Phillip's fishing guide business was back. He'd received a lot of favorable publicity for saving Claire's and my life, which had translated into a sharp uptick in his fall business.

The shooting had left El Cuchillo a paraplegic. Although it was ruled justifiable, this hadn't gone down well with Philip, who had a sensitive side to him that very few people were aware of. It had taken my friend many visits to the family sweat lodge with his father and the tribal elders before he began to put what he had done behind him.

The dramatic rescue at the cabin made the national news, and the Oregon media feasted on the story for months. A two-part article in *The Oregonian* described my role in solving the murders of Hal Bruckner, Henry Barnes, and CJ Manion, and bringing the hitman, El Cuchillo, to justice. This didn't hurt my law practice one bit. Clients were coming back and new ones calling, and for the first time in a long time, Gertrude Johnson wasn't complaining about my billable hours.

I told the press I'd gotten a lot of help from Philip, Hernando Mendoza, and even Detective Vincent Escalante, who, in truth, had probably saved my life that night in the storage locker. Which brings me to Detective William "Bull" Dorn. He didn't figure much in the press coverage. Shortly after the shootout on the Zigzag, he was relieved of his duties. Turns out he'd badly beaten a young man after stopping him and his fiancée outside Madras on suspicion of something or other. Dorn didn't realize the victim's fiancée had captured the entire assault on her cell phone camera. The video found its way onto YouTube, where it became an overnight viral sensation and precipitated a citizens' march on the sheriff's department.

Dorn's trial was set to begin the following day. Philip and I planned to get to the courthouse early for a front-row seat. Oh, and by the way, Murray Felding had managed to get the assault charges against me dropped, but he kept the five-thousand dollar retainer.

El Cuchillo, whose real name turned out to be Timothy Atwater, had been indicted on three aggravated murder charges bolstered by the testimony of Andrew Streeter. Streeter had sung like a canary to save himself from the death penalty. He'll get life in prison instead of the big IPO payoff he'd hoped for.

In all the excitement I'd almost forgotten about the files taken from Bruckner's study, the ones I'd promised myself to return. As I was sorting through them, I noticed a piece of paper folded into one of the technical reports. It looked like it had been put there to save the place for a reader, presumably Bruckner. I unfolded it and realized it was Bruckner's copy of the long lost security agreement between him and Duane Pitman. When I showed it to Alexis, her response surprised me. Instead of using it to sue Pitman, who'd just announced his plans to jump ship for the French firm, TM-E, she instructed Mitch Hannon to lure him back with the promise of a full equity share. This put the NanoTech IPO back on track. I made a mental note to buy some NanoTech stock.

I also gave Alexis the gold bracelet belonging to Hal Bruckner. She broke into tears and hugged me. I guess she really did love the guy, after all.

Claire, shorn of her cast, had gone back to her graduate studies at Berkeley. It was a wrenching separation for both of us, but we managed it. When I asked her whether she'd feel safe back at Berkeley, she gave me an exasperated look. "Dad, I got kidnapped *twice* this summer. What else could happen to me?" The night before she left the Aerie I promised that when peace returned to Darfur I would take her back to seek out Mustafa and give him the thanks he deserved.

Daina Zikaris, previously known as Svetlana Tetrovia, had gone back to Seattle after installing world-class security and management systems at NanoTech. She was worried sick about the publicity she might receive for her part in the rescue, but we managed to downplay her role and avoid even a single photograph in the newspapers. Her secret was safe with me, of course. I still loved the law, but I'd learned that sometimes there are greater considerations. Digging your own grave at the wrong end of a gun gives even a lawyer like me a broader perspective on what's important in life.

Daina and I are going up to British Columbia next week for some steelhead fishing. We're roughing it with backpacks, a tent, and a propane stove. Both the fishing and the company promise to be excellent.

To receive a free catalog of Poisoned Pen Press titles, please contact us in one of the following ways:

Phone: 1-800-421-3976
Facsimile: 1-480-949-1707
Email: info@poisonedpenpress.com
Website: www.poisonedpenpress.com

Poisoned Pen Press
6962 E. First Ave. Ste 103
Scottsdale, AZ 85251